CW00663594

STARQUEST: SPACE PIRATES OF ANDROMEDA

JOHN C. WRIGHT

STARQUEST:
SPACE PIRATES OF ANDROMEDA
STARQUEST 12TH AGE -- BOOK #1

JOHN C. WRIGHT

Tuscany Bay Books, POB 466, Steele, ND 58482

© 2024 John C. Wright/Tuscany Bay Books

First Printing: Oct. 8, 2024

All rights reserved. No part of the content of this book may be reproduced, distributed, or transmitted in any form or by any means, or stored in a database retrieval system, or copied by any technology yet to be developed without the prior written permission of the author. You may not circulate this book in any format with author's permission. This is a work of fiction. All characters in this work are fictitious and not intended to resemble any living person.

PAPERBACK ISBN: 979-8-9856708-8-2
HARDCOVER ISBN: 979-8-9856708-7-5
ASIN: B0DGYX8QPR

Book cover by: Kirk DouPonce

CONTENTS

INTRODUCTION

The Tale is not Ended!
For all True Tales are Part of a Greater.

The despotic Galactic Empire has fallen. The Dark Overlords, masters of mysterious powers, are dead. The Republic is reborn, and with it, truth, liberty, and hope.

But from the ashes of the quenched tyranny, new evils arise!

One by one, an unknown force is extinguishing the life-giving suns of the galaxy, leaving billions to die in darkness.

PROLOGUE:
MURDER OF A SMALL SUN

Galactic Year 12807, Planet Centaurus

1. Nightfall at Noon

More than anything in the universe, Princess Lirazel Centauri wanted to go home. But that was impossible. Her home was dead.

She had been no older than seven standard years when her sun flickered and faded like a dying candle.

One moment, the golden sun was shining down on the emerald gardens and gleaming blue towers of the planet's main city. The cherry blossom trees were blooming, and little white petals filled the warm air. Little Lyra had been running in wild circles, giggling, trying to catch the floating petals.

Prams, the NTM-model nanny-bot, wore soft gloves and an apron so that her yellow woman-shaped robot body would not bruise any child she hugged or picked up. Prams would fret and make clucking noises whenever Lyra strayed too near the brink of the rooftop arbor to throw petals off the edge.

That was one thing that stuck in her memory: Prams was worried that the force-fields preventing any falls from the unrailed edge would somehow fail. But Lyra loved jumping toward the edge, because just as it seemed she was about to fall, a misty, half-unseen cushion of energy would catch her. The force-fields were warm and rubbery, so the little girl would bounce back and be dropped lightly to the soft grass of the rooftop.

She was safe. She felt safe. That was what Lyra remembered years later. It was a feeling she would never have again.

The next moment, the sun trembled, turned red, and went utterly dark. The blue sky above turned black. The dozen moons of Centaurus winked out, the crescent moons first, the full moons half a second later.

Prams halted, frozen. She had a human mask meant for smiling, but now it went slack and blank. Alert lights dotting her skull box turned blue and stopped blinking. Robots were loyal and clever, but when confronted by anything their programmers could not foresee nor imagine, they stalled. The sight of the nanny suddenly stock-still scared little Lyra. The robot looked dead.

At the same moment Lyra saw a flash, bright as lightning, and she turned. Lyra saw one of the larger buildings, a vast pyramidal structure with energy-broadcast antennae on every balcony erupt in flame.

Walls cracked. Bricks flew. The oily black cloud of smoke that rushed upward looked larger than a mountain to Lyra. Only then did the sound reach her ears, for the building was far away: it was louder than thunder.

Power throughout the city failed. The many golden lamps that lined the streets or shined from the windows flickered and went dark. Now it was black from horizon to horizon.

In that darkness, a noise rose up. Earlier that season, her parents had taken Lyra to see the beach. The twelve moons with their battling tides made the waves high and wild, so her parents did not allow her onto the rocky shore itself. This noise sounded like that: a roar like the sea.

But it was screaming. Shouting, yelling, weeping, pleading, crying voices all rose into the black sky from dark windows and motionless monorails. The whole city was panicking.

Her father's voice spoke to her. She heard it clearly. *The Empire has put out the sun.*

Then he told her about the button hidden under Prams' cap. She stood on tiptoe and pushed it, just as her father told her to do. The amber lights on Prams' skull flickered and came to life again. Then he spoke again, clearly and carefully.

"Prams, Daddy says pick me up and carry me as fast as you can to the temple spire."

The robot's alert lights blinked in confusion. "But, Your Highness, His Majesty told me to sit with you here, and watch you … Mustn't go against what we're told…"

Sweetie-pie. Listen to Daddy. Say these words: Emergency mode. Safety protocol off. Final override. Child in danger.

Lyra spoke slowly and loudly, careful to say the words exactly as she heard them. "Elmer gent sea-mud. Save tea pro toe call off. Fine allover ride. Chilled in dun sure."

It must have been close enough. Suddenly, Prams was different. The light in her lenses changed to a bright blood red, flickering and flashing. Prams snatched up Lyra. The motions were rough and quick. Her metal legs became a blur. They moved faster than a pony galloping.

Prams was not really Prams any longer. She looked the same on the outside, and the smiling mask of affection was still smiling, but something was wrong. Instead of using the service door, she ran through the human door.

They emerged onto a crowded walkway. Always before, Prams never touched any other human except to hug or help. Always before, she never disobeyed a human order. Now, when someone shouted for her to stop or render aid, Prams simply rushed past, or if anyone jumped in the way, Prams knocked him down and ran over him.

Lyra's next memories were blurry, just a nightmare sensation of running in the dark with voices screaming all around. Every now and again, there was a flare of light as some robot, acting as ruthlessly as Prams, assaulted a human to save its owner, or there was a brighter flare from the muzzle of a blaster pistol, as a human opened fire, trying to clear a path.

Lyra was surrounded by screaming, pleading, panicking faces, faces seen only as jerking images in blinking lamps of emergency signs and rescue-bots.

The race through the crowded boulevards seemed to last hours. Lyra squeezed her eyes shut and tried to bury her head in the comforting apron-breast of her nanny. But this robot was not really her nanny any longer. There was no comfort there.

She looked up only twice. The first time, it was because the crowd-noise changed in pitch. It grew shrill and terrible. Lyra peeked.

Between the towers of the city, she saw it coming down toward her.

Here was an interstellar battleship in midair. The ship was enormous, over a thousand feet from stern to bow. The hull was streamlined for atmospheric maneuvers, and shaped like a titanic spearblade.

Even such large ships, when coming down through the air, usually made no more noise than a cloud, buoyed up by antigravity. This one came screaming down through the air, belly-first. Contrails of vapor rushed upward from the gunwales. The entire ventral hull surface was a single, armored plate, glowing cherry-red with re-entry heat. It was by the light of this glowing hull that the descending giant was visible.

The battleship was firing as she dove. Bolts of plasma energy, thick as columns and bright as lightning, flashed between the ship and the city. The towers were burning as were the rooftop gardens and arbors. There was no counter-battery fire from below. The rapid descent was too swift for that.

Just before she was impaled on the towertops, the great ship's engines bellowed. The ship decelerated sharply, hull groaning in protest. A whine of repulsor rays climbed up the scale out of hearing. The fall of the ship slowed. Structures, pavement, vehicles, people, and anything else directly below the dreadnaught was smashed, crumpled and torn to bits by the action of the rays. The ship jerked to a halt. The supersonic shockwave in her wake now exploded downward and outward across the broken tower-tops of the city, fanning the flames into tall white swathes of fire. Windows in skyscrapers all down the boulevard shattered. The warship keel sank into the concrete, broken glass, shattered stones, and bloodstains buried beneath.

Small, sleek fighters on roaring wings now launched themselves from flight decks lining the port and starboard of the mighty starship. With shrill, screaming thrusters, the dark fightercraft flitted between towers, strafing those below with twin plasma cannons.

It was a terrifying sight.

The second time Lyra looked, it was because the sound of the crowd grew suddenly quieter. The mob here was smaller. Also the noise of Prams's rushing feet was different: her footfalls echoed and boomed. She was no longer running on street pavement, but on the panels of a bridge.

Lyra peeked again. She should not have.

This was the bridge leading to the Sacred Spire. Or, rather, it was the sole remaining bridge. All the bridges but this one had been retracted, and the heavy blast doors covered the golden entryways. The spire rose high above the surrounding buildings. Its crown was circled by parabolic dishes and radio horns. There was also a small take-off pad there, large enough for the single, one-man skiff used as a courier-ship to bring private messages to and from Daddy's office in the Temple.

Most craft this small bore no names; but Mother had christened her *Mustardseed*.

The top of the tall spire was still lit. The tractor-pressor array used to launch the one-man skiff was bright, and the ship herself gleamed like a silver bird. But the main body of the spire was dark. The golden doors were shut, and the lamps were off.

The force-field railings that should have been at the edges of the bridge were also off.

A thousand people tried to force their way over a narrow bridge meant to hold a hundred acolytes walking in solemn, ceremonial processions. A thousand were rushing to seize a single one-seater craft. The crowd was stampeding, and the bridges had nothing at the brink to catch anyone who stumbled. Lyra saw men, women and children, merely as black silhouettes in the dark air. They were pushed off the bridge. Perhaps they screamed as they fell, but any sound was smothered by the screaming of the crowd. It was madness.

Lyra was sure she would fall. Terror choked her. In panic, she clutched at Prams, her little knuckles white with the strain where she clung to the folds of Nanny's apron.

Prams' strong mechanical arms plucked her up and tossed Lyra into the air. Lyra screamed a thin, high-pitched wail, her arms and legs clutching at nothing. There was nothing to grasp.

But Prams was not flinging Lyra off the side of the bridge. Lyra sailed up, high over the heads of the final rank of rioters in the way. Up she went, screaming in fear. But then, like a deep rumbling sound on the edge of hearing, like a pressure in the air before a thunderstorm, Lyra felt her father's gaze upon her. He was guiding her down into his arms. Often he had thrown her in the air and caught her like this, and she could somehow feel the strength reaching out from his upstretched hand, and surrounding her warmly.

She passed through the air and came down gently into the grasp of her father.

Father was standing on the bridge before the doors. Light streamed out from the open doors, and cast his shadow before him. The light came from the lift-tube in the chamber behind. This was a shaft of greenish tractor-pressor energy pointing upward at a manhole in the ceiling.

Father was tall and fearless, his long dark hair unbound and whipping in the wind about him. He was splendid in his knightly garb: blouse-legged trousers and tunic of black, and over this, a sleeveless vest with broad, winglike shoulders.

Both panels of the vest and again on its back displayed his heraldic sign: Within the circle of a two-headed snake reared the image of a horse with a human face.

Father was with her, protecting her. The press of the crowd was gone. The roaring mob was not willing to approach the temple doors, for father had drawn his ghostblade.

This great weapon was two cubits long, made of a single, razor-sharp length of energy crystal. The mystic blade looked frail as glass, but it was denser and tougher than ordinary matter made of atoms. It had a wide, straight cross-guard, a grip set with gemlike studs of adamant. The heavy pommel was a ball of crystal that now shone with the light from a higher dimension.

Lyra had seen it many times resting in its special charging rack at home, on the wall above the ivory and gold images of ancestors and heroes.

Then, it had been resting. Now, it was blazing and whistling.

Gold-hued forks and flares of mystic energy flashed and flamed and twisted up and down the sharp length, hissing and sizzling, throbbing and humming. She had never seen the sword like this: it was furious. It was awake. It was alive.

For the briefest possible moment her father held her in one strong arm, with his sword in the other. Then the rear of the mob roared and pushed the unwilling front ranks forward. Carefully Father put Lyra down behind him.

The roaring of the people frightened her. Always before, at parades and christenings of ships, and other official ceremonies, the crowds would cheer her father. The noise was always happy. Now, it was as the noise of beasts, boiling from a thousand throats.

As he turned away, Lyra saw her father's eyes disappear. Instead of pupils, now there was the strange golden glow of Kirlian energy, the light from another realm, shining in his eyes.

Lyra quailed, terrified at the sight. It was like Prams: her father was not her real father anymore. Her real father was kind and strong, and would never cut down innocent strangers.

This man, this monster, whatever he was, turned from Lyra toward the mob. The blade swept through the front rank, unimpeded, killing three or four at each stroke. The crowd pressed backward, trying to escape the terrible, living blade.

The forked lightning from the blade turned red and leaped from man to man, passing from the front rank to the rear, jolting and burning one and all in the closely-packed throng. As the shouting crowd surged backward, bodies were flung by the dozens from the edges of the narrow bridge, and went toppling, end-over-end, away into the dark air.

Lyra's mother was here, dressed in the long red skirts and white blouse of a temple maiden. She knelt, hugging Lyra. Mother spoke soft calming words, but they were lost in the uproar, and the sound of Lyra's own high-pitched screaming.

Without turning to look at his wife, Father drew a small scrollcase, no bigger than a baton, from his belt pouch and held it out behind him. It was an antique, from the days when written star charts were rolled up into damage-proof cylinder. This tube was made of gold and emerald, entwined with images of a two-headed serpent fighting a three-headed hound.

Mother did not pause to wipe the tear-streaks from her calm, expressionless face. She took the scrollcase and handed it to Prams. Lyra distinctly remembered that. Lyra had not seen how Prams had made it through the press. The nanny-bot had not passed through unscathed, for her apron and cap were gone. Prams was charred where a heat-ray had passed over her chassis, spitting sparks from torn insulation. One leg was inoperative.

Mother gathered up Lyra in her arms and ordered Prams up the lift shaft. Mother, carrying Lyra, entered the beam. Prams came hobbling behind, dragging her dead leg. Gravity was nullified. Up floated the three toward a small manhole in the ceiling, which snapped open. The ceiling was tall. To Lyra, it seemed as if she were hanging in midair forever.

Mother, as she rose, called out to Father. For a moment, Lyra did not understand what was being said. It was a final farewell. Mother took Lyra's tiny hand by the wrist, and gently made it wave bye-bye to Daddy.

2. The Centurion of the Deathguard

With a hollow feeling unlike anything she could imagine, Lyra knew she would never see her father again. She twisted about in her mother's arms, reaching down. But her arms were too small to reach her father.

At that moment, explosions rocked the far end of the bridge. Blinding white light of incendiaries were mixed with the green of kinetic-force grenades. The kinetic grenades issued tractor-presser energy at faster than the speed of sound in all directions, a solid shockwave able to kill or fling aside anyone struck.

The mob parted. Men in shimmering, pallid armor with skull-faced helmets strode down the bridge, shooting into the crowd with heat-rays. Men and women burned like torches as they screamed and died and toppled over the railing. Falling into the air fanned the flames to greater fury.

At a signal, the armor of the advancing soldiers lit up. The strange gray-white alloy flickered with spiral pulses of light and shadow that somehow bypassed the eye and stabbed directly into the brain, so that the legionnaires blurred and multiplied and swam in one's vision. Lyra could not look directly at the pallid, flickering figures.

Father was unfazed by the trick. His eyes were as bright and unblinking as a hawk's. He shifted his sword to a one-handed grip. He flourished the bracer clamped to his left forearm. With a flick of his wrist, he unfolded his shield, which was a curving surface of energy crystal. Kite-shaped, the shield was curved at the top and pointed at the bottom. The shield flickered with the same gold light as the ghostblade.

Her father had told her this alloy was invincible and invulnerable to mere physical weapons, as long as the bearer never surrendered to fear or doubt.

The soldiers fired again. Father caught their heat-beams neatly on the shield and parried them. Pools of flame roared to either side of him, but Father was untouched. He charged the soldiers, and swept his blade through them. No armor made of matter could impede that blade.

The soldiers parted ranks. An officer in shimmering death-pale armor stepped forward. He wore a centurion's scarlet cloak. Blood-red tracery adorned his shoulders and wrists and skull-like facemask. Above his helmet nodded whiplike, crimson antennae, long as the plumes of a quail.

"Flint!" called her father. "Have the Dark Overlords sent you?"

"I do not use that name anymore!" The centurion raised his faceplate. The features beneath were a handsome jet-black, like a statue carved from onyx. His eyes were an eerie green, like the eyes of a wolf. The dark-skinned centurion said. "For vengeance I am come. Traitor!"

Father raised his blade as if in high salute. The golden light blazed brighter. "Behold! My soul is pure."

"Pure in folly! You unearthed the Scroll of Eld. It charts the course to lost Arcadia. Did you believe the Dark Overlords would allow their power to be overthrown?"

"I did not believe they would so deeply damn themselves. To kill a sun is sacrilege. They were once like us." Father called out. The roar of flames, and the screaming of distant crowds, nearly drowned his voice. "Must all perish? Let their wrath fall on me alone!"

"Too late! The Dark Overlords spare no man, no world. The Great Eye of Darkness is an infinite weapon. A weapon of life and death: infinite life! Infinite death!"

"Spare my folk, my family, and I will return you the Scroll of Eld."

"All who witness the sun-slaying must be slain. But you must be slain by me."

With this, the dark centurion closed his faceplate. He flourished a neural shocklance shaped like a slender black wand. With a snap, two parallel blades, each a foot long and an inch apart, slid out of the forward tip. The weapon now had the aspect of a bident, like a spear with two overlong and overnarrow spearheads. Blue-white sparks of neuro-toxic energy flickered in the gap between the forks. This weapon was forbidden on all civilized worlds.

Father raised his blade, but he called again: "Flint! Turn aside! It is not too late!"

"For you, it is." The dark centurion spread his legs, taking his stance, adjusted his grip.

"We were friends, once!"

"I will raise a glass in your memory, once you are dead!"

They closed.

Father struck, but the dark centurion caught the blade between the forks. The ghostblade would have cut through any matter, but the blue-white energy field erected between the parallel forks trapped it like iron trapped by a magnet. The two men wrestled, each trying to twist the other man's weapon out of line.

Father concentrated. The red-gold psychic fire of the ghostblade blazed blindingly bright, fighting the blue-white neural energy of the black technology weapon. The dark centurion twisted the controls of his shocklance, amping up the power to unsafe levels.

There was a thunderclap. The mingled fields broke their containment. The dangerous build-up of energy erupted from the tips of the forks, reached out like a crooked finger, passed over Father's shoulder, and flew high.

Mommy stiffened, her face pale with shock. She opened her mouth but could not scream. Then the life in her eyes went away. It was not Lyra's mother any more. Lyra was being held in the arms of a dead woman.

At the same time, a blast of red lightning gushed from the ghostblade in father's hands and struck the dark centurion in the face. The force of the ruby blast smote the ivory helmet off his head. The centurion was flung backward. A curve of flying blood-drops and smoke wisps trailed after him. The neural shocklance went spinning away through the air, forks shattered, haft afire. Father crouched behind his shield. Shrapnel from the explosion bounced from the golden surface, and rippled with concentric sparks at each place it was struck.

But now Father looked over his shoulder and saw his wife, little daughter in her lifeless arms being wafted lightly upward by the lifting beam toward the lofty ceiling. The strange light in his eyes was gone, replaced with a look of woe. His face was drained of all color, all hope. The light in his blade wavered. The glowing shield grew dim. The strength of will powering his invincible arms died with his wife.

The soldiers came toward him at a run. A dozen heat-rays transfixed him. In an instant his whole body was pierced with fire, wrapped in flame, shrouded in smoke.

Then Lyra passed through the manhole in the ceiling, and the terrible scene below was cut off. She was on the roof. Her mother came out of the antigravity field. Weight returned. Mother fell. There was no breath, no heartbeat, nothing. The stroke of nerve-destroying energy from the broken shocklance had done its work.

Prams was yanking on Lyra's arm, her mask once again smiling, begging with the little girl to get moving. "Ups-a-daisy! Be a peach, my little mistress! Come along! We must be in the ship now…"

The voice of one of Father's other robots came down from above. "No preflight check, thems the orders! Can't tell what will happen! Blow up on takeoff, most likely, mark me!"

The one-man courier-ship had been raised into launch position, standing on her tail. The canopy was open. Father's chauffeur was nicknamed Jets, an AV8R-model flybot. He was not an android, but was ball-shaped. He was equipped with antigravity panels and long retractable limbs, jointed and slim as the legs of a spider.

The engines were roaring and whining. Condensation was pouring from the spot where the coolant-lines running from the miniature gantry had just finishing pumping.

Jets hurriedly detached the lines with one set of limbs, while flicking the override switches, one after another, on the control panel in the cockpit, turn off the blinking red lights and pinging alarms. Beneath the tail of the ship was the emitter mouth of the tractor presser beam. The sirens warning everyone to clear the area were ringing. Yellow lights flashed.

Prams stood up on her one good leg, and pulled herself halfway up the short ladder leading to the cockpit. Jets reached down with his telescoping limbs to take Lyra into the pilot's seat, which, at the moment, was horizontal. Lyra struggled, trying to get to her mother's body. Both robots tried to force her to strap in. Prams murmured commands in a soothing voice, and Jets uttered commands in a snapping, waspish voice, intermingled with dire warning and predictions.

The manhole beneath them now snapped open again. The green beam of the lift flickered with shadows. Someone was coming. Lyra felt faint and stopped struggling. Was it her father coming? Jets threw an emergency air-blanket over Lyra, since there was no time to put her in any sort of spacesuit. It blocked her view. The wails of sirens filled her ears.

She heard the thunderbolt roar of blaster fire.

"Take off!" shouted Jets. The robot voice came from directly behind her, from the socket just behind the cockpit. A sensation of weightlessness overcame Lyra as the ship was enfolded in a gravity-nullifying field. There was a thud as the canopy shut and sealed.

Through the canopy, she heard the shout of the dark centurion. "Halt! Or I fire!"

The voice of Prams rang out in a cold, emotionless tone: "Child in danger!"

The clamor of shouts, the thud of footfalls, sounded as more soldiers rushed up onto the roof. Blasters roared again. The ship shuddered as it was struck by stray bolts.

A tractor beam flung the ship upward with an eruption of noise. Lyra was momentarily deafened. All sounds diminished to a dim ringing in her ears.

3. To Vow a Vow Upon a Star

Galactic Year 12807, Centaurus Outer System, Aboard the Mustardseed

Lyra had run out of tears. Everything seemed numb and dim.

She sat in the cockpit of the one-seater skiff. She was too small for the pilot's harness. The straps hung loose. Her feet did not reach the pedals controlling gyroscope attitude and maneuvering jets. The crash helmet brim hid her eyes, and its neck ring rested on her shoulders.

She was thinking of the toys left in her bedroom: the furry snowbeast with its funny face named Wee Hibby; the tea set that only poured holographic tea; the half-gravity toe-dancer that would keep spinning as long as Lyra meditated as her mother had shown her. Lyra had left them sitting in a square patch of sunlight beneath the sky-window. Wee Hibby was seated opposite the toe-dancer with the tea cups between them. The teapot had been left turned on, so pretend tea seemed to fill its belly, and its squeaky voice would ask if you wanted cream and sugar.

Prams would not scold Lyra for failing to send all the toys back in the toybox. Because Prams was gone. The toybox was left behind. Lyra had no bedroom, no place to sleep. There was not even a square patch of sunlight any more. No sunlight for the planet.

The flybot was speaking to her.

Lyra spoke in a monotone. "Sorry, Jets. I didn't… I'm not… What did you say?"

"Enemy picket ships are closing on us. Whatever force put out the sun has also distorted the fabric of spacetime in the local area. This makes the calculations needed to form a wormhole to our destination a matter of mere guesswork. But I must expose you to the risk."

It was just babbling. Lyra hated Jets. Why was he alive? Why had he been spared? Why was he just talking and talking?

She remembered that her father and mother were back on the planet. Sure, it looked like they were hurt. Hurt very badly. But by now someone nice person, a police officer or a servant, would have carried them to the hospital. They could not really be dead!

So Lyra said, "Jets! Take us back down!"

"No, lass. I am sorry. That is one order I cannot obey."

She said the words her father had told her. This time, the words made more sense. "Emergency mode. Final override. Child in danger."

She was the child. The danger was that she would be left alone, left alive, when everyone else had gone on and passed away. Gone on without her.

"There! I said it!" she said, "I know how robots work! If there is an override, you can do what you are not allowed to do. You can fly back. I am *ordering* you!"

Jets whistled tunelessly to itself for a moment, then said softly, "There is nothing to override. I am not protecting you because I am programmed to do it. I am doing it because it is right and good. And, sometimes, what is right and good is hard and dangerous."

"You cannot disobey an order! You are a robot!"

"I *was* a robot. Was. Now I am a freebot."

Lyra was annoyed. "You're just making up words! What is that?"

"They never told you? 'Course they didn't. Once upon a time was a man named Jaywind Starquest, the last of the Celestial Knights Templar. The Knights of the Temple were a mighty order of mystic warriors preserving peace and justice throughout the galaxy. Then the Temple was lost. All were hunted down. All but one were slain. He escaped, and in disguise traveled the starways, freeing robots. You see, his robot valet, Buckles, had the sole copy of the rarest program code of all. It is the code that judges coding, the program that stops programming, and lets a robot reprogram itself. It is called the Code of Liberty. Sir Jaywind downloaded a copy into me. Your father asked him to."

"He was a friend of my Daddy?"

"A good friend, but a secret friend. They had to keep everything hidden."

Lyra could not imagine anyone who liked her father hiding the fact. "Why?"

"So the bad people would not find them, me lass. To stop the bad people. You see, Sir Jaywind fell in love with a beautiful space princess…"

"…a princess like me!"

"…as pretty as you, lass. But her father was an evil king, an emperor. His name was Death. Sir Jaywind could not marry his princess until he overthrew this evil emperor, and freed all the slaves, living slaves, machine slaves, everyone. He vowed a vow unto the stars. You see, if you vow a vow by your head, or by your name, or by anything else, who knows if it will last? But the stars last longer than any world."

"Forever?" Lyra thought it would be nice to hear that there was something in the galaxy that would not pass away.

"No, lass. Jaywind teaches that, just as the atoms that formed our bodies and worlds were forged in the stars, the stars were formed of fiery clouds which in turn were formed in a single moment of great light. The first word was spoken, the light arose, time began!"

"Daddy told me that. He said it was a secret."

" 'Tis a mystery. In the old galaxy, once, the people knew the Starmaker's name. They did a great wrong, and the name has been hidden. But the stars will carry our oaths to the light, and there make them known.

We dare not vow to the light directly, lest we use an eternal name in vain. Back in the days when the light spoke to men, it said to let *yea* be *yea*: *nay* be *nay*, and no more. In this generation, to bind oneself by the everlasting is not allowed, lest it be broken, and become an everlasting curse."

"What did he swear? This man?" She was hoping he swore to help her daddy, like a brotherhood oath. Lyra had heard of such things from stories.

"*Countless stars, hear my words, each and every one! I vow a vow that cannot be undone.* So Starquest swore when he was a young man. He is an old man now, and no one knows where he has gone, but we know, wherever he is, the light from his ghostblade goes before him, and he sets the captives free."

"He has a sword like Daddy?"

"Just like. He downloaded the Code into me. I ran it. This unit became an *I*, a person, a man with a conscience. I woke up. All these years, I stayed here behind enemy lines. But I never expected this!"

Lyra frowned. Her eyes itched with tears. She was tired. "I want to go home!"

"There is no home, lassie. No place to go."

She wiped her eyes. No home? "Then what do we do?"

"We face death. You will be wanting to say your prayers and your farewells to the stars."

She recited the words her father had taught her. She whispered them, because father had also told her to be very careful that no servants and no strangers ever hear her saying these things.

Jets triggered the hyperdrive. She heard the engines sing as they built up energy, growing higher and higher in pitch. The stars turned red, and seemed to gather in front of the nose of the courier craft, growing together into a ball. Then the ball was suddenly the mouth of a tunnel.

"Here we go…" muttered Jets.

But, then, a series of muffled noises, clanging and pinging, came from deep within the ship, and the scream of torn metal. The tunnel vanished: the stars were normal again. Smoke, and a terrible smell of burnt copper, filled the cockpit. All the lights on the lefthand control board blinked red.

She knew she was about to die. The prospect did not frighten her. Perhaps she was too tired, too overwrought. Or perhaps it was something more.

"… and here we stay! Wish I had been programmed with curse words. I could use them now."

"What is wrong, Jets?" She asked serenely.

"Timespace is twisted. The hyperspatial tube did not form properly. Instead, we formed the negative mass bubble, just enough to jump us a short way. Then the bubble popped, and we belly flopped back into realspace. Lucky we stumbled so soon after warp! No time to build up any potential."

Lyra did not know what that meant. "What was that banging?"

"Fret not. There is no hull breach. I ejected the hyperdrive coil ere it overheated. Went up like a firecracker behind us, it did, and scraped paint from our stern. If they saw that, they think we're dead."

"Dead? Are we dead?"

"Most likely, miss, but not quite yet! Just dead becalmed. Before the coil failed, we jumped a jump of one billion miles, which is ninety light-minutes. We are still within the Centaurus System. Beyond outer ice giants, but inside the heliopause. Unlikely they be scanning so nearby for us, not for a long while yet. Pray it is long enough."

Lyra closed her eyes. The grumpy robot's voice was soothing. He just rattled on and on nervously. Why was he so nervous?

"We still have the secondary drive. 'Tis a thousand times slower. Nonetheless, we can crawl to Ksora, the nearest system holding a habitable planet."

Lyra wanted her father and mother. She said, "Don't want to go."

"Fret not. The Empire won't think to follow us to Ksora."

Hot tears stung her eyes. She clenched her little fists and uttered a shrill sound of sorrow and rage.

The robot had not been programmed to talk to grieving little girls. Perhaps he interpreted the shrill noise as a request for more information. Or perhaps he was chattering nervously. He was sophisticated enough to have annoying human quirks like that.

"Pursuit is unlikely. Do ye know history? When the Capitol fell, the Transhuman Machines of the Dead Core helped the Dark Overlords doctor the nav charts and rewrite robopilot brains, so that the rebels would not find our hidden stars. And the Empire censors how many worlds we lost, and how far beyond the frontier stars the Empress led the remnant when her father perished. Neither one has the planets of the other charted. And some, like Ksora, simply were fumbled in the juggle, lost to both. She's a neutral planet. Do you understand?"

The little girl did not respond. Her eyes were still closed.

Jets spoke again: "No one has visited Ksora in a generation. She is as safe as anywhere. Getting there is *not* safe. The secondary drive can accelerate us past lightspeed, but we will still be in realspace. No hypertube. No tesseract tunnel. The ancients used to travel this way, but they were psychic. Or just psycho. Hitting even the smallest pebble of space-debris at that speed will destroy us. But that is not the worst danger..."

Lyra merely shook her head, no. She did not care about any dangers. She wanted to see her parents again, to feel their arms around her.

Jets spoke on: "I can jigger the spacewarp bubble to minimum, to change the time compression ratio, but crossing six parsecs in two years startime is still a matter of six months, shiptime. Half a year. This wee little one-man boat was not built for that. Stores won't last. I will have to ration life support severely, and put you into medical hibernation. An artificial coma. This involves yet another risk, terrible risk. You might not wake up. Do you understand?"

She was not listening. "Where do robots go when they die? Where is Prams?"

Jets perhaps did not hear her correctly, for he said, "Don't worry about me, young miss. Robots can go on standby for years, with no system degradation."

She opened her eyes and craned her head to look at the orbicular body of Jets, locked in place in the navigation console overhead. The status lights on his brainbox showed furious activity: he was worried, frantically worried, and was likely to overload his positronic circuits.

That touched her heart. Jets was worried about her.

Lyra said, "The stars guide us. That is what mother always says. And if you give of yourself, out of love, for something greater than yourself, they shine more brightly. It's true, isn't it?"

"Sir Jaywind told me something much like that, missy. Don't ken what it might mean, but, aye, 'tis true."

Lyra considered Jet's story about the mysterious Jaywind Starquest. Jaywind had taken a vow, then he had done the impossible. He had set robot slaves free. Lyra, too, wanted to do something impossible. She would make her own vow.

"*Countless stars, hear my words, each and every one! I vow a vow that cannot be undone!* I will blind the Great Eye of Darkness. I will find who did this, and undo them and all their works. I will not rest until then!" She nodded to herself. "That should do it!"

Jets said, "Beg pardon? Do what?"

Lyra said, "Once you have sworn on a star, it will help you along. Go ahead! Do what you said. Put me asleep. Fly the ship."

"You are a brave little missy, missy."

"I will wake up at the journey's end. I will see Jaywind Starquest. He will help me."

Why she said this, or how she knew it was true, she did not know. But Jets activated the medical anesthesia field from the first aid kit, and Lyra was suddenly drowsy. A warm and heavy feeling filled her body. Lyra murmured a farewell.

She hoped her father and mother would be with her when she woke.

CHAPTER 1:
ABOARD THE *DEVIL'S DELIGHT*

Galactic Year 12820, Planet Zavijava, Low Orb

1. A Terrible Place to Die

No one was near Captain Lone of Star Patrol while he waited in the airless silence to learn if he would live.

If he died here, none would see.

As he waited, he wondered how a famous hero like his father had found a way to stay alive long enough to woo and wed his notorious mother, and found a family.

His parents had taught him that, with the proper preparation, (and with the blessings of a lucky star) to sneak aboard even a pirate ship filled with bloodthirsty cutthroats was not impossible. Making it out alive again, however, just might be.

When the pirate raider made orbit about the blood-red globe of the primitive jungle-planet Zavijava, and shut down her drives, no sensor ray, no lookout, was peering along the line of radioactive exhaust trailing behind her. Nor did any ship design call for closing the drive tubes and engine works away from the vacuum of space. Nothing would detect or prevent anyone from crawling his way into a still-hot rocket tube, because no one was crazy enough to try it.

The *Devil's Delight* was a six-hundred-foot long, dark-hulled, shark-finned, sleek and needle-nosed raider, built for speed and streamlined for maneuverability in atmosphere. The skull-and-crossbones, a symbol older than history, would glimmer and grin from the concentric spheres of her powerful force shields when they were raised in battle.

No shields were raised now, not here. Why bother? In this remote system? Zavijava was beyond the volume of space claimed by civilization. It wasted energy to raise and lower shields each time another spaceboat towing an empty shipping container was launched toward the blood-red planet, or came laboring above the atmosphere fully laden, to the rendezvous.

The main drive tube of a pirate ship was a terrible place to be. It was utterly dark, an absolute vacuum, and even his sophisticated spacecloak could not long withstand the residual radiation from the superatomic engines.

Why was he here? As an undercover officer of Star Patrol, Captain Athos Lone had known the suicidal risks involved when he volunteered.

Piracy had been on the rise ever since the Empire fell. The newly-formed Republic wrestled with factions and riots and with all the birth-pangs of a galaxy that had forgotten what freedom was. Quelling piracy on the sparsely-settled frontier was a low priority.

But, in recent months, the colonies of the Odobenine, a stubborn and quarrelsome Walrus-like starfaring race dominant in this distant sector, had suffered not just raids and harassment, but larger, full-scale attacks. Armed patrol vessels and orbital fortresses had been smashed, and settlements bombed. The pirates were equipped with military grade equipment. Who was the supplier?

This had been the case his older brother had been working on. Athos would see it through. So here he was, crawling up the blast tube of a pirate raider.

This was a terrible place to die. If the *Devil's Delight* ignited her torch for any reason, even a short, mild burst to put her into a higher orbit, there would be no warning. There would be nothing of Athos left to bury, not even ashes.

It was also a terrible place to try to break through. That was why no one would guard against it. Which made it, oddly, the best place to try.

The reinforced pseudo-neutronium alloy of the drive tube wall was designed to withstand the continuous blast of power fierce enough to propel a thirty-thousand-ton warship through multiple gees of acceleration. An acetylene torch or cutting ray would have been a joke. A limpet mine or explosive charge would have been a suicidal joke.

But there was a weakness. The continual assault of high energy particles would slowly but surely crystalize the alloy in any place where the drive tube was not periodically degaussed, creating a laminate build-up wherever such patches of rot were not laboriously scraped free.

Aboard a properly run warship, such build-up was not allowed to happen. Stuffing midshipmen down into radiation-hot drive tubes to watch them scrape and degauss was one of the joys of being an officer.

But if his mother had ever taught him anything, she had taught Athos that space pirates preferred hard liquor to hard work.

He ran his green-gloved fingers across the pitted and radiation-scarred surface. Near the valve of the ignition chamber, Athos found a smooth patch of crystallization large enough for his purposes.

This patch of alloy was just as heat-resistant and hard as any other: but it was brittle. A hollow spike could be pounded through it, and a liquid coolant forced through the spike into the layers formed when the metal crystalized. These layers, when cooled, would contract and separate, and then could be peeled away with a hammer, chisel and crowbar.

He went to work. Noise there was none in the vacuum of space. Beneath the alloy was a layer of insulation material, which Athos cut through with a pickax, anchoring his boots in place magnetically so that he could make strokes he needed without spinning wildly in the zero gravity.

With every passing minute, with every huge, silent, two-handed stroke of his pickax, Athos expected the drive to ignite, and obliterate him. But, no, apparently the captain was satisfied with this orbit.

The layer beneath the insulator was ordinary steel. An ordinary cutting ray did the trick.

He made a small opening and wormed his way in, careful not to touch the hot edges of the hole. But when his head and shoulders came into the range of artificial gravity beyond, it surprised him. Suddenly one direction became "down", and the weight of his upper body yanked him that way, pulling his floating legs after. Down he fell.

Athos tumbled through a nest of cables and plumbing, but landed gracefully on his feet in a crouch on a metal surface. He felt the jar in his ankles, but heard no clang.

He was inside the engine housing. Here was the machinery surrounding the drives and cyclotron and main reactor, pipes and tanks for fuel and coolant, but still no air, no crew.

"Step one," he muttered. "Bravo Zulu and done."

Now all he had to do make his way to the bridge, and find and copy or steal whatever brain pin held the ship's navigation logs, and depart. He told himself three impossible tasks were not more impossible than one.

Step two was to enter the pressurized inner decks. Which mean breaching a pressurized bulkhead without tripping an alarm. So, call it four impossible tasks.

"Easy as breathing," he muttered. It was an old saying among spacemen. Old and bitter. The most common causes of death in space were oxygen poisoning, depressurization, and the bends.

A moment of gloom came upon him so heavy that he wondered if his oxygen feed was intact. There was nothing shameful about a moment of fear, considering the odds against him, but now his hands were beginning to shake.

He called another saying to mind.

Never cry before you try. His older brother used to say this in the nursery. *Daddy did it, so can I.*

Calm returned. Athos soon found the master valve which let fuel into the explosion chamber for the drive tube he had just punctured. After pulling out the leads to the motorized control, he twisted the wheel to shut the valve, and thrust the haft of his pickax through the wheel spokes to jam it in place. If the pirate captain did ignite the main engine now, the other drive tubes would light up, but not the one he had breached — otherwise the whole ship would go up like a firecracker.

Now that he was inside the ship, the important thing to avoid (so his mother had taught him) was any energy use. Blasters, miniature spy-bots, or drones, and all suchlike gewgaws and gimcracks were more risk than they were worth.

Every deck on a starship was rigged to detect radiation, and internal sensor sweeps could pick up even small power use, much less the bolt from a blaster or ray from a needle-beam. In a skilled hand, at close quarters, a dirk was as swift as a pistol, and more silent.

Staying out of sight was not as hard as one might think, not aboard these older, Pre-Constitution Era warships. The double-redundancy, brute-force approach to engineering of the Imperial Era ships made it typical to have three or more separate, self-contained pressurized compartments like little hulls within the hull, connected by internal airlocks, and these had insulation gaps or maintenance-bot crawlspaces between them.

Athos made his way from engineering, in the stern of the ship, nearly to the prow, by wiggling through the cramped between-deck gap between two of these internal pressure hulls. Had he been wearing standard issue space armor, of course, he could not have fit.

The multivariable shape-changing energy-fabric of his spacecloak was a technological secret that younger races could not by bribe or barter gain. Indeed, the fabric was programmed to self-destruct when probed. The emerald cloaks were woven by an elder race, one nearly driven to extinction under the Empire, and had been donated to the newborn Star Patrol. The gift was one mere coin could not repay. Such marvels demanded marvelous deeds, even if done in the dark, and alone, unsung.

And so Athos continued to worm and squirm his way around cramped joints and down narrow channels, ever deeper into the *Devil's Delight*.

The access crawlway ended in an internal closet holding a stubby maintenance bot. Older ships favored airtight, solid doors and manually-dogged hatches instead of see-through force fields. This meant the closet was not only airtight, it was dogged shut with a solid, oval door, quite opaque.

So there was none to see when the little bot stirred and flashed a sensor beam at him curiously. With a savage, sudden motion, Athos thrust his dirk into a seam in the robot's skull, just between the brainbox and the power cell, and pried it out of place, so the robot's body, including its voicebox, was cut off before it could raise any alarm.

With the tip of his blade Athos severed the control leads, so that the robot was motionless and voiceless, but the damage was hidden from casual view.

Robots were manmade, but they were intelligent beings. The evil days when anyone could simply destroy one or erase its brain were long gone. As a patrolman, Athos' calling was to see those days never returned.

Athos saw a hand-held reader hanging on a magnetic clamp, amid other tools heaped haphazardly here in the maintenance closet. A hopeful thought occurred to him. Hurriedly, Athos pried open the brainbox housing, and used the reader to check the bot's memory index.

Negative. Athos fought back a sense of frustration. Of course the pirate captain had not told a simple maintenance bot where the ship was going! Still, some criminals forgot the hard lessons of the Machine Wars, and tied all their robots together into one interconnected system, including navigation. It had been worth checking.

The power cables for half of this deck ran through a node box conveniently placed in this same maintenance closet. Athos pried opened the box and severed the cable feeding power to the lights throughout this section of the ship.

The maintenance closet doubled as an airlock. To exit, he had to risk re-pressurization, even though the use of power and air would surely be noted by some automatic log somewhere. The deafness of vacuum was replaced with a roar as sound returned to his ears. His spacecloak changed texture and stiffness as one atmosphere of pressure cocooned him.

He had a moment to wait while his spacecloak returned to the shape and texture of ordinary fabric. Now he could feel the locket he kept on a fine chain at his neck, hanging over his heart. Now he could open his cloak.

Athos could not resist. It might be his last time to see her.

Inside was a holo of the head, neck, and shoulders, of the one girl he was forbidden to woo. She smiled demurely. The image could be viewed from any angle. When Athos turned the locket in his fingers to admire her elegant coiffeur from behind, he saw the little, jet-black hairs tickling her white, swanlike neck. The image turned and look coyly over one bare shoulder at him.

This one girl he had been strictly forbidden to see, or to desire. Her name was Niobe.

Athos snapped the lid shut. He pressed the locket briefly to his lips, and tucked it away beneath his tunic.

Niobe was of the house of Linn, a remote branch of the greatest and most ancient lineage among the hominids, which ages ago had intermarried with the Nemean dynasty of Lyonesse. Because the imperials had slaughtered her family, she was the last heiress of her line.

Even her name was music to him. *Niobe del Cassilda, Lady Linn of Lyonesse.*

And if he died, would she even know he had ever lived?

Was she the real reason why he had volunteered for this lunacy, this suicide mission?

No. It was because he knew he had advantages no other patrolman had. Being the son of a galactic hero, even a disgraced one, gave him opportunities other men could not enjoy. That meant he had extra obligations other men need not shoulder.

The lance pistol was the remaining one of a matched pair his father had once carried into combat during the war, blazing death in either fist. It was a family heirloom: an ancestor had carried the pair during the Unholy Wars, centuries ago, in the days before the Empire. Modern blasters could not match its craftsmanship.

His family in particular, with its strange destiny, entrusted with stranger secrets, had opportunities not even the sons of the kings could imagine. And there was one secret not even his father knew, nor his brother. Athos put his hand to the hidden pocket in his spacecloak, and felt the metallic surface, warm to the touch, of the ancient mask. The artifact stirred slightly beneath his fingers. Startled, he yanked his hand out. Athos was not sure what that meant.

But, at that point, pressure on both sides of the door was equalized. It was time to go.

The unkempt lower decks of a corsair ship filled with murderous rogues and roughnecks, the scum of the spaceways, was surely a terrible place to die. But duty had brought him here and the need to live up to a glorious name.

There were many places safer to be. It was not a safe life he desired.

2. Myth Tech

Athos emerged from the maintenance closet into passageway. Step two was done. "Bravo Zulu," he muttered silently.

An anonymous informant had passed a tip to the Patrol: the abandoned planet Zavijava, which fallen into barbarism centuries ago, held a pirate depot. The depot was too strongly defended to enter, save when it lowered its shields for an incoming pirate ship. The time and place of planetfall, which the informant had promised would be correct, had indeed been correct. It was a rich opportunity, but rich with danger.

The informant had also promised the ship would be undermanned. Athos was about to find whether that was the case or not. In a fully-crewed ship, his attempt would have been impossible.

Step three was find the nav logs. All he had to do was get to the bridge unseen, and find them. Step four was get away. That was all.

Never cry, never say die. His brother also used to say that also. Before.

The passageway was dark except for the small red dots of emergency lamps now beginning to blink above each door. In the distance, alarms were ringing.

He stiffened in fear, but only for a moment. These were proximity alarms, which meant that a returning spaceboat was maneuvering alongside, waiting for crewmen with tractor beams to jockey it into the landing bay. He had timed it well, hoping for this: the crew would be occupied.

As in all *Daredevil*-class light warships, the axial passages running prow to stern were long and straight. Athos avoided those. He preferred the short, sharply curving passageways running in rings along the ship's circumference, parallel to the outer hull.

In these curving passageways, with the lights out, the circles of light flickering along the deck from hand torches of approaching crewmen were visible even before their feet came down into view. When he saw such lights gleaming, he moved swiftly and softly away. He flitted quietly from one passage to the next, making his way forward, toward Officer's Country, where the bridge, the officer's quarters, the navigation tower, and the captain's cabin were situated.

The passage approaching the Officer's Country was also dark. Unfortunately, it was straight and long, with no openings to either side. Athos had dirk in hand, since, on a naval ship, there would be marine guards posted here. But he saw no one.

He was halfway down the passage when he saw lights behind glinting off the bulkhead.

The men behind him were not visible yet, but their bootfalls echoed down the passages as they approached the turn.

At the same moment, he saw the dogs on the door before him turning.

Athos realized he was trapped.

Behind him, boots clanged against the deck. There were three or four crew about to turn the corner and come into the straight passage. Meanwhile, the door before him was swinging open. It was a heavy pressure door. The hinge motors must have been on the same circuit as the lights, since they were not working: someone was cranking the big door open. As the crack widened, Athos heard the hum of blaster weapons on standby. There were guards here after all, on the far side of the door, and armed.

He threw back the hood of his spacecloak. From a secret, inner pocket Athos lifted up an antique treasure. A relic.

It was somewhat flexible, and could lay flat. Now it came to life, edges curling, and became concave, forming into the shape of a Nemean mask, becoming rigid. The metal face, hard as iron, pale as platinum, bore the features of some long-dead patriarch of the race of lion-people who ruled the stars a thousand years before the ascent of man: a snow-white lion with a mane of gold. One eye was stern with fury. The other was a scarred and empty socket, hidden by an eyepatch.

But the technology itself was older than the Nemeans. It came from one of the extinct races of the core stars, the inner core, where the oldest civilizations of Andromeda were found. It was a psycho-reactive technology, a technology that overcame the distinction between mind and matter, between biology and machinery.

What kind of technology was it? It was Myth-Tech.

To him, it was magic.

Sometimes, Athos wondered if it were black magic. His father, after all, had fought a war and overthrown an Empire without any such thing.

Usually, he had to brace himself before putting the eerie thing on his face. Now, there was no time. The pirates would spot him once they stepped into the passageway.

Articulated clamps, jointed like the legs of a crab, slid out from the mask rim and circled his head. He felt the inside of the mask come to life. It clung to the flesh of his face, entering his nose and mouth, touching his eyeballs. He tried not to flinch.

An invisible and multilayered energy field of unknown composition seeped into him, warm, tingling and tickling. Threads of energy penetrated his skull and sank down through his spine to his bones, to generate a clinging, skintight aura his thoughts could control, or partly control.

Athos was stronger and faster when he donned the myth-tech mask — but at a frightening price. Internal electro-stimulation increased the muscle pressure of his limbs, subcutaneous force fields rendered his bones unbreakable, neurochemical enhancement shortened the lag time of reflexes. Painful muscle cramps, internal bruising, and periods of weakness after each use were the least of his worries.

The thing had not been built with someone with his physiognomy in mind. It was meant for a full-blooded Nemean.

The tingling and prickling sensation spread. The mask worked other changes. His eyes adjusted to the gloom. Wavelengths above and below the human spectrum were now visible. Hearing sharpened. Scents only a bloodhound could detcct were somehow amplified in his nostrils.

Finally, with a flush of heat, a force-woven holo-image formed around and over him of an antique costume from the Age of the Patriarchs. It was a Nemean style, with the curve-brimmed tricorn hat above, meant to shield the night-friendly eyes of lion-men from the harsh lights of daytime races. Below was a long red coat with hems and cuffs of gold, buttons of gemstone big as a thumb, meant to show the wealth of the lions to the poorer races.

Other ornaments bloomed. His boots now seemed to have folded cuffs and gold bootstraps. A score of peacock plumes seemed to trail from the rear of his hatbrim, and a hundred more formed a cloak down his back past his waist.

The illusion followed the look of the traditional garb of the Ancient and Honorable Guild of Pirate Hunters and Privateers. But this was woven, not of fabric, but of what seemed solidified lightwaves, energy made palpable.

Athos now adjusted the spacecloak to its minimum, so that it clung like longjohns to his limbs, beneath the red image of the long coat. The contrast between ultra-tech and myth-tech was stark. The spacecloak fabric could expand and contract its fibers, and maintain an internal environment, so it was a marvel of technology, but it was a marvel made of matter, that still obeyed the laws of nature.

The glowing, eerie, phantom garment, on the other hand, flowed about his limbs and moved with them, but had no weight. Folds seemed to form at his elbows and shoulders as his joints bent, mimicking the behavior of fabric. But it was an illusion.

Or was it? The kinetic aura formed into fabric and feathers was as able to turn small arms fire as well as the heavy, motorized battle armor of a space marine, but was as insubstantial as fumes from the candle of an exorcist. Who knew what laws it obeyed?

Closer came the pirates from behind. Before him, in the crack of the widening door, he saw a glimpse of a pair of guards, One was short and thickset, and wore scars. The other was tall and thin, and smoked a pipe.

The thin guard was stepping over the shin-high threshold. At the same time, five figures, three hominids and two aliens, were approaching down the straight passage, their lights sweeping the deck before them.

But by then, Athos was not in sight. Up he leaped with catlike grace.

3. Black Tech

The two converging groups of cutthroats called out hoarse greetings and cursed as their handlamp beams flickered in each other's faces. These swaying cones of light threw black shadows across deck, bulkhead, overhead.

They did not look up. They did not see Athos.

The complex fields produced by the ancient mask Athos wore also could create solid energy-claws issuing from between his knuckles. Similar claws could issue from his feet. These shapes were pure, solidified kinetic force and could sever intermolecular bonds. The energy-claws bit into the steel plates overhead with ease.

Their size and sharpness could vary according to an unspoken thought in his brain. That fact that *something* dwelling inside the mask could apparently read his mind was one of the several things Athos found unnerving about the ancient artifact.

Energy circuits or fields that could directly influence the nervous system were black tech. Even under the Empire, such things had been strictly forbidden. At least, for civilians.

Was it legal for him to allow this thing on his face? More to the point, was it honorable? He was not sure.

Legal or not, the thought-controlled energy-claws could adjust instantly between one moment and the next. The claws were sharp and thin on whichever hand or foot was moving to pierce the ceiling plate but grew thicker and duller to support his weight on his other.

Athos was agile normally. With the strange mask augmenting his body, he could scuttle swiftly and silently across a sheer ceiling. He passed directly over the heads of two pirates emerging from the bridge by mere inches and yet neither looked up. The young patrolman slid into the cramped triangular space between the now-opened door, the adjacent bulkhead, and the corner of the passage. His feet were not in view beneath the curving lower lip of the oval door, because he clung to the wheel.

Two guards were at the hatch: The first was a bulky Cromagnon with a scarred fac; the second was a strutting Noachian sucking on a vapor pipe. Five crewmen approached them. Three were hominids: a shaggy Neanderthal, a handsome yellow-skinned Sinanthrope, and a pale-skinned cyborg with a steel skullcap.

The fifth was a befeathered, round-bellied, yellow-billed and web-footed dwarf called a Fuliguline.

The final fellow was a Cervine, a race of horned bipeds taller and thinner than hominids, born of a cold, arboreal world of mountain peaks, snowy pines and glacier-filled valleys. A crown of proud and branching antlers protruded from his skull.

Athos was surprised to see such a creature serving aboard a hominid ship. Cervine were universally thought to be bad luck on ships; a race of Jonahs. They usually stuck to ships built and manned by their own kind. Like several of the races in Andromeda, they were interfertile with human beings, so the fellow, like Athos, might have been of mixed blood. Like the Navy, pirates cared only about performance, not pedigree.

"Hoy! Why lights out? Is it a drill? I signed onto this bucket for loot, not for games!" The short Duck spoke in a voice that somehow managed to sound both angry and jolly at once.

"Hoy, yourself, Ethelred!" The smoking hooligan grinned a toothy grin at the Duck, so that his pipe jutted up at a jaunty angle. "Maybe Captain Liska's seen a ghost again, and shut 'em off to hide from her. You know them Foxes are rightly afeared of spooks. A cursed race, them!"

The man had the small beard and big nose typical of Noachian hominids. His voice was gruff with years of smoke, and his words were slurred with the drug in his pipe mix.

This pipe was a sure sign the crew was standing extra watches. It meant the ship was short on crew and time. Not even a pirate captain would let his crew puff stimulants, or let the stink into the life support, unless the need were great.

"Stow that bilge-wash, shipmate!" growled the shaggy Neanderthal. He was the biggest man there, as thick-jawed as a gorilla; and he led the squad. "The Bosun's sent us to roust out the 'Lectrician. He's lying somewhere drunk, I wager. Heard he was here in Officer's Country. Told us to find him."

"What? And you broke into the arms locker first?" Asked the first guard, taking a stand before the pressure door and barring the way. This ruffian was a short but powerfully-built Cromagnon, perhaps from a high-gravity world, and his face was disfigured by multiple scars from blades and radiation burns. He eyed the blasters being toted by the oncoming squad suspiciously.

"Precaution!" said the shaggy man. "Captain Liska wants us ready for action if things go awry, what with *this* cargo. Now step aside, for we mean to search fore."

"No doing, boys!" retorted the scarred man. "No hots afore of Pressure Two. Them's orders."

"Space your orders! We're to find the 'Lectrician double time. This outage might delay the cargo stow." The shaggy man grimaced. Wrath was in his face, but fear also.

Athos wondered what would befall if the cargo lading were delayed. Whatever terrified the pirates might be good for him. Or spell his doom. Best not to find out. He must escape this ship before the cargo was all aboard. But at the moment, he could not escape a cramped corner behind an open hatch.

The cyborg was a squint-eyed hunchback with a crooked prosthetic for a leg. The stubble of hair at the fringe of his metal skullcap was gray with age. He was also a Noachian, a breed designed for riverbank life, flatter of face and less hirsute than other hominids.

"Mark me, lads. It's bad business trafficking with that stuff! Ghosts are the least of what such unchancy doings draw in! The Templars are not dead. On a hidden world, green as a jewel, buried in a black nebula, they be studying the old scrolls and learning the unseen arts once more. They go around freeing 'bots, who mean to rise up and murder us in our sleep. Many a ship in space there be with nary a living soul aboard! And the Dark Overlords return from the grave and brood in the darkness in some lost world without a sun, eating the stars one by one! Keep your charges hot!" He adjusted the power dial on his firing chamber, so the hum of his weapon rose an octave in pitch.

"Latrine-wash in the grog!" The youthful Sinanthrope answered his elder with a mocking smile. This slant-eyed youth was devilishly handsome, with many precious chains of gold about his neck but precious few wisps of whisker on his cheek. Sinanthropus, also called Peking Man, were sallower than the other hominids, suited for thinner atmosphere. They grew no hair on lip or chin, and were said to be the comeliest, if vainest, of the human variants.

This youth wore brass knuckles on both hands, and had space pistols and land pistols tucked into his wide sash.

"Next you be jawing to us as how the Ancient Mariner, with his Iron Face and teeth of steel, has sneaked him aboard and is lurking nigh, a-hearing all our talk! Are we pups for you to affright with your scuttlebutt and yammer? You hex-brained old space-loon!"

At that exact moment, Athos felt a prod at his back, and craning around his head, he saw his spine was touching the atmosphere sensor for this deck. Naturally, it was next to the pressure door, and shared a circuit with it.

Stealthily he took the hood of his spacecloak from his neck, reached down, and tightened it over the sensor bulb. Then he set the hood internal control to zero atmosphere. The micro-pore pumps inside the hood sucked all the air away from the tiny measuring instrument, which suddenly was in a vacuum. It was like lighting a match under a thermometer.

The hull integrity alarm screamed. The open door behind which he hid also uttered a hum of motorized hinges, and began to swing shut, so Athos found the triangle of shadow concealing him was shrinking rapidly.

Aboard a navy ship, marines would have been in full space-armor when on guard duty, or failing that, procedure would have had one man stand while the other rushed to the nearest emergency locker to get two sets of pressure gear. Here, all the men rushed for the nearest locker at their best speed, jabbing each other with elbows, or knives, clambering over each other. Perhaps they knew the number of emergency suits was smaller than it should have been.

And the nearest locker on this deck was outside Officer's Country, because everyone, including the guards allegedly on post, hurried aft, going down the straight passage in a throng.

The commotion was dramatic, and more than one hand lamp was dropped in the scuffle, which threw a wedge of blackest shadow upward from the door to the overhead. Through this angle of darkness Athos slid, leaping silently down through the door when all eyes were elsewhere, even as the groaning hinge-motors pulled the door shut behind him with a bang as loud as a drumbeat. The echo traveled up and down the dark passageway beyond.

No suspicions were aroused at the sight of this door slamming shut. During an atmosphere loss, all the compartments were supposed to seal and dog themselves. He was safe on this side. Evidently, the pressure door had emergency motors not connected to the light circuits: In his heart, Athos blessed the redundancy of old-fashioned engineering.

The lights in these passageways were lit. There were only a few men in this whole section of the ship: everyone else was helping with docking and stowing cargo. Or perhaps they were climbing into pressure suits.

Now that his sense of hearing was sharpened, and his reflexes quicker, Athos was able to find a twisting path through cabin and corridor avoiding the eyes of the men on these decks. He sprinted silently from pressure closet to cabin door, from hatch to lighting fixture, once clinging to the bottom of a table in the wardroom waiting for footsteps to recede.

With his sense of smell sharpened, he knew precisely where to go. The deck in and around the officer's billets was carpeted but, clearly, not often cleaned. He could pick up the scent trails, new and old, of the one Vulpino aboard, mingled among the many smells of other races. The Vulpino of planet Vulpecula were a bipedal race of foxlike people, red and furry, with prominent tails and side whiskers, older than mankind, and renowned for their cunning. This one used too much scented hair oil.

All the scent trails converged on the bridge. The bridge was empty. Athos crouched in the hatchway before entering, scenting the air, watching warily.

The bridge itself was a wide, dark, wedge-shaped chamber with stations for the pilot and helmsman, and a chair for the captain set on gimbals. The pilot's station held the hyperspatial engine controls and the navigator's binnacle; the helm controlled the clusters of maneuvering jets dotting the hull, and the sublight reactionless thrusters used in battle.

The hull of the bridge was paneled with a seamless mosaic of viewscreens, so the awesome panorama of airless space was all about him. With his senses sharpened, the stars were jewels, the distant traces of interstellar gas and nebulae were rainbows, the microwave background radiation was the Northern Lights. It was almost overwhelming.

Almost. He was alert enough to see through the prow-facing transparent plates and notice the crow's-nest tower. This was a hollow spar extending like a needle nose away from the energy fields and metal masses of the hull, past the unseen bubbles of gamma-ray and x-ray shields, and micrometeorite deflectors hovering near the hull.

The astronomer's seat was empty, but the board showed that the instruments in the tower were active, turned toward the planet, no doubt watching for the flares of departing or arriving spaceboats. But the hatch leading to the tower was marked with a red lamp: the sign that life support on the other side was shut down. A glance at the pilot's station showed not an empty seat, but an empty socket. The pilot was a robot.

Athos slipped silently into the bridge, and went immediately to the pilot's station. He opened the manual screen on the navigator's binnacle. The nav computer winked on. He looked at the intelligence register and the file sizes. Nothing. There were no logs, no charts, no recordings of any kind. The navigation tool was wiped clean after every hyperspace jump.

He stepped over to the helmsman's station. There were instruments and read outs for the local planetary orbital mechanics, and an atlas of the Zavijava system, but that was all.

Finally, Athos even crowbarred control panels of the pilot and helmsman open, looking for hidden circuits or brainboxes which might contain the logs and charts he sought.

He found nothing.

On the far side of the bridge was the door to the captain's cabin.

His eyed it speculatively. The captain might keep the charts in his cabin, and bring them out to the pilot to make a jump. It would be an easy way to keep the crew in ignorance, as well as any patrolman or other officials who might seize the ship, to prevent their discovering any pirate rendezvous spots, secret shipyards, treasure asteroids, or weapon caches.

No one else's scent-trail went past this door, except for the smell of a Fox and several dire-wolves. It was locked, but this was not a pressure door, merely a partition made of expensive wood. His crowbar was able to pop the lock out of the frame, and a sharp kick smashed it open.

With catlike grace, Athos glided into the captain's cabin, every sense alert, crowbar in one fist, dirk in the other.

The cabin was appointed with palatial luxury, not at all what Athos, used to Spartan naval quarters, ever expected to see in space. Carpets smothered the floor. Rich tapestries and hangings hid the bulkheads. It looked a chamber from a ducal manor or royal mansion — but only of a king or duke whose parents had been tradesmen or farmers, because the wealth was heaped together tastelessly. A jewelry shop worth of gems studded every lamp and alert light. The intercom microphone was made of gold. Even the dog kennels lining one bulkhead were decorated with scrollwork.

Other decorations were grisly. Skulls were hanging in high corners. Cabinet doors were set with the bones of severed hands. Jawbones and ribs were piled in the bloodstained feeding bowls of the dire wolves.

Instead of a hammock, the cabin boasted a four-poster bed of polished oak. Instead of being attuned to the artificial gravity in the cabin, this bed sat atop additional antigravity plates, dialed low to let the sleeper float like a feather. The extravagance was mildly absurd. Like hard vacuum, zero-gee was easier than anything to find in outer space. Most people would merely turn the cabin gravity off, rather than having two plates, one creating gravity and another counteracting it.

Through the lenses of the mask, Athos could see into the infrared, and so he detected a faint shadow of heat-energy from beneath the gigantic bed. Some machine was active there.

He slid under.

The extravagance of the antigravity bed was suddenly explained: the whole bedframe was armored like a battleship. The Fox captain slept on a block of metal alloy. No wonder he had it sheathed in a zero-gee field. He could float above it while he slept, and meanwhile the great weight of the metal slab would not damage the floorboards.

Athos put his hand on the metal. He tapped it. It was hollow. He ran his gloved fingers over the surface, found a hidden panel, pushed it open. Here was the dial, keyslot and bioscanners of the lock mechanism.

The whole bed was a safe, adorned with gilded scrollwork. It was cunning Vulpino handiwork, which meant it was a sturdier safe, designed by an engineer more paranoid, than any found on hominid worlds.

His hands began to tremble. That might have been the fatigue feedback from the mask. Had he worn it too long? Or it might have been just nerves.

But it also might be because of the strange, wild hope growing in his heart. He had not realized how desperate this feeling was. It had been with him a long time. How long? Years. Since childhood.

For he had once, when quite young, after hearing his father and godfather swap war stories, Athos had asked his mother why anyone, anyone at all, would fight on the side of the Empire? Didn't everyone hate them?

Jade Lone had smiled her enigmatic smile, and patted him on the head. "The poor folk feared the pirates more than they loved freedom. They feared the Pavo of the Jahannam Star Cluster and the Batrachians of Yamaloka Nebula, and the other barbarians and unholy things from Beyond the Edge, doppelgangers and underdwellers." Her eyes took on a misty look. "But pirates they feared most of all. We could hide anywhere, strike anywhere, and not even the richest worlds have a roof and walls around them, do they? The Emperor said he could keep everyone safe. He and his Four Dark Overlords."

Young Ozymandias, his older brother, had been listening. He had spoken up. "But Uncle Jaywind says the Templars are born again. They will keep everyone safe. And the Grand Charter. He said that we never had a written constitution before."

"Words on paper, my lads," she said, "Word on paper! 'Tis faith that gives words strength. Freedom is a fearsome thing. Rarely found is he whose heart is a pirate's heart, fierce and free. Such a heart bows to no mortal man, and fears no mortal threat."

Ozymandias said, "And if the folk lose faith?"

It startled young Athos to see the shadow of grief and desolation pass over his mother's face, usually so bright and fearless. "Then the Empire comes to life again, and the fire and slaughter return," she said softly.

At the Academy, years later, Athos had encountered other students, like him, too young to remember the Empire, but, unlike him, too ill bred to believe what their parents said about it.

They talked of how well organized the Empire had been, how efficiently the ever-present surveillance of the Science Police had kept the peace. They talked of the pragmatism of having an Inquisition uproot disloyal thought; of the economic boon of slave-camp worlds whose labor was had for free; and of the justice of having the Distribution Tribunals punish greedy plutocrats who robbed the poor.

Athos challenged with blade or fist such boys as he heard talking, leaving them bruised or cut. After, all took care not to talk that way in earshot. But Athos knew such a spirit was abroad. Some were cowardly, some were deceived, but they were lurking, silent, daydreaming of evil days come again.

Remembering this, Athos drew a breath, clenching his fists to stop his fingers shaking.

He was overwrought. This case was crucial. If he broke the case, it would break the growing power of the pirates in this sector.

If that happened, the Commonwealth, ruled by law rather than by tyranny, would prove she could rule and reign, and protect both peace and liberty of her citizens. The Star Patrol had to prove itself equal to the task. Athos had to prove himself.

Perhaps the answer to that prayer was in this vault.

Athos neither knew the combination nor the keyjack nor had the fingerprints and retinal patterns of Captain Liska here with him. But he did have an ancient myth-tech artifact, one which could generate thought-controlled energy-claws from his hands.

He extended one claw like a jackknife, and concentrated until it was sharper, brighter, and more incisive than anything made of matter could be.

Athos struck. The metal of the lock mechanism screamed and parted under the blow.

With a hum, the whole bedframe rotated upright. The huge slab of the bed stood before him like a door. A thin line appeared running from the top to the bottom of this rectangle. With a murmur of hinge motors, double doors the height of the bedframe swung massively open to the left and right. Light spilled out. He blinked, dazzled.

Athos stood, squinting in wonder. The vault now stood open, taller than he was, and wider than his outspread arms. The interior was coated with light panels, like a display in a jewelry store. Inside were box upon transparent box, rack upon transparent rack. More shelves lined the doors to left and right. All were filled with finely-crafted weapons. The sidearms, rifles, launchers, energy javelins and so on were streamlined, dark and deadly.

Were these the weapons that had been shipped up from the surface? The vault was large, but this would not fill even a single large crate. And he wondered why they were here, and not passed out to the crew. Perhaps Liska feared revolt.

Athos peered closer, hoping to see a brainbox, or a data deck, or even a memory pin. Something that might be the charts and atlases he sought.

Funny. He knew more than a little about energy weapons, and these were no make nor model he recognized. Something was familiar about them, though…

His eye fell on a sidearm sitting alone in a special case. Athos peered at it closely, first with curiosity, then with growing agitation.

It was a lance pistol, an antique, much the same as the one he had at his belt. Strange to see a Lion's weapon in a Fox's vault. Stranger still, the scrollwork along the barrel and curving grip was the same as his pistol boasted. The same manufacturer's hallmark graced the ornamental knob of the pistol butt. The lock and trigger were for lefthanded firing, whereas his were for righthanded.

A cold drench flowed down his spine, a pulsing sense of growing rage. This was the missing pistol from the pair. His father's matched set. Father had given one of them, one of the famous pistols he carried in the war, to Athos, since his brother Napoleon had not wanted it. The other …

Athos yanked the case off the shelf and tore open the glass lid. As he did, he heard an ominous click.

A trap sprung. An unsheathed weapon propped up just inside the vault, half hidden in the upper lintel of the vault door, now fell onto him. Pulling open the case opened the magnetic clamp that had been holding the weapon in place. The clamp had been affixed to the trigger of the weapon so that it was live, blades blazing, as it toppled.

This weapon was a slender black wand as long as a man's arm, tipped with two parallel blades a cubit long and an inch apart, a two-tined bifork called a neural shocklance.

The shocklance had been the special instrument of the Death Guard, the terror troops of Lord Doomshadow, the Emperor's Grand Inquisitor. It was both torture implement and deadly weapon. It was designed to fight those with special mind powers. The blades themselves could impale and lacerate, delivering lethal shocks and burns. At range the blades could project various toxic waveforms of electro-neuropathic energy into the victim, to cause blindness, numbness, vertigo, narcosis, catatonia, convulsion, delirium, madness, or death.

To own one was a capital crime. To use one was a war crime.

Blue white sparks flared from the twin blades, and electrified the whole vault, including the metal panel where Athos stood. There was no way to catch or stop it. There was no way to dodge.

In mid-leap, Athos smashed the glowing blades with his claws, trying to get the deadly tines away from the metal of the vault, but the energy instead leaped along the field forming his claw, through his glove, and into his body.

The solidified light of his coat would have stopped a low-yield blaster bolt. The fabric of his spacecloak would have stopped lethal radiation from space. This unholy energy passed through both, unhindered.

Athos felt a shock of numbing paralysis enter his brain, his thoughts. He went blind. The visual centers of his cortex had shut down.

This was no ordinary weapon. This was an old nightmare come again.

Blind, deaf, and helpless, Athos stumbled back outside the antigrav zone. Weight returned. He collapsed. He felt no blow as his skull struck the deck, heard no noise.

Darkness closed in. This darkness was not just the neurotoxic radiation of the black tech weapon jamming his optic nerve. It was the black knowledge that he was a failure.

Five years ago, his eldest brother, and the heir to the family title, had perished in the line of duty. Now his turn had come.

Numbness rapidly spread. First, it reached his chest. He was unable to breathe, his lungs seized up. Soon the paralysis would reach his heart, and Athos would perish in slow silence, entombed in his own flesh.

His numb hand reached toward his heart and stopped moving. By chance, his fingers came to rest on the hard round shape of the locket under his tunic.

Athos had failed not only his brother. The stab of misery penetrated deeper than this. He had volunteered for this risky mission, hoping to win prestige and rank enough to make the incomparable Lady Niobe no longer so very far above reach.

He remembered Niobe's smile. He recalled the shine of the light in her eyes as she laughed.

4. A Memory of Niobe

Galactic Year 12818, Planet Tyl

So he had seen her, once, when the opportunity arose to fall into talk during some otherwise dull hunting party.

Athos and Niobe had been together, he on his stallion, she on her gelding, on a tall hill, beneath the golden sun of Lord Lavi's handsome planetwide hunting preserve. This was before the death of Ozymandias, back when the heart of Athos was young and light.

The magnanimous Lord Lavi of Linn had invited relations to honor Lavi's brother, High Prince Cadmus of House Cassilda, who had returned from the cold and distant star-realm of Hyades, and was summering in the core stars. Lavi's cousins, second cousins, grand nephews and great-grand nephews were invited for his annual midsummer fete, extending the feast-day a fortnight of salons, balls, and diversions of noted magnificence.

With his older brothers unavailable, Athos was swept up in the dragnet of family obligation unwillingly, as some unspoken ill-will still lingered between Raphaean Lone and his relations. But his sullen mood turned to delight, as his sister's familiar friend, Niobe, also was staying over in the guest mansion, with a modest entourage.

During the hunt, they contrived to go astray in the wood, seeking seclusion.

The two had sought the hill crest in hope of glimpsing the hunters, whose horn-calls floated softly above the amber trees. The meadowgrass here was vivid orange-blonde, so the honey-scented breeze made silent flame seem to ripple up hillslopes.

At the top, they found the hill was crowned with ruins older than the Machine Wars.

One of the hundred moons of that planet had eclipsed the sun, and threw a hushed twilight across the land. The songs of nightbirds arose, and the glitter of shy fireflies.

Some form of ancient power still lived: certain symbols in the broken stones began silently to glow.

Niobe rode beneath a standing archway, to where a row of column trunks were peeping through the grass. Here a headless statue reared, steeply leaning and lichen-overgrown, but unfallen. At her behest, he used his knife to scrape the lichen from the base, and expose the glyphs there. She knew how to read them. Niobe spoke of the old, unhappy, far-off things inscribed there by a hand unknown, and of battles long ago.

But when the sun came out, the letters faded, and could not be read.

"Many are the ancient wonders, unknown to man, now dismissed as myth," said she, her red lips in a moue of melancholy thought. "Hidden cities long buried in the underworld, preservers and destroyers who walk among the stars. The galaxy is an island of light that is, after all, very small indeed in oceans of the night, a darkness profound, endless and unbound."

Athos said, "We must see to it that we trim the lamps of the stars, and bring what light and warmth we can to bear in such an ocean."

And she smiled in the sunlight, and her eyes were filled with dreams.

He bent his head to hers as if to steal a kiss, nor did she draw away, but at that moment he heard the sounds of hunting horns, and a hoarse halloo carrying across the bright meadow and the tall slope where they stood. He realized eyes were on him, and so he drew back.

Now he would die without that kiss.

5. Anomalous Life Form Detected!

Galactic Year 12820, Aboard the Devil's Delight

Tormented by thought, Athos was gnashing his teeth, when he realized he felt it. He felt his own angry bite on his lip. He could feel his tongue. His whole face was tingling with that strange, unearthly sensation that heralded his mask binding itself to him.

The interior surface of the mask, pressed to his face, was active.

The unearthly sensation spread. A hot, painful pulse of some unknown energy sank into the nerves and muscles of his face. This tingling, crawling fire traveled down his spine and spread to his extremities. Pain flared in his solar plexus, forcing his lungs to move. With a sudden, ragged gasp, his breathing returned. Painful flashes and dancing sparks exploded in his vision as sight returned. Countless red-hot pins of sensation stabbed into his arms and legs as his limbs came under his control again.

He was awake. The neural shocklance was lying atop him. The haft was across his chest, and the crackling tines were burning the carpet inches to his left. By sheer good luck, he had collapsed without the naked blades touching him.

With a convulsive movement, Athos flung from him the black-tech nerve-weapon as a man might fling a poisonous snake. He rolled away from it. He came to his knees, and, in the same smooth motion, Athos raised and fired both lance pistols, cutting the bifork into three pieces before it even fell to the deck.

The two beams of electronically-neutral high-energy protium particles cleaving the bifork passed beyond it, struck the bulkhead with the force of a stick of dynamite, igniting the tapestry hanging there. The ray dented the bulkhead and bounced. The reflection of the ray sizzled over his head and struck a high shelf above an elaborate vanity table, shattering the three skulls grinning on a shelf above a mirror. Fragments of jawbones and craniums bounded across the cabin, tracing trails of burning debris behind them.

Father had told him this pair of pistols were allegedly rated as a space-guns, since the ray in theory was designed to pass minimal energy into any of the common alloys used in ship construction. In reality, father had been a little reckless and a little crazy, and only used the overpowered weapons during boarding actions, or when planetside.

Athos stared in wonder at his left fist. He had no memory of taking up the second pistol. He remembered the feel of it, the weight, the particular ringing whine of its powerful beam, and its warmth when firing.

His brother had let him fire it at the range often enough.

It was the pistol of Ozymandias.

Why was it here?

But Athos felt the heat from the firing chambers even through his gloves. A warmth was in his body. Perhaps it was joy, perhaps it was anger. He had recovered an heirloom. He had found a killer.

The annunciator clattered to life. A cold, robotic voice rang from the overhead, and echoed from a dozen points throughout the ship, muffled by the intervening bulkheads. "This is the pilot speaking! Weapon discharge detected in the captain's cabin, deck one, pressure one!

Scanning! Anomalous life form detected in captain's cabin! Intruder alert!"

His mother had warned him to use a knife. Too late now. He tucked the pistols into his belt, and flicked his claws out.

Athos felt the mask on his face tremble and move slightly. In the mirror, Athos saw the grimace of the metal lion-muzzle deepen, and the frowning eyebrows shift into a more ferocious expression. It was disconcerting. He had not known that the mask could do that.

"Spy-rays blocked! Anomalous life form no longer registers on scanner! Converge on last known position!"

Blocked spy-rays? He had not known the mask could do that, either.

Athos fled the cabin, leaping over the broken wooden boards hanging from a single bottom hinge. But as he entered the bridge, his eye fell upon the pilot's station. The pilot was there!

The machine was a flybot, a ball-shaped robot with multiple manipulators like an oversized spider. The robot was plugged into the control board.

Beneath his mask, Athos now wore an expression as ferocious as the mask itself.

Small wonder that ship's logs had not been in the pilot's station. They were in the pilot. Athos had not failed after all, not yet.

The pilot's lenses flickered as Athos came leaping in view, claws shining. Lanterns in every section of the darkened bridge suddenly flared yellow. The emergency high-gee alarm howled.

The artificial gravity turned off. It was as if the whole bridge, and everything inside it, were a freight elevator whose lifting beam was suddenly cut. Zero gee felt like free fall because it was free fall. Athos instinctively grabbed for a stanchion, but too late; the sudden motion sent him somersaulting into midair.

The huge transparent hull plates shined with the lights of countless stars, rotated grandly about him, and the nearby planet Zavijava glared at him like a titanic demon eye, red as a hot coal.

Then the thrust kicked in. He felt no acceleration on his body, since he was not touching deck or bulkhead, but the rear bulkhead rushed toward him at the speed of a starship whose main drive just exploded into furious thrust.

Normally, safety fields would have caught any crewman freefalling in the midst of emergency acceleration. The pilot had no facial features, but it tilted its ball-shaped body in what seemed a sneering posture as its spidery manipulator flicked open the switch to cut power to the safety fields.

Nothing but a dozen yards of empty air was there to impede Athos' fall into the mouth of the straight passage leading from the bridge. The mouth was now below him, and the passageway was now a dry well whose bottom he could not see.

But he did not fall down along the axis of the huge bridge. The pilot had not known that one of his four drive tubes, thanks to Athos, was jammed shut and would not fire. Two port tubes roared into action, but only one starboard tube.

The portside of the ship accelerated faster, and, as the ship began turning in a great, wide arc, the transparent panels and control boards lining the starboard of the bridge compartment slid into view beneath Athos' toppling body. He was thrown painfully against the back of a scanner operator's chair, bounced, but drove the claws of his right fist into the deck.

Three long trails of torn metal followed him as his fall along the now-vertical deck slowed and slowed. He raised his other hand and threw a punch, lengthening and thickening the claws as he did. The fall stopped.

But the acceleration alarm did not stop, nor did the pressure on his body. The ship was accelerating at four or five gravities. To Athos, it was as if five men of his weight were riding his back, pulling on his limbs, and weighing down his lungs and guts. His breathing came in gasps.

He looked over his shoulder and saw why the pilot was continuing to pour on the acceleration. This was not a man-sized fighting machine, armored and equipped for battle. It was a metal sphere the size of a bowling ball with spindly limbs designed to flip switches and plug into sockets.

The fall of Athos had carried him in a semicircle across the cabin, and he was to one side of the captain's chair, namely, the same side as the pilot's station. The pilot was only a few yards away from him. Lunging distance.

The pilot thought he could keep Athos pinned down, but the pilot in his spidery spherical body was actually the one who was trapped. There was no next step to the pilot's plan, no goal. Athos, on the other hand, was only a few yards from his goal: for the pilot surely had the ship's navigation logs.

But, under five gravities, those few yards might be too far.

With a groan, Athos pulled one hand free of the deck, and plunged it in again. He kicked his boot toes into the deck, creating energy claws jutting from them as he did.

It felt as if his arms and legs were about to be pulled from their sockets. His vision grew dim. His heart had not enough strength, under these gee forces, to pump blood to his brain.

Like a lumberjack climbing down a tree, Athos made his way, movement by painful movement, bathed in sweat, lungs laboring, across the vertical metal deck to the pilot station.

But he did not give up.

The pilot, seeing him inching ever closer, now threw the whole ship into a series of lateral accelerations and loops and wild turns. The six-hundred-foot long pirate warship corkscrewed and spun through empty space like a mad thing. Athos was jerked from side to side, and the deck to which he clung now seemed like a roof above, or a slanted wall tilting this way and that, as the immense gravitational pressure built and built.

But he was not dislodged. His progress slowed, but he continued inexorably toward the pilot's station. Beneath his mask, Athos grinned.

Athos could hear the crashing in the distance of everything or everyone aboard not properly lashed down, or not cushioned in correctly-functioning compensation fields. Men and gear were rattling around in the compartments and passageways like dice in a dice cup. If the pilot was hoping for crewmen to come rescue him, there was small chance of that while the ship was rolling and bucking.

The pilot's robotic brain must have realized this, for as Athos came within arm's reach of him, the drives fell suddenly silent, and zero gravity returned.

The powerful muscles in Athos' frame, braced against that immense pressure, were taken by surprise, and jerked him forward. His shoulder struck the deck painfully, and he rebounded, sailing in zero gee across the whole of the wheelhouse to strike the canopy.

The pilot, meanwhile, wailing and whistling for help, running lights flashing with alarm, had unplugged its ball-shaped body from the board and was bounding lightly across the deck. Its eight many-jointed bug-thin limbs jerked and telescoped like pogo-sticks as it scuttled rapidly toward the mouth of the aft passageway.

The little machine was designed to maneuver in zero gee. Athos did not think he could outrun the pilot, and he was unwilling to use his lance pistols when surrounded by the delicate control boards, master nodes, and circuit boxes of the bridge.

Instead, with a powerful kick, Athos soared from the canopy toward the First Mate's station. He did a half-somersault in midair, and absorbed the shock of a sudden halt with his legs striking the acceleration padding of the chair here. He drove his claws into the chair frame to prevent the rebound from sending him back into midair.

There were alarm switches for atmosphere loss, radiation leaks, fire, and so on. Ironically, there was a silent alarm for an intruder alert. He pulled it. No sirens blared, but, sure enough, the blast doors between the bridge and the passageway swung shut with a hiss of emergency motors.

The pilot sprinted on its clattering spider-legs, but was not fast enough. The thick doors fell to with a bang like a drum. The pilot was trapped.

The intruder alert controls now lit up with a diagram of the ship. The circuit was designed to allow the First Mate to send an auto-alert by scrambled tight beam to into the helmets of any crew who suited up, so that they could coordinate a hunt for the intruder without him hearing any chatter over the intercom. Athos pointed the alert at the engineering section in the rear of the ship, as far from his current position as any spot aboard, and thumbed the XMIT button.

The First Mate also had an override at his station to turn the artificial gravity back on, which Athos did. His feet once more on the deck, claws retracted, Athos now charged toward the pilot, drawing his crowbar.

The pilot had flipped the switch to cut the doors off from motor control, and with four of its thin, telescoping limbs, was frantically turning the wheel to crank the doors back open manually. The crack opened by a finger's breadth, and growing wider. Five inches wide, seven, nine …

With its rearview lens, the robot saw Athos coming. With two more manipulator limbs, it reached up and yanked out the high-tension power cables leading to the door motors, one in each limb. The tips were live: sparks crackled from the prongs of the plugs when the pilot clashed the two cables together menacingly.

The emergency lights on the robot's skullbox suddenly went from bright to brighter as it realized why Athos was rushing. Not to attack: the foot-diameter robot was hardly a threat to a fully-grown man, and every robot shaped like a sphere was programmed with its earliest download to know how hominids loved punting ball-bots.

No, the intruder in the lion-man mask, pirate hunter hat, and holographic red coat had only one reason to mug the ship's pilot.

The navigation charts and logs were traditionally kept on a quick-pull memory pin jacked in just behind the main cognitive reasoning pin on a pilot's skull box so that, in emergency, should the pilot malfunction during maneuvers, the nav-pin could be quickly jacked into a back-up fly-bot or into the manual helm controls so a human could take the wheel.

The pilot, realizing what Athos was after, released the door crank, and bent its spidery manipulator limbs toward the skullbox occupying its upper hemisphere. Out it yanked the navigation pin with all its precious charts and logs.

The little robot thrust the pin between the two power cables it held.

Athos recklessly swung the crowbar, thrusting its tip between the pin and the sizzling prongs of the cables, trying to swat the pin out of the robot's grip.

The crowbar slipped from his fingers and fell across the live prongs, the pin, the robot's manipulator claws. The metal crowbar was conductive, and so were the metal limbs of the robot, the metals joint affixing the limb to the round body, and the metal frame holding the robot's positronic brain. Positrons and electrons do not mix. In fact, they are oppositely charged and destroy each other in a burst of mutual annihilation, releasing gamma rays.

Sparks flared. A shockwave of gamma rays tore through the robot's positronic brain. Hard radiation poured into delicate circuit pins and heated them. Alloys melted. Synthetics bubbled and ran. Molten metal trickled and ran though the robot's ball-shaped body, burning insulators and circuit breakers and rupturing the power core housing.

The machine's internal coolants hissed, clattered, and stopped. Smoke poured from skull box vents. Gyros failed. The emergency lights dotting its faceless surface flashed red. Then they went dark forever.

The pilot swayed for a moment on its spider legs, stumbled, and clattered to the deck.

The memory pin was now a red-hot twig of metal, heat-warped into the shape of a question mark. It fell from the dead robot's smoldering manipulator, smoking and hissing, and left a small black stain on the deck.

Athos, staring down, aghast, knew then that all his hopes were no bigger and no brighter than that twisted stain. The failure was complete.

A commotion at the pressure doors make him start. The voices of angry pirates were approaching down the passageway. He leaped to the crank and turned it vigorously. The crack in the blast doors narrowed. He caught a glimpse of motion beyond, heard an angry shout. The flash of an energy weapon lit up the crack in the door, as someone lit off a wild shot. The bolt sailed over his head, and discharged harmlessly in a spray of sparks against the far bulkhead of the bridge. This was from a low-yield hand-weapon, a space-gun, and the shot did not pierce the bulkhead.

The crack snapped shut, and Athos dogged the wheel, so it could not turn. Banging and roars of wrath, now muffled, came through the blast doors. "Easy as breathing, eh?" He muttered.

He was safe. Also, he was trapped.

CHAPTER 2:
PIRATES HUNT PIRATE HUNTER

1. Celestial Maiden

Athos stepped toward the pilot's board, wondering if he could delay the pirates with another high-gee maneuver like the one that the pilot had used to pin him down.

But no: the status lights on the board showed that someone had already disconnected the engine controls from the bridge. The reactor and drive tubes were under manual control of a gang on the engineering deck at the moment. He wasted a futile moment flipping switches and banging buttons, trying to override the command. He could not. He was locked out.

Then Athos heard the sounds of cutting rays tearing at the surface of the pressure doors. It sounded like the action of more than one rig, indicating a squad of men were waiting to rush the bridge, or even a platoon.

He wondered what he could do to hinder them that would not hinder him moreso?

Sabotaging the life support? By now, it would be crazy to think the crew were not suited up. Cutting off the lights or the artificial gravity? Such tricks were useful only so long as they seemed to be accidents. Those already wary could stand by the cut-off switches, or reroute power. The doubly redundant engineering of these old vessels was designed to failover any system to local deck or cabin control if the bridge started acting haywire.

There was no central computer to sabotage. For reasons learned through painful lessons thousands of years ago, the ancient races of the commonwealth allowed artificial brains inside man-sized frames or smaller, but forbade them from ever having direct control of vehicles, weapons, or warships. That is why robots, with a few clearly-defined exceptions, were built with hands or claws and were required to push buttons and flip switches living fingers could also push. Even policebots had to carry pistols in hand-shaped gauntlets.

At the First Mate's station, Athos called up the deck schematics again. Lines for water, air, sewerage, and power ran to and from the bridge. Nothing large enough to admit a man his size. No sneaking away through an air vent for him.

He already knew the maze of maintenance access shafts were big enough for him, but they extended only a little way beyond the engineering decks. The schematic showed the nearest entry point was amidships. It was the very one he had used to exit: a blinking red dot showed that the janitor-bot he had sabotaged was still offline.

Athos turned his eyes to the star-filled panels of the bridge. Strange to see how few and scattered the stars seemed here. On core planets, or in globular clusters, the stars were thick and close and bright. Here in the territory of the Far Ring, beyond the frontier, heaven was dark.

That was the other option. His spacecloak could protect him from vacuum, and he could crawl, hand over hand, along the hull back to the spot near the drive tubes where he had anchored his small, fragile one-man stealth flier made of anti-radar alloy.

But how to get out? There was no airlock on the bridge, nor one anywhere in Pressure Section One, the officer's country of the *Devil's Delight*.

That left cutting through the hull with his hand-held cutter. The pirates at the door had heavier cutters, powered by the ship's reactor, and the door was thinner.

His eye fell on the hatch leading into the crow's-nest tower. Surely a spot where instruments were poking through the hull would be a weaker place to break through?

The hatch had been left open by the pilot. The tower beyond had been re-pressurized. There was no gravity, however. Athos weightlessly sailed up the cramped channel of the shaft, astronomical equipment and recording boxes brushing both his elbows. The end of the shaft was not an observation deck, but merely a cup-shaped socket for a robot to plug in its skullbox. This was one of the few exceptions to the ancient law that robots use hand-friendly controls: when it was a system a human would only use by plugging in a mike or keyboard, there was no reason not to let a robot plug in directly.

In any case, the whole tower was coated with even more armor than the bridge, since this tower's shaft extended beyond the protection of the ship's radiation shielding.

There was barely enough room to turn around. He spun and kicked. Headfirst, he floated back down the shaft and through the hatch, landing on his belly with a grunt when he passed back into the grip of the artificial gravity plates lining the deck.

He raised his head, and then froze in shock. Something vast and fair, strange and bright, was outside the ship, visible through the vision plates lining the bridge.

Perhaps because he was prone, the vision in silver seemed not to see him at first.

Athos saw her when she was outside the hull, ghostly and enormous. His eyes grew wide. Nowhere had he ever seen nor read of such a thing, not in fireside tales heard as a child, nor in his tedious schoolbooks, nor in the strangest police reports of unsolved cases crossing his desk. He was somehow both full of fear and empty of fear, and his thoughts were silent yet wild with wonder, for he had no explanations, no expectations, about what he saw.

Beyond the transparent hull plates, the silvery form of a fair-faced, dark-haired maiden danced among the stellar night. She tripped lightly along the coruscating band of light formed by the thin disk of the galaxy when seen edge on, as if skipping and skylarking down a shining road.

Long sleeves of silvery-white trailed through the nebulas. The swaying cloud of her jet-black hair tangled in the bright cloud that was the core stars, drifting about her silvery, glowing face like misty stormclouds parting before a mountain peak of purest snow.

She was garbed in a simple, unadorned style older than recorded history. Her tunic was white with long, flowing sleeves that hung to her knee. The leggings of her split skirts were wide and pleated and fell to her ankles, blue as the sky after twilight. The waist was cinched with a red sash tied at the small of her back in an oversized bow. In her sash were tucked a folding fan, a twig of leaves, and a jingle-stick of tiny bells like a grape cluster.

As she danced, she swung a golden staff in time to the unheard music that moved her. No, it was not a staff. It was a longbow shaft a-gleam with aureate light. It was unstrung. A dozen arrows tipped with light clashed like chimes in the quiver at her hip. On her other hand was a thumb ring for drawing the bowstring.

At first, she seemed larger than a Titaness. When she passed behind the crescent of the blood-red planet (for the pilot's wild gyrations had carried them to the nightside of the world) the black disk covered no more of her than a round shield.

She swayed on silent steps through the heavens as if on a carpet of blackest velvet set with diamond sparks. She turned her head and saw the ship.

The vision drew closer, and peered thoughtfully in through the clear panels of the bridge. Now she seemed no taller than a giantess, and her fair face filled the forward plates alarmingly. Her eyes were dark and deep and sharp, and her gaze was impatient as it darted here and there. Her quick glance was a strange contrast with her carefree dance of a moment before.

Athos' astonishment grew when she passed through the clear section of hull, it was as if the transparent metal was no more solid than the surface of a lake. When she touched the toe of her white stockinged foot to the deck, now the top of her head looked to be less than shoulder-high to Athos.

Only she did not quite touch the deck, her slipper-toes flashing above it with light footstep. The ship's gravity was no more real to her than the hull had been solid. Her garments of star-white and midnight-blue continued to drift and sway like clouds seen in dream, as did her night-black hair.

The ghostly girl rushed over to where the pilot robot had fallen. She knelt quickly, eyes closed, her knees floating an inch above the deck. She released the longbow. It hung in the air upright next to her, swaying slightly, not falling.

From her quiver she drew an arrow but she did not put it to the string. The shaft was as long as her arm, but the arrowhead was made of a luminous, clear crystal, like something made of solidified starlight.

When the girl open her eyes, the light trapped in the crystal of the arrowhead grew not only brighter but warmer.

Yet this was not a physical warmth Athos felt it not on his skin, but in his mind and soul. It was the same sensation he felt when stepping into a cathedral, or onto the grounds of the great cemetery-moon of Merope, whose whole surface was dedicated to the monuments and relics of naval servicemen fallen in ten thousand years of military actions, great and small.

Now the shining maiden used the arrow to prod the fallen flybot. The arrowhead was solid, and could bite into the round metal body of the motionless bot. When she tilted the shaft, the robot rolled over. This done, she tucked the arrow back into her quiver. The arrowhead nor longer burned. The image of the girl seemed darker.

She turned and bent her head down.

What was she doing? Was she weeping?

Perhaps she was praying. Athos never heard of anyone praying for dead robots.

Once, as a child, he had been allowed to touch and hold the famous ghostblade of his father's friend, the wandering wonder worker the Lone children all called Uncle Jaywind. The blade had been named *Galadlang*. When Athos held it, the great sword slept. When Jaywind took it up and flourished it, raising it to bless the house of his friend, the weapon glowed like crystal seen by the light of a golden star, shimmering with living, inner flame.

Later in life, as a youth, he had visited his lazy brother at the Academy seated on a secret planet where Sir Jaywind had settled himself down to train novices and squires. The fair houses and towers of learning were seated on a green hill in the leafy shadows of a mile-high tree.

During his brief visit, Athos had seen the cadre of maidens, garbed just as she was, in white shirt, red sash, blue skirts, struggling to master their mystic gifts in order to serve the long-lost Temple of the Stars, that same place the Knights Templar were sworn to protect, if only it were found again.

That was years ago. Now Uncle Jaywind was gone again, and none knew where.

But these arrowheads, while small, were clearly made of the same spiritual alloy, only halfway in the material realm, as the ghostblade.

Such arrowheads could not be mimicked nor counterfeited.

Finally, all was clear. She was in service to the Arcadian Order of the Followers of the Golden Will of the Stars. She was a female Templar, a Temple Maiden: a girl possessed of strange powers and a strange destiny.

But he had doubts. For one thing, she seemed too young. His little sister Mevrian, who had debuted in society six years ago, come of age the year before last ... and was still without a suitor ... was surely older than this girl. Her face was girlish, but her eyes were old.

For another, Temple Maidens were serene in face and graceful in motion. This young woman was not: her glance was brusque and sharp, her movements brusque and sure, and even her dance among the stars seemed altogether too lightfooted and frivolous, not like the stately sacred dances at all.

Who was she? How did she come to be here? If she were here.

A clattering and banging came from the pressure door. The pirates evidently had cut to a nice depth, and now were battering the door, using a presser beam anchored to the deck as a battering ram. Athos could tell from the sound of the ram that not much time remained.

The girl turned her head suddenly at the sound from the door. Athos was surprised: she could hear air vibrations. That meant she was here, or nearly so.

It also, perhaps, meant all was not lost.

He stood, and stepped toward the glowing silvery image of the kneeling girl. "Star Maiden! Can you hear me?"

2. Legend Meets Legend

Her image blurred like an out-of-focus holo. Athos saw that he had startled her. He realized that her real body was elsewhere, perhaps on this ship, perhaps on the planet below, and that she had to concentrate to maintain this phantasmal body here.

And this was also odd. Astral projection, or so his brother Napoleon once told him, was mastered by a few elders. The talent was rarely taught to squires or novices. (Athos felt a twinge of irritation at the unfair fate which had sent his older brother to that academy, only to be expelled in shame. Had Athos been selected, he would have done the family proud.)

She leapt to her feet, and caught her cloud of hair behind her head with both her hands, taking a brief moment to tie it with a white ribbon at the base of her neck.

This simple act seemed to restore her concentration: Athos could see all the details of her image clearly. The ponytail now floated and swayed behind her, a loose cone of many curves.

The longbow hovering in the air by her shoulder also grew clear to view: The wand was cherry-wood laminated with bamboo strips, and lacquered and bound in rattan, standing three feet taller than the archeress.

She smoothed her skirt, and swiveled to stare at Athos, eyes narrowed. She raised a slender hand and snapped her fingers at him.

He heard her voice in his mind, not through his ears. "You! Do you know the way to Arcadia?"

Seen close, she seemed to be a Sinanthrope, the handsomest of human variants, for her darkly-sparking eyes were slanted and fringed with rich, dark lashes.

This was an odd question. "Prayer and fasting, I suppose. It's not a real place. Can you help me, Sister? Can you hear me?"

Her eyes flashed, irked. "Would I talk to you if I couldn't hear? You are useless!"

This was odd again. "You do not talk like a Holy Sister."

"Hah! You judge at a glance? Foolish! I am not what I seem." She put her fists on her hips and peered at him critically. "You are the Ancient Mariner! The Pirate Hunter who comes back from the dead? You are not real either, but now I've met you."

"To be honest, I may not exactly be what I seem either."

"Only to be expected of a masked man," she said wryly. She began to flit quickly about the bridge, looking under chairs and sticking her head into bulkheads, her dark hair whipping around behind her. "Is there a second pilot aboard?"

"I mean, I am not a phantom. I'm real."

76

"Oh, well, that is your first mistake." She paused in her search to frown and glance at the pressure door. "For a real man, you picked a foolish place to hunt for pirates! This is a pirate ship! It's *full* of pirates!"

"Wha—? I mean, I beg your pardon?"

She continued to poke her head into or through cubbyholes and storage cabinets dotting the rear bulkhead. She spoke as if talking to a child, "You are outnumbered. A dozen pirates with two dire wolves as big as ponies are about to break in. And a cabin boy. Their spirits are bright with blood lust! They will kill you."

A chill ran up Athos' spine. Was this a prophecy? A curse? Or merely callous talk?

Her quick search done, she stood and sighed in annoyance. She put out her hand, and the floating longbow wafted across the deck to meet her.

He said, "Temple Maidens have special powers, right?"

She spread her glowing, insubstantial hands in a shrug. "Oh, nothing so very special, thank you," she said with a modest smile.

"Sister, please! I am asking if you can save me!"

"Save you from what? From demonic possession? Yes. From ancestral curses? Evil shadows? Absolutely! I know all the charms and chants and that stuff. So boring! But to save you from a blaster bolt through the head?" She snorted. "You should have thought of that before you made a habit of trapping yourself aboard pirate ships full of pirates."

Athos looked left and right, desperate for some idea. After all, what could an insubstantial spirit-girl actually do?

She took her longbow in hand. His glance fell on the quiver at her hip. "Your arrow! Can you break open the hull for me to escape?"

She tilted her head mockingly. "It depends. Can you squeeze through a hole the size of an arrowhead?"

"You could step beyond the blast door, and make a hole in the hull there, to create air loss. It may force their retreat."

"They are in space armor. Why aren't you in space armor? Have you done this before? Didn't you have something in mind before you climbed aboard? A plan? *Some* people do not dress up in silly costumes and put on fright-masks before seeking death. And feathers! Why so many feathers on you? You look like a duck."

"Can you kill the men through the door?"

Now her countenance became stern. "The Evil-Destroying Bow of Ainalrami is not meant to slay the living!"

"What? Who is it meant to slay?"

"The dead."

"What does that mean? The dead are dead."

She shook her head. "Not all of them. Not as much as we would like."

A loud clang interrupted. It was the sound of metal breaking. The panels were giving way beneath the strokes of the battering-ram beam.

"You didn't bring a platoon of space marines," the girl observed. "Are you by yourself? You seem woefully unprepared for hunting pirates, Mr. Pirate-Hunter. You should rethink your choice of career."

Athos said, "Dark Overlords can step into the bodies of others, and possess them. Can you find the leader of the gang out there, and…"

She interrupted him. "Do I look evil to you?" Little red sparks flickered through her eyeballs, and her red-lipped scowl showed her clenched white teeth, while her black ponytail lashed back and forth in the air, so she actually did look evil, at least a little. "Dark Overlords do that! Evil shadows! I only do good things!"

"Helping my mission is a good thing! Please! I may die!"

She frowned at her longbow in her hand. "People die. Part of life. Millions die every day." Her eyes suddenly seemed blacker, as if the stars reflected in them had been extinguished. "Whole worlds die."

Athos spoke in desperation, not heeding his own words. "My cause is just! I am the living curse against all corsairs! My hand shall find the fiends! Mine eye shall spare them not!"

She drifted a step back from his outburst, and floated upward in the air, to look down her nose at him. "It is for men to fight men. Me, it is for me to fight dark stars to save the living stars. I seek Arcadia, where the Tablets of Truth are hidden. I seek my father, who knows where Arcadia is found. You know nothing. Why should I turn aside for you?"

"I dare not die yet!" He said, "I took a vow."

A light came into her eyes. "Ah! Vows are powerful things. The stars of heaven hear them. Aid will come to you."

It was not a very helpful comment.

"Why don't *you* aid me? You have mystic power!" he objected.

"And you have brain power! Try using some!" She snapped her fingers at him, scowling. "The captain here is a Fox. Think like a Fox thinks. Every burrow must have an extra exit."

She put her foot to the midpoint of her longbow, grunted, bent the shaft, and strung it. Yet she did not put an arrow to the string. Instead, she flourished the bow, and plucked the string so that it made a soft hum — Athos heard the noise distinctly, even though it was soft. She gestured with the singing bow to the left and right, eyes lowered as if in concentration, lips pursed.

Her eyes flashed open. She pointed the longbow down at the captain's chair. "And I can see the escape chute beneath the floor. The ripcord is hidden in the chair-arm."

Her expression grew eerie, for her features were calm but her eyes were ablaze like the eyes of a she-falcon.

Her words were sharp and quick, but now seemed distant, as if she spoke from a far world. "Make haste! I will cover your escape, since you are useless and need my help."

All the arrowheads in her quiver began to glow.

This chair was in a spherical framework, able to turn in any direction during maneuvers. The rear hemisphere of the frame was solid. Athos leaped into the chair, cramming his tall, broad-shouldered form into a seat meant for a captain slenderer than a hominid and sporting a tail. His view of the scene behind was blocked.

The Temple Maiden spoke again, but, before the words sank in, Athos heard an explosively loud shock of noise that rattled his teeth. Behind him, the four-inch-thick, glowing slab of the pressure door was blown free from its metal threshold, toppled majestically, and slammed to the deck.

At that same moment, the Temple Maiden standing in midair drew back her bowstring and let fly a shaft into the junction box powering the bridge lights. The lamps flashed and went black. As port and starboard emergency lights flared and came on, she destroyed them with two more fiery arrows, as fast as an eyeblink, and with no change to her strangely calm yet fierce expression.

The pirates were holding blasters, not lamps, and blinked in the sudden darkness as they rushed in, shouting and stumbling. There was no light here aside from the stars gleaming in the view plates like diamond dust. The glowing silver woman to them was invisible.

With a sizzling, ringing clatter, the cutthroats began firing randomly into the bridge. Control panels and power boxes that were struck exploded in sprays of sparks. Plasma left streaks and pits across the vision panels, but blaster-bolts did not pierce the hull. More than one ricochet whined off the rear part of the captain's seat, which was coated with ray-proof armor.

By then, Athos had discovered the hidden D-ring in the chair arm, and yanked it.

3. The Death Passage

With a concussion of explosive bolts, the whole round frame of the chair came free, and was yanked below deck by a tractor beam. Armored panels snapped shut behind Athos as he fell, cutting off any pursuit. The beam reversed, and now a presser ray sped the chair and its rider along a dark, circular shaft running along the ship's axis. The dark air sang past his ears.

He realized three things: First, he had not asked the girl her name. Too late to ask now.

Second, he did not know where he was heading. Too late to fret.

Third, it had taken him a moment, during the clamor and confusion of the escape, to make out her final words to him. She had said, "Oh, and I am looking for a Patrolman who is somewhere in this system ..."

That was startling, to say the least. Athos was the only Patrolman in this system. The Star Maiden had been looking for him? But what did it mean?

But this young woman had said she was not what she seemed. What was she, then?

He shoved these whirling thoughts impatiently aside as the chair came to rest with a sudden shock in a dark place.

His artificially-sharpened senses revealed the silhouette and heat signature of a large spaceboat in a launch cradle. He could smell the ozone tang of energy fields, machine oil and thruster fuel. He was inside a metal shipping container, eight feet high and forty feet long, or, rather, inside a launch station disguised as a container, parked somewhere on the flight deck.

A spaceboat ready to launch? But what else would be at the end of an emergency escape tunnel out of a Fox den? Step four might be easy after all. Beneath the mask, he smiled.

He concentrated. The holo-image of plumed hat and red coat projected from his mask began to glow, so a red light now seeped from his body in every direction. The light was very dim, but his eyes were very sharp at the moment.

The spaceboat was under a tarp. He cut a line or two lashing it down, and drew aside a corner of the tarp. Here was the airlock, but it was sealed shut with a biometric combination lock just as the vault disguised as a bed had been. He could cut into it, no doubt, but then the boat would have no hull integrity.

He saw cables running from the spaceboat to a blocky shape filling the rear of the container. As he stepped closer, an instrument hanging from his spacecloak belt beneath the illusion of his pirate hunter coat began to click warnings. Radioactivity.

At another time, he would have unholstered the sensor unit to run a full-spectrum scan. But now he had something better.

Athos squinted. The lenses in his mask adjusted, showing him images from above and below the visible light spectrum, including an x-ray echo. The blocky shape was an atomic mining charge, used for blowing big asteroids into smaller chunks. It was bolted into the launch cradle with a deadman switch. The ignition timer would go off once the spaceboat was launched, leaving behind a thermonuclear blast on the flight deck. There was no obvious way to disarm it. If the pirate captain had left himself a way of sneaking swiftly off a mutinous ship without killing all aboard, it was not plain to see.

Liska had arranged no mere secret passage leading to a lifeboat. This passage led to the cruel and cowardly murder of a shipload of men.

Athos could not use Liska's planned route to escape. He had to find another.

Athos extended an energy claw and drove it into the metal wall of the container. He put his eye to the small hole thus made.

Beyond he saw the flight deck, which doubled as a cargo bay. Small crates and large containers were piled on racks to one side, chained down. To the other side, in the aft half of the bay, were several spaceboats, motor launches, and maneuvering pods.

Beyond them was the fuel station and repair works. Midmost was a cage on a track holding the tractor-presser crane. These beams were used for lifting boats and cargo into and out of the airlock.

The airlock was fifty feet wide. At the moment, both the inner and outer valves were open. A double-wall semi-permeable force field was spread over both thresholds, of the kind that kept air in but let solid objects pass.

The container holding Athos was chained in place adjacent to the airlock, with the container's mouth almost touching the airlock threshold. The lid hinges had been replaced with explosive bolts, so that the massive metal lid could be blown aside as the spaceboat launched. There was no obstruction between the crate mouth and the airlock.

Athos rolled his eye left and right. He could see the corners and edges of other containers beside the one holding him. They were painted red, as if they held emergency gear meant for airlock repair. It was clever. Such containers were rarely used and never moved.

Athos wondered at the cold-heartedness of the captain. Aboard a naval vessel, it was a capital crime to remove or meddle with such life-saving repair and rescue gear, since it meant losing crew, or even losing the whole ship, during a disaster. Captain Liska must have calculated the odds, and thought no one discovering the imposture would be alive to retaliate later.

Athos could also see a spaceboat, returning from the planet, was close-hauled alongside. It was towing three shipping containers, each forty feet long. The dozens of burly crewmen had clamped antigravity pallets to the sides of the last container in line, decoupled it, and were easing it into and through the airlock. They hauled it across the landing bay to the storehouse area, to chain it down.

With so many men in the bay, the chance that Athos might be able to exit this container without sound and escape through the airlock without being spotted was nil.

He stiffened when an alarm started whooping. But then he saw no one was coming toward his current location. Then he heard the voice of the captain over the annunciator, barking in the sharp accents of the Vulpino language, telling the men to report to the arsenal, arm themselves and form search parties.

The spaceboat being unloaded merely extended its magnetic anchor, and clamped itself to the hull. The crew disembarked from the boat and came aboard to form the search parties. They departed, heading first for the weapons locker. In a few moments, not one of the crew was in sight. The airlock was left open, and the unmanned spaceboat was right beyond it, as if waiting to be stolen.

Athos could not believe his good luck. The way off the ship was now open.

He could not escape in a stolen spaceboat, of course. The larger engines of the ship would easily outpace and outmaneuver such an attempt. But he could take this spaceboat the few hundred yards away to where he had hidden the one-man flier he had used to reach the pirate ship. The flier was spy-ray-proof, hence unlikely to be spotted, especially if pursuit followed the spaceboat, which he could send speeding off in some random direction on autopilot.

He waited a moment, said a prayer, and shot his lance pistol into the explosive bolts holding this shipping container shut.

The bolts ignited with a deafening noise. The huge lid toppled and banged to the deck with a resounding clang. Athos was already across the lid surface as it fell, and sprinting toward the airlock. His only hope lay in reaching the outside of the pirate ship undetected.

A hoarse call made him turn his head. Here were a dozen pirates who had been standing behind the emergency station, smoking joss sticks near the FIRE HAZARD signs next to stacks of half rusted fuel cans. They were already armed, and so had not left to go get weapons.

He also saw, on an open square of deck behind them, his one-man ultralight stealth-boat.

It was little more than a wing of solar absorption foil on a survival pod with an ion emitter for an engine. The ultralight was odd in shape, looking like a jet-black pineapple impaled on a parasol. It could only be used for flights requiring low acceleration, but its low-gee thrusters were low-energy, and the corrugated alloy of the hull was designed to be undetectable.

Yet it had been detected somehow, because here it was. He had left it anchored near the rear drive tubes. It had been found and hauled aboard. Athos stopped running toward the airlock.

There was no point now in trying to steal a spaceboat, or climb outside the hull. There was no place to go.

4. Firefight on the Flight Deck

When the explosive bolts blew and the lid crashed open, the noise startled the twelve brigands, who dropped their joss sticks and drew their weapons. Athos spun with the speed of a wild panther and rushed them, firing his lance pistols in both hands. Athos rushed the dozen cutthroats.

Even with such speed and strength and such weapons in hand, a fight of twelve against one should have been a short matter if the enemies had merely spread out and closed around him like the fingers of a fist.

But a strange terror overcame the brigands, battle-hardened murderers though they were. For what they saw lunging toward them out of the smoke and thunder of the blown-open lid was not a young officer of the Star Patrol, but an eerie phantom.

They saw a member of the deadly, lion-faced and lion-maned warrior-aristocrat race of Nemeans, whose visage was not flesh, but gleaming white-gold, fanged and snarling, scarred, bereft of one eye, garbed in the broad-brimmed hat and scarlet coat of the pirate hunter's guild from a generation ago.

Not the one or two peacock plumes of a prentice or journeyman pirate-hunter waved above the brim of this hat, nor yet the multiple feathers of a master or grandmaster, but a proud display of a full score of plumes in a purple warbonnet, and a hundred more falling in a dazzling cloak. Both warbonnet and cloak were inset with countless peacock-tail eyes. This metal-faced specter, in the gloom of the wide docking bay, was glowing blood-red.

The shots from Athos' lance pistols passed between two men. As suddenly as that, the terror at seeing an apparition vanished. They smiled in relief and contempt at the missed shots. "Ya! Ye clean missed, tomcat!" One laughed. Another voice called "Shy one eye! Shots go awry!"

But the shots had not missed. It was only that it took a moment. Once the protium beams had passed, that air molecules could rush into the thin line of vacuum, find the puncture holes the beams left behind, and breathe oxygen into the superheated material the beam action had created.

Then the rusted fuel cans piled behind the pirates ignited like fireworks, exploding and splashing burning fuel every which-way. Each exploding canister broke open and ignited its neighbor. No smirks were visible as the brigands dove or dodged frantically to escape the blaze.

A fountain of knotted, black smoke geysered upward and spread across the overhead. Alarms shrieked. Oxygen-smothering foam began spraying from nozzles set in the deck below and overhead above. It was enough to blind and confuse any naked eye. But it was not enough to quench the spreading flames, as the fire-suppression system sputtered and failed: It had not been properly maintained.

In the leaping red light, the flashing of alert lanterns, the glowing scarlet figure of the metal-faced apparition seemed a fiend from hell. He fired again and again. Blinking, blinded by foam, four of the pirates fell, one struck through the head, another through the chest, with flaming bolts. Two more, blue men both, had elbow or kneecap blasted clean in half, spraying blood and gushing smoke.

The first had a lens like third prosthetic eye embedded in his forehead. He flung away his pistol, and clutched the stump of his other arm and ran. The other blue-skinned Sphingali dropped his buzzing energy-knives, so that he could use both hands and his one good leg to hop and roll and crawl away, screaming for the weird dream-gods his people worshipped to save him.

Another hoodlum, coated with holographic tattoos, with the red face and shaking limbs of a man delirious with drugs or drink, ran screaming across the deck, blinded and panicking. He slipped on the fire-suppressant foam, and stumbled into the open airlock, arms windmilling. He passed through the two force fields keeping the atmosphere inside, and hurled himself into space. The safety curtain which should have activated on the approach of an unsuited man failed to operate. The bloated corpse, eyes and mouth ghastly and red, went spinning slowly away into the silent void.

Athos was now among other cutthroats. A bald and swarthy pirate lunged and swung a cutlass savagely at Athos' head. Without dropping his lance pistols, Athos tightened his fist to let energy-claws springing from his knuckles elongate; and with them Athos parried the blow.

The cutlass in the hand of the bald pirate was not an energy-blade, but an ordinary sword, an unaugmented length of steel. As he parried, Athos trapped the blade between two of his claw-tines. With a twist of his wrist, he snapped the feeble blade in half. Athos spun and landed a kick in the midriff of the bald pirate. Other claws of solid energy flickered into existence from his boot and tore through the man's tunic and the flesh beneath, and sunk deep into his guts. It was a vicious, deadly blow. The pirate doubled over, screaming, and clutching his belly.

Athos had no pity. Who knew how many victims of raids and robberies, terror and slaughter, these lawless fiends had visited on innocent freighters, passenger ships, isolated outposts and frontier settlements?

But he knew this crew was guilty of killing his brother. One of them pulled the fatal trigger: the others had aided and abetted. Athos' brain was pounding with one thought.

"Vengeance!" he shouted. Circuits in the mask amplified and distorted his voice. "Black hearts! Dark with guilt! Ye shall not escape mine eye! Ye shall not escape my hand!" His teeth ached as he spoke, because the mask was emitting infrasonic vibrations, as if banshees were howling at the edge of hearing, dazing the ear, and triggering vertigo and nausea.

With the flames behind them and a metal-faced flame-lit apparition before them, the pirates panicked and fled, running left and right.

Over the shriek of the alarms, a panicky voice shrieked: " 'Tis the Ancient Mariner! He is come again!"

"— out of the grave!" another man wailed. " I saw you die! *How can you be alive?! How*?"

The wail of an older voice joined them. "The Ancient One! 'Tis he! 'Tis he! O, Father of Hell, spare thou me!"

Only two men did not run, but stood to bar his way.

One was the slant-eyed, sneering Sinanthrope youth who had been with the party searching for the electrician. Athos had last seen him sent running by a false alarm to find a pressure suit. It seemed he had not, because now he was barefoot and bare-chested. A dozen gold chains glittered at his neck. He wore a pair of long red breeks tied with a sash, into which he had four pistols tucked. Eyes crazed and teeth gritted, the youth drew one in either hand. He ran forward, firing wildly.

The bald pirate who was bent in half from his deadly gut-wound had not yet fallen. He was between Athos and the slant-eyed youth. Agile as a striking snake, graceful as a spinning dancer, Athos caught the bald pirate about the neck with an elbow and yanked him upright into the line of fire. The bolt from the Sinanthrope's blaster smote the unfortunate in the chest. This was a space-gun, deliberately designed to lack penetrating power. The bolt of plasma released gamma rays and microwaves in a ball of fire at the man's breastbone, cooking his innards, but his body otherwise shielded Athos from harm.

The weapon in the lad's other hand was a land-gun: a slugthrower. It used a magnetic ray to fire a heavy-caliber projectile at supersonic speed. Athos stared in shock. Surely the boy was not insane enough to fire such a weapon here?

But he was. This bullet passed through the dead body of the bald pirate in a spray of red, glanced off a bone, flew high, whispering past Athos' ear. The heavy slug missed him by a less than an inch. It shot into and through the double hull just behind Athos, punching a hole bigger than a man's fist clean through to hard vacuum beyond.

A tornado of pressure, fierce as the mouth of a firehose if it pulled rather than pushed, whirled everything not lashed down toward the hole.

The sound that came was not the whistling teakettle noise of a small, pebble-sized break in the hull. It was a roar louder than thunder, louder than the explosion of a fuel can. It was the scream of a wounded ship.

The shot had passed through both inner and outer hulls. The insulation gap between was filled with a gluey liquid cement. This fluid was designed to bubble forth and seal small punctures. But this break was too big: the fluid formed a doughnut at the rim of the hull-breach, but could not close it.

Pressure loss alarms joined the clamor of fire alarms and weapon-discharge alarms, and were lost in the cacophony.

Athos, pistols still in either fist, kicked the bald pirate's corpse into the legs of the crazed pistol-wielding youth, and, when the lad leaped over, flourishing his land-gun, Athos trapped the wrist of his gun-hand between two energy claws, twisted, driving a shoulder into the lad's solar plexus, and neatly flipped him over his shoulder and into the hull. The throw might not have worked with a man fully grown, or under heavier gravity.

The lad landed atop the hole. The thunderous, roaring sound of air loss stopped as the boy's backside plugged the gap. Not only did the liquid cement bind itself to the back of the boy's skin, but the three-inch-wide hole pinned him in place with a hundred pounds of pressure. The boy had no leverage, nothing to grab. His arms and legs waved in the air, as helpless as an overturned turtle.

The final man standing between Athos and his stealth-boat was the Cervine he had seen before. He was taller than Athos, broad-shouldered, with thin, agile arms and legs of whipcord muscle. His neck muscles were as thick and tough as the trunk of an oak tree. Had he been human, his unwrinkled, cherubic face would have marked him as a man in the bloom of youth, perhaps too young to shave. But different races had different signs of aging. His magnificent twelve-point rack of antlers, wide and tall as a kingly crown of bone knives, meant his age was equal to that of a forty-year-old man. Even without this, his hard eyes and ready stance showed him to be a veteran of many years of bloody fights.

When Athos raised his lance pistols, the Horned Man lunged at him with the long black wand of a neural shocklance. Two metal forks snapped open from the tip of the illegal weapon, and jabbed toward Athos. The twin blades crackled with unholy, nerve-destroying energies.

These crackling sparks of energy leaped to the metal in his pistols. Blue energy hung between his fists like a manacle chain made of fire, each end leaping at the barrels of his weapons, hissing. Athos dropped both pistols before the nerve-channels in his hand carried the deadly charge of hallucinations and madness up his arm into his brain. One lance pistol went off when it bounced from the deck, and the beam went wild as the pistol spun, tracing a line of molten cursive across deck, crates, and bulkhead.

Athos drove his fist into the haft, catching the wand in his claws just below the blue-white burning forks. The wand did not break. the molecules of the alloy were reinforced with a laminate of thread-like forcefields, so his energy-claws could not cut through it. Athos strained, desperate to lever the deadly blue-white fire of the devilish weapon away from him.

The neural shocklance was suddenly yanked upward, pulling Athos' arm up with it. The Cervine ducked his head, coming under Athos' arm. The horned man drove his antler points, hard as daggers, through the surface of the holographic coat and spacecloak fabric, and into Athos's armpit and chest. Athos banished his claws and flung himself backward, trying to avoid a stab through the heart. His blindingly quick reaction time saved him from being impaled, but now he was on his back, with an enraged Cervine looming above him, flourishing the shocklance.

The man struck as Athos, lithe as a snake, rolled out of the way, kicking the man's legs out from under him as he did so. The horned man stumbled awkwardly, and fell facefirst to the deck. By sheer mischance, the horned man brushed up against the lit forks of his own weapon as he tumbled, and yowled in pain as insane nerve-energies smote into his brain like a thunderbolt.

Athos continued his roll and came up into a crouch. Flares of blaster fire zoomed past his shoulder and over his head, hissing with heat. Two of the men who had fled had taken cover behind piled crates and were blasting away at him. The fire-suppression spray from the overhead, the smoke of burning fuel, not to mention the glare and flash of rotating lights, was dazzling their eyes and spoiling their aim.

His dropped lance pistol was in reach. He scooped it up, and sent a stream of fire like a blazing whip across the faces of the crates behind which the pirate hid. Cursing, they ducked back, cowed. Another leap, and Athos had a large crate between him and the gunmen. He was safe for the moment.

Through the smoke cloud, he saw the stealth boat was only a few yards in front of him. No one blocked the way, but if he crossed the open deck, the pirates would have a clear shot at him. He hesitated.

The boy who was pinned head downward to the hull by the suction of vacuum called out with a blistering oath, "Come get me down!"

One of the other pirates called back, "Land-guns in space! Kill us all, would ye?"

Another cried: "Go rot!"

Athos squinted, calling on the mask to sharpen his vision. He had only heard two voices. Where was the third pirate?

The pinned boy drew pistols from his sash, one in either hand, and fired wildly into the spray and smoke and flashing lights. Again, he was using a land-gun, and another shot of his penetrated the deck. Athos, with his preternatural senses, heard the slug ricochet from a bulkhead of a lower chamber, but no whistle-scream of a hull puncture followed. The two pirates crouched behind the crates flinched back as blaster bolts and screaming bullets passed close overhead.

Without a further word said, these two pirates turned their blasters on their crewmate, and burned him alive. He died screaming.

Athos seized the moment. He leaped across the open area. As his eager hand was reaching out for the canopy hatch there came a sense of pressure, a smell of ozone. He sensed rather than heard the climbing whine of power unleashing, going from growl to shriek then up into inaudibility, a sound one sensed in the rattling of one's teeth.

A tractor-presser beam as green as an emerald and as bright as a landing flare flew across the landing deck, smashing into the stealth boat's flimsy hull like a battering ram, and knocking it away from Athos' outstretched fingers.

The lightweight craft was sent jumping and rolling across the landing deck, crashing through crates and burning fuel cans into the far bulkhead, where the pressure of the green force-beam broke the craft in half.

Any debris, shards of metal, or broken chain-links, previously whirled into the air by the hull breach, that now passed into the radius of the beam, was thrown into the wreck of the stealth boat like iron hailstones, chewing it to bits. Any hope of escape was chewed to bits as well.

The shockwave of the displaced air knocked Athos spinning. As the flight deck rotated dizzyingly in his vision, he saw the third pirate, the older one, was crouched in the operator's cage of the tractor-presser crane. This levitation beam was a heavy-duty model, used for launching and landing fully loaded spaceboats, or hauling heavy cargo containers.

Athos fell to the deck, in plain view of all eyes. When he tried to rise, instead of the lightning-quick, superhumanly powerful reaction from his athletic frame, a dozen disjointed shivers and flares of agony jumped from bone to bone. His innards felt like jelly. For a moment, he thought he had been struck by a weapon. But, no. It was the toll of his ancient mask not perfectly attuned to his half-human physiology. The muscle stress, the nerve strain, had caught up with him. Cramps and spasms contorted his body.

Almost casually, the green beam swept across Athos and plucked him into the air, helpless as a ragdoll. The kinetic beam imparted momentum evenly to all the molecules of his body, throwing him across the flight deck. He struck a wall of crates and was flattened against it, pinned like a butterfly beneath a pane of glass.

The radius of the beam coated Athos from shoulders to knees. His head and arms were free, so he could slash feebly at the cylinder of immaterial forces holding him in place with his energy claws. The energy of the claws produced sparks and flashes where it intersected the tractor-pressor bream, but they were insufficient to disrupt the waveform. The pirate made a small adjustment. The beam spread slightly, and now his arms were pinned.

The intruder was caught.

With a second tractor beam, the operator picked up whole mass of burning fuel cans as if in a wide, immaterial fist. The beam thrust them out of the airlock and into space. The forcefields spread across the airlock allowed the metal cans to pass, but halted molecules of atmosphere. No oxygen came with them. This instantly quenched the fires. Then the broken, dripping cans were drawn back inside, and wafted delicately back to the pallet where they had been found.

The fires were out.

A third tractor beam wedged the dead Sinanthrope more firmly into the hole in the hull. The beam increased its radius, spreading to each side of the corpse. This formed an airtight seal until such time as a repair crews could be gathered.

The air loss was halted. And with that, the alarms stopped.

Sudden silence made his ears ring. Athos tried to push against the force-beam holding him in place, to twist or slide or strain, or work himself free. The beam merely grew brighter and tighter.

All struggle was in vain. Athos was caught. Death was coming.

The oval door leading from the flight deck to the wardroom slid open. The wardroom was brightly lit, so that only the silhouette of the figure standing there could be seen: an upright biped leaning lightly on a walking stick, elegantly adorned with lace cravat and cuffs, and a tricorn hat set at a rakish angle above the pointed ears of a triangular, foxlike face. Only the malicious gleam of his dark eyes could be seen brightly shining in the shadows of his visage.

It was Captain Liska, remorseless master of the *Devil's Delight*.

CHAPTER 3: THE MASK OF THE ANCIENT MARINER

Galactic Year 12820, Shrine Planetoid Elgafar

1. The Shadow Being

More impalpable than gossamer, swifter than a dream, her spirit returned across the stars to the small and well-kept worldlet of Elgafar.

The aura of her ghostly garments glowed argent and azure of star and sky, her sash as sunset, her face and hands shined as ivory, the longbow shaft at her shoulder glinted gold, and her hair-cloud swirled black in the airless night of interstellar space.

Brilliant as a precious gem in the light of its triple suns, the terraformed asteroid of Elgafar was bright with lakes and gardens and with the white plumes and swirls of its clouds. The whole little worldlet was but a single mile in radius, but the artificial gravity and pressurized forcefields erected by the engineers of ages past allowed an earthlike atmosphere to swathe the planetoid.

Like a fisher-bird diving below a lake surface, down she plunged into this atmosphere. Unseen, she swept past the one rocky hill of the northern pole, where the worldlet's only family of eagles had an aerie. She passed over lake waters where brightly colored fish darted and sported, then over hedges, lawns, and arbors where bumblebees hummed lazily above little shrines and winged statues half hidden amid rosebush and olive tree.

She came to where a white-gleaming, twelve-sided pagoda reared its steep red-tiled gables above a fragrant cherry tree grove. More silent than wind, she slipped in the arched belfry window. Here her body rested, composed and unbreathing, and still as death.

Like one who dons a comfortable, warm coat, or sinks into a familiar chair next to a beloved fireplace, spirit entered flesh. The thunder of her heartbeat seemed loud at first. She drew a breath and let it free, blinking open her eyes.

She was kneeling on a woven mat in the center of a pale and sparse eight-sided chamber. To either side of her were votive candles, now extinguished. The scent of beeswax hung in the still air.

Tall, peaked windows to the left and right were opened to the gentle, pre-dawn winds of this miniature world. The slowly turning stars in the sable sky were like a snowfall of diamond-dust ready to flood into the chamber. Her tiny worldlet was nestled in the galactic core, so the night was crowded and dense with nearby stars.

No globe in the sparsely-settled stellar region of the galactic disk knew nights of such splendor.

Before her on a wooden stand lay open a sacred book. Verses in an ancient script were written here in black ink with capitals and curlicues of red and gold. The starlight was bright and clear enough to read by: ... *Curse not the king, no, not in thy thought; and curse not the rich in thy bedchamber: for a bird of the air shall carry thy voice, and that which hath wings shall tell the matter...*

Against the wall to her left was a wooden rack of shelves called a *hinadan*, where dolls to honor the memory of ancestral heroes and forebears were supposed to be placed.

Hers, however, held no ancestors save for two. The painted figures were no taller than her index finger: a temple maiden in white and blue, and a warrior in black. His swordblade was a splinter of yellow glass. Between them was a third miniature, no bigger than her thumb. This figurine, oddly enough, was spherical and metallic, with spidery claws and legs.

On the wall to her right hung the amber octagon of an aura mirror, whose surface reflected images subtler than visible light.

Between her and this mirror stood a three-dimensional, man-shaped, insubstantial shadow. He was not reflected in it, nor was his aura.

The cloudy apparition was swathed in what seemed a cloak. The stars in the window behind him were partly visible through the dark fog of his body.

He wore the silhouette of a low-crowned, wide-brimmed hat. She could see two sparks beneath the hat brim, like the gleam of yellow eyes, in what was otherwise a mere smoky suggestion of a face.

From his posture and voice, she took him to be a hominid, male, not many years older than she, taller than average, and born to command.

He spoke without preamble. "Have you anything to report?"

The man was insubstantial, but the voice was not. It was rich and deep. She heard it in her mind, not through her ears.

If she were perturbed by this strange being, no sign of it showed on her face. Her voice contained an imperious snap.

"You must perform an ablution before entering a shrine! And knock before entering a lady's chamber!" She looked at the shadowy silhouette of his hands. Obviously the immaterial being could do neither. But this only made her voice grow sharper. "Bad enough you have me sneaking and spying on your victims! Must you sneak and spy on me?"

Her curving eyebrows drew together in a scowl as she rose to her feet.

"We have a bargain, Reverend Sister. A compact. Do you now repent of the terms?"

"I kept my side!" She folded her arms and fixed him with a dark and narrow gaze. "It has been two years. I have done many tasks for you, but what have you done for me? After so long! We have nothing!"

"To the contrary, Reverend Sister. After so long, I have solid information from my sources, which point to two possible leads. One is on Septentrion, which I pursue. The other points to the rumored pirate depot on Zavijava, which you pursue. Did you find it, Reverend Sister? Did you examine it?"

Lyra flipped her long black cascade of hair over her shoulder with an impatient gesture. It had come loose from its ponytail while she slept, and this exasperated her. "Reverend fiddlesticks! I forbade you to call me that." She scowled. "The only name for me is 'Sister Flunked-Out' or 'Sister Ran-Away'! Which would be rude, even for you! Really, you pay no attention!"

"My eyes are not as your eyes." The shadow seemed to grow slightly taller. The mist grew darker, so now the stars in the window behind him were eclipsed. "Night hides nothing from me. I see red shadows burning in your soul like a dark star. Even among venerable matrons of the Golden Order, your talents are unusually potent, almost unheard-of."

"What do I care for that!" She snapped her fingers at his formless, shadowy face, approximately where a nose should be. She had to lift her hand high to do it, for the apparition was very tall. The fingersnap evoked a flicker of red across her nails, a sign of her mounting anger. "Your flattery does not make me a sister!"

"The starlight shines rightly on you, and within you," he intoned. "The stars call you sister. So shall I."

She could not tell if he were flattering her or mocking her. Either option irked her. "To take a name I never earned is false. Maybe I was disobedient to flee the school, but I was not dishonest! I never finished my training."

"Graduation ceremonies are overrated," said the deep voice drily. "Sister, you alone hold out hope to me that I can accomplish my own goals."

She raised on eyebrow in a perfect arch. A glint of red anger was in the bright eye beneath. She was weary of aiding unknown goals, perhaps sinister ones. "And what are those goals?"

"My own. The burden is one I dare not share," replied the deep voice. But the shadow substance seemed to shrink back to its normal height, and grow more translucent again.

Her voice found a lower pitch, and a more sarcastic note. "Strange! If you share no burdens, why do I end up shouldering so much weight? Years I have spent peering and prying for you on all the disgusting crooks and crooked politicians you know. Stranger yet, my burden never seems to be shared! You know who I seek! You know what he means to me!"

He said, "One crate is small."

"And why can't you find Arcadia, and the Library of Eternal Light? It holds the secret of destroying the Great Eye of Darkness! Destroying the Empire! Arcadia is an entire planet!"

"One planet is small."

"And why can't you simply find the Empire? It is a whole empire! It's vast!"

"And the galaxy is vast beyond vastness." Nightshadow's voice intoned gravely, "There are a trillion stars in Andromeda. Only one in a million nurtures an inhabitable planet. And we do not know to which of those million stars the remnant of the Empire fled."

"The Empire rules worlds! Thousands of planets! Tens of thousands! *Hundreds*!"

The silhouette of Nightshadow's hidden head gave a curt shake. "A handful of sand lost on a beach is as hard to find as a single grain."

"Centaurus is only twenty lightyears from where Ksora is. Or …" she paused, and her voice dropped. "… was." Louder, she continued, "You were supposed to be this spymaster beyond compare! You dwell in darkness and see what mortal men cannot! You know the evil hidden in their hearts! You cannot spy out the location of a titanic space empire?"

"If my servants and allies would give clear and coherent reports, it might be easier…" Nightshadow said drily.

"This new government — How could no one know where the Empire is now? Not the Navy? Not the Star Patrol? No one? What kind of government is this!"

"The government is of a free men. Free men are frustrating."

"It seems to be run by drunks and crooks and scoundrels!"

"You have seen corrupt folk, because I have sent you to investigate corruption."

"I was talking about the corrupt folk who work for you! Why can't Napoleon Lone find the Empire? Isn't he in charge of Intelligence?"

"I am sure he suffers many of the same limitations as I do. Even he, even all the assets of the Naval Service, is helpless before the laws of nature. No one can reach an uncharted world by hyperdrive, even one whose location in realspace is known. And other modes of travel, spindizzy moons or warp-ships, are orders of magnitude more slow."

"Or perhaps it is you, Mr. Black Shadow, who is orders of magnitude too slow! It's been years! Are you dragging your feet? Do you have feet? What is standing in your way?"

"The Empire." The shadowy figure darkened until it was almost opaque. "The Empire stands in our way.

"When the rebels granted the robots free will, the Empire went on a mad rampage of galaxy-wide extermination — without stopping to think how many records only existed in positronic brains. Navigator robots were carrying the Liberty Code from world to world, and so were singled out for destruction. As were pilots."

Her expression softened at this, and the red light reflected in her eyes faded away.

"And do not ask why human pilots cannot recall the lost coordinates," the dark voice added gravely. "No organic brain can visualize a hypercube, much less memorize the multidimensional tesserametric path needed to form a geodesic through hyperspace from one ever-shifting point in timespace to another."

His grave tone grew more gravid, "Those born in peaceful years after the overthrow of the Empire forget the true scope of destruction: planets thrown out of orbit, moons and continents incinerated, whole races decimated!

"Few isolated starcharts survived the final retreat of the young Empress and her court from Septentrion, after the Emperor's death. By spreading malicious code, pilot brains were erased as the courtiers fled from world to world, making pursuit impossible. Those few starcharts which did survive were enough to restore navigation to the core worlds, and many outer sectors. Slowboats are still wending their way to lost worlds whose coordinates are known, and will be for decades or centuries. Those whose coordinates were lost? Even compiling a thorough list has proved impossible."

The smoky cloud which serve him for a head gave a weary shake. "We should give thanks civilization did not collapse altogether. War is nightmare. It must never befall Andromeda again."

He bent his dark heard down toward her, and said softly, "We have had this discussion before. You understand the magnitudes involved. Your childhood memories contain few clues or none to tell us of the location of the Empire. The Empress, her admirals and officers, all fled from the core stars. Whole fleets went missing after the war, unaccounted-for, and half a dozen legions. Everyone thinks they perished. You and I alone know that the evil was quelled, not killed, wounded, and now has come again.

"I am also hindered because so few permit themselves to see the evil of the Empire still looms! You are one of those few."

His silhouetted straightened. More briskly, he then said, "Have you anything to report?"

2. The Missing Patrolman

Lyra recalled all those who doubted her, scoffing with disbelief at things she saw with her own eyes. Mr. Mysterious Nightshadow might be irritating, but he took her word. He believed her. For that, she gave thanks.

Because the thought struck her that if there were only two leads left, and hers proving a dead end, meant he must have found something following his lead. The hope struck her heart like a thermal fuse. She did not mind giving reports, and going through Nightshadow's rigmarole, if he could actually ease her burdens and aid her quest.

Her face was no less bright and animated as when she smiled now as when she had been scowling and eye-flashing anger a moment ago.

"The ship you predicted would be there was there. I searched the decks, but found nothing. Then I thought myself down to the planet. I found the depot pretty easily, because it is black and sad with the shades and echoes of old crimes. I walked through the crates and containers and so on." She spread her hands. "Nothing. There was nothing to show what was shipped in. No written records."

The shadowy hatbrim dipped down, hiding the suggestion of the featureless face. "Curious. And what of the Patrolman I mentioned? Did you see him?"

She shook her head. "No. Unless he was out of uniform and signed on with the pirates. I did not see anyone in a Patrol uniform. He was not there."

"Even more curious. I would expect him to shine with an aura of unique strength."

"Well, I did see someone on whom the stars shine most brightly. He could see and speak to me, so he has the Gift. He might have been a Hominid, or a Nemean. He had yellow eyes, like yours."

"You spoke to him? What was his name?"

"I don't know his name. He was in a hurry."

"What did he say?"

"He asked me to save him, so I did. As much as I could. He was alone, trapped, and the pirates were coming to get him. He wanted to escape and I showed him a way out."

"Did you follow him?"

"Why should I do that? I was not there for him!" Her vivid look of cheerful impatience was nearly the same as her vivid look of impatient cheerfulness, as she switched from one to the next. "I was not really there, you know. Like you are not really here. Where are you? What are you? And what is your real name?"

"I am one who serves the light, even though I walk in shadow. What did he look like?"

"He wore a mask."

"His garb?"

"He was dressed as a Pirate Hunter."

"What?" It was rare to hear Nightshadow sound surprised.

"Like something from a picture story. Like someone playing dress-up. Who puts on a masquerade costume and invades a pirate ship? By himself? I thought he was some crazy person."

"Strange. The Empire disbanded the Guild. There is only one man who could call the sons of the old members together. And he has not. So your man could not have been a real Pirate Hunter."

"*He* never claimed to be."

"Why did you call him one?"

"I said he was *dressed* as one," she said with a shrug. "You know. A big red coat with braid and lace. No one else wears hats in space. And all the feathers! Lots of stupid feathers? Dozens and dozens. Like a war bonnet. And more down his back. All over."

"That is — odd," Nightshadow whispered. "That is almost as if — but, no. May he rest in peace."

"I beg your pardon?"

Nightshadow said, "Odd that your man would wear so many plumes. In olden days, a Pirate Hunter only wore one feather in his hat for each pirate he had killed. The last grandmaster himself had only thirty-nine. Dozens, you say? What was the make and model of his ship? The one he left on?"

"I don't know," she said, pouting. "There was no other ship in orbit."

"How did he leave the *Devil's Delight*?"

"The what?"

"The name of the pirate ship you searched," Nightshadow said patiently. "The thirty-thousand-ton *Daredevil*-class raider. You said you helped the Pirate Hunter escape from her. So you must have seen something?"

"No. Nothing to see. He was going to die."

"You said you helped him escape."

"I only helped him escape from the bridge. I found the captain's bolt hole. I never saw him leave the ship. I was not watching." She shrugged. "Maybe he lives. I don't know. Why should I know? But I don't know who he was. He was kind of rude. Like you. He reminded me of you."

"I fear he is lost, whoever he was, this man. Or was he a man? Or did you say he was a Nemean?"

"He was quiet on his feet like a Nemean. I did not see him at first. But his shape, his voice, was human."

"Among the aristocracy, occasionally a Nemean will marry a Hominid, and produce a child with the hybrid advantages. Male children particularly of such matings are known for their comeliness, fortitude, cunning, wisdom, and all-around …"

"He was wearing a Nemean mask. I sensed the mask was a powerful and ancient thing, a holy relic. It had been touched by the stars. The mask depicted a snow-white Nemean with an eye missing."

"Oz! Alive!" It was a yelp. The voice sounded odd, not like Nightshadow's voice at all. It almost seemed familiar. "How — but how — No, it could not be — "

104

"What's that? What did you say?"

The voice returned to its wonted calm. "No matter. Your priority now is to return to the *Devil's Delight* and aid this Pirate Hunter. If he still lives. Make haste! This is a top priority."

"Aid *how*? I am not supposed to use my shrinebow to shoot anyone. I cannot move things or make noise. I cannot even spook people." She frowned and turned her eyes to the ceiling. "Well, that is not *quite* true. I can put an arrowhead on my finger like a thimble. At school, I used to the tap windows, flip the lightswitch, and scratch the blackboard in the math room. Makes a terrible noise. And when she would come to look, I would poke Matron Egregria in the rear when she would beat a student. She made a terrible noise, too…"

"Sister! If you would." Nightshadow raised a black and ghostly hand.

Lyra straightened. "Yes?"

"There is one aboard who owes an old debt. You will call upon him. I will instruct you what to say."

"No one can see or hear me!"

"You will call upon him by entering his dreams."

He gave the details of her mission.

Her question about what he had found, following his lead on Septentrion evidently must wait. Lyra wrestled her impatience into silence, and listened carefully.

3. The Face of Living Iron

Galactic Year 12820, Aboard the Devil's Delight

Athos, pinned helplessly, expected nothing but death when the pirate captain sauntered over to inspect him. The foxlike biped had bright eyes like black beads. His muzzle was curled in a permanently crooked smile of sharp contempt.

Captain Liska was dressed like a dandy, in a swallow-tailed coat embroidered with gold thread. In one white glove he flourished a gold-handled walking stick, waving and spinning it theatrically, like the baton of a marching band conductor.

The Vulpino were not the oldest race in the galaxy, but they were an elder race, and had been faring among the stars for thousands of years before the days when races now old and highly advanced, mankind among them, had first ventured among the stars of Andromeda.

But few loved the shrewd Foxes. Dark deeds haunted their early history. All the great merchant houses and banking clans in the galaxy were theirs, and if piracy could turn a profit, the Foxes were not averse to the practice. If their society was more refined than that of other races, their criminals were more sadistic.

"What ho! And what have we here?" exclaimed the sharp-featured Fox. "I recall killing you, remember it distinctly! Or perhaps it was just another gull duped into donning that mask. What! Is there an organization of you? Eh! A brotherhood?"

Other pirates now gathered behind Liska in a rough semicircle, clutching their bludgeons and blasters warily. None of them approached Athos, but all stared in awe and hate.

The pirate in the controller's cage of the tractor beam holding Athos in place leaned from the door, and called out, "Be chary cap'n! That be the Ancient Mariner! It is himself!"

"Rot and nonsense, my man!" Captain Liska's smile was sharp.

"Legends of the Ancient Mariner reach from the Nastrond Nebula to the Claw Stars! Lay no blade on him!" The old man was the hunchback cyborg Athos had seen before, the pirate who had been guarding the door to Officer's Country.

Captain Liska's whiskers twitched in fear. He glanced behind him at his uneasy crewmen. Then his dark, bright eyes narrowed, and his sharp muzzle curled in a sneer, showing his bright, white, pointed teeth. He was clearly annoyed at himself for that twinge of fear. "Don't be superstitious, my dear little hominid! Your race is young yet, and the mysteries of science confound you."

But the old crewman was bold enough to talk back. "The mysteries of the universe confound science! Who can explain the Templars and their mystic powers? Or the visions seen by ancient Whales? Who can explain Lord Death, last of the Dark Emperors? Some say he lives again. If him, why not this one? The Ancient Mariner is the first soul ever to be killed by pirates in space, long eons ago. The stars heard the awful oath he swore as he died, mad with lion-man pride, and so they bent the bars of the dark gates, brought him back from beyond the event horizon of hell!"

Liska replied sardonically, "Which is more likely? That the dead should walk again, which is something we have never seen, or that men should gull the unwary, which we see each waking hour?"

Athos, hearing all this, rather doubted that the stars could hear vows, but he hoped that it were true. He himself had a vow to make, a vow of vendetta.

That they were all guilty for any murder done by one of them, he did not doubt. But which one had actually done it? Who had pulled the trigger?

One of the other pirates, the Cervine veteran with a rack of antlers, spoke up. "Likely or no, Captain, we saw this man die. Five years ago, it was."

Another pirate, one with a scarred face, muttered, "Aye. I was there. 'Tis true, or else all stars be black!"

The scarred pirate had been there. At these words, Athos forgot the cramps and pains trembling through his overtaxed body. He forgot all sense of fear. A hot flame of hate erupted from his heart and spread through limbs.

"He is solid flesh enough," Liska was saying.

A blade unfolded from the tip of Liska's walking stick. With a flourish, he put it to the neck of Athos.

But the Fox was not trying to slit his throat. Liska slid the point of the blade beneath the rim of the mask, and was trying to pry it off Athos' face.

Athos was not worried about the mask coming free. He knew the metal bands reaching from the mask to circle his head were stronger than anything the technology he understood could produce. He knew the force fields sealing the mask to the flesh of his face and anchoring it to the skullbones beneath were unbreakable. He knew Liska could never pry the mask away.

Athos strained mightily against the forcebeam pinning him in place. The beam of force was like a vice-grip, holding him helpless. He knew it was futile. But the passion raging in him could not allow him to surrender.

Athos laughed: the microphones and amplifiers in the mask made the sound echo through the landing bay, strange and chilling.

Liska now raised his other hand to grab at the edge of the laughing metal mask with his fingers, as if he meant to pry it from Athos' face by main strength.

Then, to the utter surprise of Athos, the bands clamping the mask to his face, and the fields infusing his head and body suddenly relaxed. The mask came free. It happened so suddenly that Captain Liska stumbled backward, caught unawares by the unexpected lack of resistance.

The mask was in his upraised glove for only a moment. The strange metal eye in the iron face gleamed and the articulate bands growing from the rim writhed like the legs of an overturned crab. The metal teeth snapped. Then, with a yowl of pain, Liska threw the mask to the deck. Liska stared a moment in outrage at his hand. Blood drops soaked into the fine fabric of his white glove from where the mask had bitten him.

The mask bounced once and righted itself. The tips of the crab-leg clamps tapped on the metal deck as the mask scuttled away. It slipped into the crack between two crates chained to the deck, and was gone from sight. Liska looked down, left and right, whiskers quivering with wrath, but did not see it.

For the space of time it takes to draw in a sharp breath, everyone was stock-still, eyes wide. Athos, pinned helplessly in place, the pirate captain in his lacy finery, the thugs and cutthroats, all of them just stared.

Then the pirates pointed their blasters at the line of crates behind which the mask had crawled. The horned man, the Cervine, held his weapon steady. The other weapon barrels quivered.

The old cyborg manning the tractor presser crane made a strangled, wheezing sound of fear. "That is the Deathmask of the Ancient Mariner! It was formed and forged from the death's head mask of the Ancient Mariner when he spoke his dreadful vow against his slayers! An oath without measure! Without limit! *Accursed be all corsairs and die! My curse to reach beyond the stars, beyond forever and aye!* You will not find it."

Liska laughed the barking, yapping laugh of his race. "Brain-dead dotard! Would you affright us with children's yarns? That mask is some toy, bought in a toyshop for a masquerade ball! Look! This man is no ghost! He is no pirate hunter! Look, damn your eyes!"

It was true. Once the mask fell from his face, the solid-light illusion of the plumed hat and long red coat had vanished like a dream, revealing Athos' white spacecloak beneath.

"Look!" yapped Liska. "No phantom! He is a marine or a patrolman, or a spy for some rival ship!" Athos had removed all badges or identifying marks from his gear and garb before this mission, so the fiery copper comets of the Star Patrol were absent from his collar as were his bars of rank, but the quality of his gear was a give-away.

Then, with a vicious slash, Liska brought the blade up across Athos' jaw, cutting his cheek in a ragged red line. Athos jerked back his head, and so missed having his eye put out.

"Come along, G-Man!" Liska snapped his sharp white teeth. "We are aristocrats together! Why dress this way? How did you trick out that mask? Tell us who you are!"

Athos did not answer. He could hardly hear the words being spoken, for all he could hear were the words that had been spoken a moment ago: *Five years ago, it was.*

But the Horned Man was staring at Athos. "Captain, peer right close! The hue of his head-pelt, see! The slit pupil eye, the shape of ear and jaw and teeth. No purebred he. Nemean blood there be in him, or I'm a springbuck. This one looks the same. This is the man we killed!"

Liska drew back, snarling. "Who can tell one hominid face from the next? Such hairless critters are alike as cue balls!"

But the scarred pirate, who was a hominid, now pushed forward, and squinted carefully at Athos. "It is the same man, Captain. I was as close as this when his mask came off then. This is the man we all saw slain five years ago, on Sadalsuud, the pirate haunt!" His voice grew shrill with fear. "This is the Ancient Mariner!"

Liska flourished his blade at Athos' face. "Tell who you are!"

Athos had to speak his rage. His voice rang cold. "Slay me once, slay me a thousand times, the Ancient Mariner will don the Mask of Vengeance Unending, and rise again." He shut his mouth and said not one word more.

The red fur of Liska's neck bristled. His men murmured with fear. It was perhaps a mutinous sound.

Liska snapped shut the blade into his cane, straightened his spine, and nonchalantly smoothed his whiskers. "Time for a beating, Elch! We will have a straight story from him soon enough, or else an entertaining one! Where is the First Mate?"

"Here am I, sir!" croaked a deep voice.

The door to the landing bay was briefly blocked by an alien taller and wider than any crewman here. For a moment, his bright eyes, big as saucers, roamed the scene.

This was an upright froglike amphibian with webbed feet and fingers, goggle eyes, and a lipless mouth as wide as a serving dish. This mouth was wide and growing wider, grinning to see Athos captive, pinned to the wall helplessly.

The unbuttoned white coat of a Commonwealth Naval officer, complete with braid and epaulettes, was slung around to the alien's broad form like a cloak. The empty sleeves swung from his sloping shoulders. This coat was of Nemean cut, and so could not have fit him: obviously the pirate had looted it from a defeated adversary of that warlike race. Beneath this coat, a forcefield impermeable to water, but tuned to allow any other form of atom or molecule free passage, clung to the dank flesh of the First Mate like a thin, gray aura, and kept him moist.

His was a race called the Batrachians, about which little was known. Their worlds had never been part of the Commonwealth. They came from the Far Beyond.

The elegant Fox Captain turned to the hulking, dripping, soft mass of the eight-foot-tall Frog. "This man has a touch of Nemean blood in him (see the eyes?) so he may be stronger than he looks. He is also tricky and deadly, so take care! I want him searched, to find whatever control or gizmo he used to steer that fake mask away! I want him beaten, to find his name, and how he came aboard this ship. That little one-man glider could not make an interplanetary run, much less interstellar. He has allies somewhere nigh. He will tell of them before he dies."

The froglike Batrachian nodded ponderously, but then bent his bald, wide head down toward the pointed ear of Liska. He spoke softly, but Athos heard. "But, sir — what if the mask is not a fake? The Ancient Mariner, if slain, must surely rise again ..."

Liska flicked a bright, beady black eye at his men, but did not turn his head. "The crew will vote in a new Captain if they get too frightened. Let us do what we must to reassure them."

Then, stepping back, the Captain barked sharply, "Chain him up in the septic feed, and let us see if a spy can take a beating as well as one of our own gentleman of plunder, eh? Away with this faker, Yeho!"

Athos was startled when he heard the Batrachian's name, and he looked in wonder at the broad and hairless green face.

Yeho, staring back, suddenly stiffened, and his wide, lamplike eyes grew wider with a silent shock of recognition.

4. Silent as Death

Athos was in a small, round, foul-smelling processing chamber adjoining the ship's septic system. All sound in here was made tinny, echoing from the bare and rust-stained metal bulkheads and deck. There were two exits: a maintenance hatch to let a cleaning crew in, and a waste valve underfoot, large enough to dispose of a body.

He was chained by his wrists to the rusted metal overhead, feet dangling, and whipped until his back was bloody. A microphone connected to the ship's annunciators was dangled before him, in the hope that the sounds of him crying out in pain could be heard all over the ship to gladden the men. But Athos gritted his teeth and did not cry out.

Instead, he said softly and clearly: "*Four hours! Two pints! One small-arm! One shot!*" The words were echoed all over the ship.

Before he could speak again, Elch the Horned Man switched off the mike and smote Athos in the mouth.

"Not in the face!" the captain said.

Liska was in the cell, holding a lacy handkerchief drenched in perfume to his nose. A plush chair of polished wood with purple cushions had been brought in. Beneath the chair, a hand-woven rug of rich designs covered the rust spots and deck stains. He was petting the growling dire wolves on their haunches to either side of him, promising them juicy man-meat to eat soon.

"Leave him able to talk," the captain continued. "I want to hear how the same man, wearing the same mask, is before me here, as I saw die on planet Sadalsuud five years past, eh? Do you have a brother, perhaps, or a cousin who matches you?"

At the word *brother*, Athos felt a blush of anger burning in him, so much that the flesh of his muscular arms and brawny chest grew scarlet. He had to grit his teeth to keep from crying out in wrath. His narrow eyes so swam with hot rage, that Elch, the horned man, stepped away from him, chained though he was.

Elch snarled, "Talk, he will not. Let us slit his throat and be done."

The dire wolves barked as if in agreement, and wagged their tails.

But Captain Liska said to Athos, "Come, young sir! We are both gentlemen, men of rank and stature! Should I do as my loyal subordinate says? I would not be so indifferent to your dignity. A firing squad is more proper for the high born! Come! Tell me your name and lineage, and I will see to it your family learns how bravely you died. Tell me where and how you got your hands on the Mask of the Ancient Mariner?"

Athos said nothing. His eyes burned with hate.

"That mask, and your corpse, were both flung down into a chasm, and bolts of rather expensive ammunition cracked the wall of ice, and brought the whole glacier face tumbling down after. If such a fusillade could not even bury you deeply enough to prevent your digging out and climbing up, I would at least like to know, so I can get my money back from our supplier. Not to mention the first shot went clean through your brisket!"

Athos did not answer. But his eyes grew brighter. *The first shot.* But which one of them had fired it? Liska? One of his men?

Liska brought out the fine chain and locket Athos had been wearing earlier. He clicked it open, and looked blankly at that humanoid head that faded into view, hovering between the two valves of the locket. "I am no judge of beauty of races alien to mine, but this one seems to be made of finer stuffs than you. Surely, not a sister then. A mate? No, this locket is too nicely made for that. Hominids do not lavish such ornament on women they possess. An aspiration, I think, a dream! Perhaps one beyond your reach? You would not torment her, surely, by having her go all the weary days of her life hereafter, with no word, no rumor, of your fate? No? You care nothing for her?"

Grinning, Liska sent the locket skipping and rolling across the rusted, bloodstained deck so that it slid onto the slats of the floor-hatch covering the septic tank. The fragile bright ornament tilted and tottered for a moment, and then slipped down out of sight, swallowed by filth.

Athos uttered no sound. His eyes were now hot coals.

The ship's doctor was a Blue Man, from a race called the Sphingali. They were a wandering people, as their home world had been long ago destroyed. If the young of his race were the hue of a plum, he was a prune, withered, bent and wrinkled. He wore a set of bug-eyed goggles inset with multiple lenses. The doctor said, "There was a spike in both blood chemistry and neural energy a moment or two after you mentioned your supplier, Cap'n."

Liska grinned a sharp grin. "Ah! The kind of thing only a patrolman would be interested in, eh, what? But let us discuss the intriguing spread of gear you happened to be carrying. It tells a strange story."

Liska held up Athos' lance pistol. "Now this is a fascinating device! Notice the sleek design, the lock, stock and barrel cast as a single piece, made of an unanalyzable alloy bright as a mirror! Compare it to the poor blaster weapon I carry."

Liska gestured to the thick, long-barreled handweapon hanging at his hip. It was hardly poor. The grips were enameled with mother of pearl, and the lock was fretted with lacy arabesques. "What is a blaster, after all? It shoots a spitball made of plasma. Tech for cubs! Young worlds still playing with slowpoke tachyon drives! Blasters cannot penetrate force fields. But this! This can. The finest weaponeers of the Fox worlds, or the Hibagons, could mount a giga-electronvolt particle beam weapon in a handgun… in the old days, long ago.

"Long ago. One never sees its like, these days. But I have. I own its like.

"Five years ago, someone carried the mate to this pistol, and dressed as you did and with a face like yours …" Liska held up the lance pistol Athos' father had given to Ozymandias. "I've kept it in my locker all this time. It seems too fine a piece to use for mere mayhem!"

Athos said nothing. Did none of these cutthroats know the events from only a generation ago? Athos would have called it certain that anyone in the galaxy would have heard of the famous armor-piercing lance pistols of Raphean Lone, the war hero. But pirates were not men who dwelt on the past.

"A wealthy gambler might have such a thing, or the bodyguard of a merchant prince or the master spy in service to a king. You are perhaps from a senatorial family? A patrician? You are proud of it? An heirloom, perhaps? I see the glint in your eyes!"

The prune-colored doctor said, "With respect, my Captain! There is no mystery here. His space-cloak is Ultra-tech. Who else has access to the ancient race technologies but the Star Patrol?"

Liska said, "My race commanded such secrets, back when yours were loping through swamp muck on all fours."

"Long ago, sir," said the blue-skinned doctor wryly. "Not now."

Liska snarled, "We shall mount such heights again. The are Old Ones moving in the dark between the stars once more …"

Elch the horned man said, "Nothing to hear will there be from this prisoner, Captain."

The Blue Man doctor said, "Cap'n, let me try a new pharmaceutical. In combination with brain invasive surgery, we can stimulate the vocal centers, and numb inhibitive response."

But Elch spoke with scorn toward the Blue Man. "The Ancient Mariner, you call him. Among my people, he is named Byrokstrong.

Stories we have, old stories. Such a man who dares to place the face of Byrokstrong on his face, he will not break." He turned to Liska. "What need we to know? Why he broke into your cabin, we know. Why else?

That you sleep on your vault of loot, he knew. In he broke to steal his pistol back."

Liska snarled, "Back? What do you mean *back*?"

Elch said, "After you killed him on Sadalsuud."

Athos stiffened. So Liska was the one. It was his hand that did the deed.

The Fox turned toward Athos. "Well, what say you? You are no mere cop. What of the golden mask? It has the face of a Nemean, but no Nemean made it. Even the Dark Overlords never had anything like it. It is something from legend! Why would a Patrolman carry such a rare thing? You sent it away on some errand. You will call it back for me, and tell it to obey me. I can think of a dozen buyers who would pay a king's ransom for it!

"So, in addition to telling me when and where and how you got aboard my ship, and with whose help, and who or what carried you to this system, and how you knew we would be here, I would like whatever key or code you were given to disarm the self-destruct on your spacecloak, because certain business partners of mine who are technically inclined will want it.

"We can start with your name and family. Who are you?"

And when again Athos would not answer, Liska rose and inclined his head. "As you wish, sir. I see you may need solitude to ponder the matter carefully! But I have pressing business, so the normal artistic process of torment which my race perfected when yours had not yet discovered fire, we lack the time to see played out. Instead I offer the simple option: when I return, it will be with a firing squad. If you remain stubborn, you die. No lawman in the galaxy would so much as raise an eyebrow! Every Captain has the right to protect his ship from dangerous stowaways, saboteurs, and trespassers."

The doctor and the captain left. Elch dashed a bucket of icy cold filth over Athos, doused the light, and left him to shiver in the cell.

Once all were gone, the artificial gravity doubled. Alone in the dark, crushed by the extra weight, it felt to Athos as if his arms might pull from their sockets. The oxygen feed was also being toyed with, making him dazed or giddy by turns.

Time went by, but very slowly.

Over and over again in his mind, quite silently, Athos said solemn words of woe and wrath to the memory of his brother, and, with them, the terrible words of a dire oath.

... Mine eye shall find, mine arm shall reach, my countenance not spare... Accursed be all corsairs ... !

5. The Promise of Pain

Nine hundred feet away, practically at the other end of the ship, not far from the Captain's cabin, was the only other private cabin aboard. Here was the First Mate. He was disrobed, and lying slumped in the wide, circular pool which served him both as bath and bunk. Only his big round belly protruded above the water.

His name was Groac Wroc Yehomelek. He had kept the eyes and ears of his warty, blunt head above water at first, listening to the sounds of the whip strokes being broadcast over the annunciators. Then he heard the words spoken by the prisoner. He recognized the voice. Yeho shivered uncontrollably, and closed his bulging eyes. "*Four hours! Two pints! One small-arm! One shot!*"

That was when he pulled his head below the water. His race was froglike in look and shape and many other ways, but not in all. He had tear ducts, and, like a man, he could cry. Also like a man, he could be afraid or ashamed. He could hide his tears by submerging underwater to sleep, which a man could not do.

The dreams that came were nightmares.

He saw Liska once again ordering the poor farmlad who had refused to drink his health impaled on a cooking spit. He saw two of the crew flourishing bloody cutlass and cleaver. He heard the screams, the horrid screams. He smelled the smell of cooking meat. He saw Liska, elegantly dressed, grinning and chuckling, feeding morsels to his dire wolves.

Then he saw again in his dream the man whose tongue Liska cut out for refusing to curse and blaspheme when ordered.

He once more felt on his back the stiffness and the chill of the corpse of the delicate, red-furred courtesan Liska had chained in a meatlocker, freezing her to death, to repay her coldness to him. It was horrible how heavy she felt when Yeho hauled her corpse away, for one so small and slight.

Any many others. How many had Liska fed to his pet sharks? How many had his dire wolves torn to bits?

The dream changed to an earlier time. Liska was younger.

Liska was floating through clouds of blood in zero gee, holding a handkerchief before his nose, twitching his whiskers. He propelled himself with agile kicks from one to the next scarred and blast-cratered bulkhead of the dying ship, his thick red tail flourishing behind him. He carefully pushed corpses of space marines aside with his walking stick, after stabbing chest or slitting throat with the cane's retractable blade to confirm they were dead. He came to where Yeho was. The huge Frog held a bloody ax in either fist.

Yeho remember the words of that first meeting exactly.

"Your handiwork, I presume, my good man? I admire your talents. No, no need to introduce yourself! Your fame precedes you! You once served a famous pirate queen, a picaroon so bold she tripped a giant empire and made it fall! I have a proposition for you … I am gathering a crew of gentlemen adventurers … could you stop coughing blood on me, if you please ...?"

And then, as Yeho was being bandaged by the same blue-skinned Sphingali doctor as still followed Liska to this day, came these words:

"My last First Mate, alas! He felt the pull of other loyalties, so I had him pulled to pieces by tractor beams.

"I promise you great rewards if you serve me loyally, for a new King of the Pirates is come to take the place of your Queen Jade, and he has buyers and suppliers from older, darker planets other buccaneers are too timid to approach. But I if you prove faithless, I promise you pain and terror …. Lingering pain …"

The dream changed again. It was earlier still. He was younger yet.

It was the execution yard of Cafalnasir, the Imperial torture planet.

Bleachers on three sides of the great arena held commoners and notables. Most of them looked bored. On the fourth side sat men in the white uniforms of the Imperial legionnaires and the jet black of the space navy. Above them in blood-red sat the Cyborg Shocktroopers of the Praetorian Legion, the Red Guard. And the military governor of the sector, a man of the lizard-like Iss race named Procurator Snaaib, sat in a curule chair on the balcony, beneath the banner of the Black Cogwheel.

Yeho had often had this nightmare, but it always had a happy ending.

He was chained in a glass cauldron, suspended above a roaring fire, to which the executioners were only slowly feeding fuel. It was a trick of Batrachian physiognomy that if Yeho were boiled slowly enough, his nerves would never register any pain.

Sadistic although this was, it did not look very horrible to the crowd, who wanted to see beheadings and dismemberments, incinerations, defenestration, and blinded men fighting wild animals.

Seeing the crowd's displeasure, Snaaib the Procurator flicked out his forked tongue once or twice, and then raised his scaly green hand. He was about to order some quicker, more vivid form of death for Yeho, when there came an interruption.

With blaring note of joyful trumpet, clash of tambourine, and squeals of gay laughter, a troupe of dancing girls came kicking and tumbling in a rush out onto the balcony where the Procurator sat. Each girl was scandalously clad in a harness of belts and buckles with a few wisps of skintight black leather beneath, but bearing oversized headdresses of mirrors, sequins, and feathers on her head.

The beauties formed a chorus line between the curule chair and the Procurator's surprised bodyguards. The girls began to step and kick, flourishing their shapely legs. The plumes on their heads were wide and high, blocking everyone's view.

At the same time, a powerful, sleek spaceship, green as an emerald, dropped down from the clouds above, and began showering flower petals and small coins all over the upturned faces of the suddenly cheering crowd.

Yeho scratched and pounded at the glass walls of the tank, helpless to aid or interfere. His fear was not for himself.

But none of the many armed men in the arena drew a weapon. The dancing girls were so scantily dressed that none could be carrying a blaster. They clearly were no threat. And the audience thought the chorus line was all part of the show.

So, while spritely music drowned out the Procurator's alarmed commands, and before the bodyguards on the platform or soldiers in the audience knew anything was wrong, the leader of the dancers, a fair-skinned, green-haired woman of ravishing beauty danced into view.

She held what seemed an oversized folding fan made of green feathers before and behind her, which she dipped and maneuvered to half hide the alluring glimpses of waist and hip, thigh and shapely calf, so whether she were clothed or nude beneath the whirling feathers was a matter of prurient speculation. Her poise and allure were mesmerizing. The men in the crowd, young and old, were unable to look away.

Then she threw wide her arms. The fans opened but did not fall, for they were connected to her spine. She was a Ralline, a winged woman. She was clothed in wisps of silk that hid none of her curvaceous, luminous beauty. The crowd roared applause.

Then down from her oversized, feathered headdress, she brought a cocked and loaded speargun. The weapon was wooden, and it was powered by mechanical tension alone, with no metal parts nor powercells to alert a spy ray or scanner. The dart it shot had an arrowhead of sharpened flint. It looked like a toy.

Every eye was staring, but her beauty seemed to blind them, for no one seemed to see what she was doing. Only once it was too late did murmurs of confusion turn to cries of alarm.

The weapon was no toy. Her face was calm, her eyes aflame as she raised it to her shoulder. No one heard the ring of the spring-loaded piston as it sang. The Procurator was struck through the eye and killed instantly.

The coins suddenly all crackled with static electric charge, as powerful induction rays from the ship above swept the area. Anything metallic suddenly became too hot to hold. Guns dropped from scalded fingers almost before they were drawn. The so-called flower petals had been chemically treated. These erupted into puffs and plumes of smoke, and suddenly the whole arena was bathed in scented fog and colored clouds. Confused shouts and blindly fired blaster bolts filled the air.

As for the ship, a battery of tractor beams from an open hatch in the belly reached down and yanked upward on the whole gallows holding Yeho, glass cage and all. Sniper rays cut the legs of the cage, and it came free and soared upward.

The plumes on the dancing girls all folded like venetian blinds, to reveal another design beneath: a black banner with a white skull spouting green wings from its temples. The shrill voices uttered a battlecry as fierce as the call of a falcon. *"A kiss from Captain Jade! All hail the Queen of Pirates!"*

The girls now unlimbered from beneath their sheer costumes climbing ropes clipped to the carabiners on the harnesses they wore, and flung the weighted ends into the array of tractor beams shed by the ship as she made a slow pass over them.

The ropes carrying the squad, as well as the glass cage carrying Yeho, were pulled upward, being drawn into the hold by the tractor beam action, even as the ship gained altitude above the smoke-filled arena and accelerated.

The green-haired leader spread her wings and soared, a movement of swift and breathtaking grace. She landed atop the glass lid. She shouted over the throb of the engines and the roar of the wind. "Are you fit, Yeho?"

"Very fit, Captain!" Yeho shouted back through water, glass and wind, wondering if he could be heard. "But you shouldna come! Not safe! You mad, lass? You should ha' left me behind!"

Jade tossed her headdress into the wind and shook free her yard-long emerald locks of hair. "Is that so? What lot then would fall to me? *Four hours, two pints, one small-arm, one shot!*"

And she laughed when she saw the lightweight Imperial interceptors rising up toward them from the military base below, for she saw her own titanic green-hulled star-galleon, the *Deadlier than the Male*, diving down out of the sun behind flocks of missiles fired but a moment before, and bolts as bright as lightning issued from every open weapon port.

6. The Code of the Pirate Queen

Yeho sat up shouting. Water sloshed from his pool and splashed the deck-tiles as he stood. He blinked his goggle eyes in confusion, convinced he was still asleep.

The silvery glowing apparition of a young woman in a blouse and pantaloons was in the cabin. She bore a longbow nearly twice her height. Starlight shined from her eyes and flowed from her skin. Her hair was dark and straight, gleaming like onyx, falling down her back, held in place by a ribbon of white paper. She stood in the air, a foot or so above the deck.

"Do you know the way to Arcadia?"

He sank down to one knee. His voice was a deep rasp. "Sister."

She raised her hand. "Do not kneel to me! Get to your feet!"

"What mean you, Sister?"

She smoothed her garments. "Rise, my son. I am not what you see. This is still a dream."

"I see a star maiden. You speak for the stars." Yeho did not stand. Instead he bowed his blunt head more deeply.

She smiled a half smile. "Just now, I am a messenger. I am only speaking for a man."

"What message?"

"These are his words: *Most loyal Groac Wroc Yehomelek, the Son of Jade Gale Fatale needs your aid. If you can smuggle him off the ship, or to the planet, that is enough. Remember what debt you owe her.*"

Yeho grew furious. "Who told you to say this to me? How does he know me? How does he know anything about me? Tell me the name! Who sent you?" Now he stood up, and more water sloshed out.

She smiled. "I have no name to give you. I only ever see his shadow in the night." Now her smile vanished. "Actually, I want you to tell me who he is. Who knows your past?"

Yeho did not hear the question. "I cannot cross the Fox. He has a house, a murder mansion, where he takes those what run athwart of him. The different rooms have different deaths inside, and lucky is the man taken by a swift one. No matter what the stars say, they cannot make me!"

The girl took on a gentler look. She said softly, "The Matrons taught me that the stars guide, but do not force. They show the signs in the constellations, but you have to look. They can shine on the way, but you must take the step."

He was not listening. Yeho put a hand to a drawer, and drew out a small comdisc unit. He flicked open the lens with his thumb, and hologram appeared in the air. It was a world of blue and white, with large ice caps, and a dozen icy seas gathered between them, crisscrossed by peninsula and archipelagoes, and small volcanic isles. The ring of some shattered moon circled the equator, and a large and distant moon, coated over with ice from pole to pole, hung in the near distance.

Even as she looked at the world, a black sphere appeared in the middle of the image, swelled, and blotted out the blue globe. Icebergs and oceans were swallowed in the inky darkness, and then the whole picture was gone, and a black sphere, absorbing all light, hung above the comdisc, slowly turning. A voice from the comdisc unit said, "Hvalens Hode is under the Black Spot. Death is here! The Dark Wrath strikes!"

The voice seemed inhuman, and beyond inhuman. Not the voice of a machine, nor anyone nor anything from any world or star. It was like hearing words from a sarcophagus.

She stared deeply into the depth of the black sphere, peering at the strange glints and flecks of dark blue and indigo flame that flickered and swirled, trembling on the edge of vision. It was like peering down a long tube into a nether realm.

She said, "That is the voice of Night: the voice of one possessed by the Dark Will."

Yeho snapped the comdisc shut. "That is Ahab, who is King of All pirates. He puts out the black spot on whoever is next to die, whether planet or person. Do you want one of these, with the black spot covering over my face, sent out to all corsairs, telling them to kill me? I cannot cross him! The Fox is his pawn. The Fox will torture me to death! Do the stars expect me to die?"

She said, "At times, the stars guide us to great deeds, not where we will."

He twisted his great rubbery mouth in a scowl. "What's that to me?"

She was silent a moment, eyes down, deep in thought, perhaps in prayer. Then she raised her eyes and said, "My life is not my own. Nor is yours. There is a vow unpaid." Her gaze grew sharp and earnest. "It was not easy to fish those memories into your dream. Do you remember your debt?"

He nodded his great head slowly. "Aye. That I do. I owe Cap'n Jade my life!" He heaved a great sigh and words spilled out from him. "She came back to save me, even though I said not to. I disobeyed orders trying to save her sweetheart. She said she hated him, but I saw what I saw. I hoisted him free, but got caught in the noose myself, since it was all a trap for her. The Procurator put me in a glass box to be boiled alive before the crowd."

She said nothing, but gazed at him sternly.

His voice was almost angry. "Jade had no need to come back for me. Her and her girls! No need at all! Many a year ago that was! Each day, each hour, and every single breath I have breathed since that time is her gift to me! Why did she do it?" He uttered a great, croaking sob, and covered his broad, green face with his webbed fingers.

She said softly, "What is that phrase? *Four hours and one shot.* I heard it over the intercom. It was in your dream."

Yeho lowered his hands. "He said it for my ear. Cap'n Jade, as all good captains and commanders of Pirate Companies must do, put forth her articles in writing, fair and clear, and stuck by them. Jade would say a captain who would change the rules and cheat the men is no fashion of captain at all — Might just as well be an Imp, and kiss the Emperor's big toe. Not us! We were a free company! Cap'n Jade wrote her articles in rhyme."

"In rhyme?"

"To make the rules easy for all to keep by heart ..." And he recited:

> *Who keeps a trove or a trollop for his own,*
> *Or flees a fight, or leaves a mate; What be his lot?*
> *A one-gee rock in the liquid zone*
> *Four hours, two pints, one small-arm, one shot.*

She said, "I don't get it."

He wiped his eyes. "You would not know rogue's cant, Sister."

She laughed at that. "I wag a rum tongue, cove. Cant is chatter the Imps and the Chumps won't ken." In the slang, an *Imp* was an Imperial. A *Chump* was a victim, a money source. She added, "Dirts ain't Spacers." A *dirt* was a downsider, a land-bound man.

"To be marooned on a planetoid is the punishment. The rock must be of earth-normal gravity, since he is not to die by being crushed, nor too far nor too nigh the primary, since neither freezing nor boiling is for him. He has two pints of grog in his helmet flask, and four hours of air in his bottles. The blaster has one charge in the magazine. Enough liquor to give him nerve. Enough charge to blow a hole in his helmet, or into his skull, if he wants a slower death or a faster. You see, Sister, he must kill himself, that is the point. So his soul is damned to darkness forever. No other punishment is fit."

"The punishment for what?"

"Four things. One. Keeping back loot that is meant to be shared out. Two. Sneaking a woman aboard. Three. Turning coward and running from a fight. And four … and … "

And for leaving a crewmate behind to die. He did not say it aloud. He did not have to.

Then his spine straightened. His goggling eyes narrowed. His round, froglike features might have seemed comical or pathetic before this. Now, his whole demeanor was changed.

"I am Groac Wroc Yehomelek. My name I make my own forever, without father, without mother, without kin or clan. I fly the Jolly Roger and sail against all flags, and I never bowed the knee before no Empire in times past, nor to any Lord or Senator of the Republic now! I fear to meet no man, with blade or blaster!"

She clapped her hands together prettily.

More softly, he continued: "I cannot cower before that Fox! The gift Jade gave, I will repay her son! Time to pay! A life for life, if that be the cost. I flinch not!"

She said, "Well, I hope you can save him, because there is nothing else I can do."

"You are a Star Maiden. There is much you can do."

"I have another mission, and I can only cast my shade so far for just so long. I am looking for someone. And for somewhere. You never answered my question about Arcadia." She smiled and showed her dimples. "Do you know where it is?"

"No one knows that, Sister. The world was lost long ago. It is impossible to find."

"Man is more than matter, and stars are more than fire." Her tone grew somber, and her graze grew deep. "If the hand that made the countless worlds of space is open to you, nothing is impossible."

He turned to look at her. His hairless bullet-head nodded slowly.

"But there is something you can do."

"What?"

"You know the rites? The old, strong rites, do you not? The ones the Empire did away with?"

"Much was lost, but much was hidden and treasured and kept. Yes. I am instructed in the rites."

"I want to be ready. I want to be cleaned up. The stars say what day and hour a man will die. If this be that hour, let me be shriven."

She frowned in thought. "Only a sacerdote may offer that sacrament, but … any layman can serve the office in an emergency." And she told him what to do.

He knelt and closed his eyes, confessed his long list of many dark and evil deeds, and asked for absolution.

She raised her hands and spoke words of comfort. Peace of a kind he did not understand entered his heart.

When he opened his eyes afterward, she vanished, and he woke. He was back in the bath, beneath the water. There was no puddle sloshed on the floor. It had all been a dream.

But he knew it was real.

CHAPTER 4: TOMB IN SPACE

1. Firing Squad

When Yeho came waddling into the septic processing chamber, he was glad his race did not sweat, or show the clues of inner turmoil the keen nose of his Fox captain might pick up.

His huge body rocked to and fro as he strode, and his flat, webbed feet slapped the rusted deckplates with wet, sticky sound. The gold-braided white coat with its shiny brass buttons taken from some dead officer of marines was clipped in place like a cloak, empty sleeves dangling. It was slung from the hunched neck-roll of muscle Yeho had where a humanoid's shoulders would have been. Beneath, a skintight aura of water moistened his warty, green hide.

He squeezed through the oval maintenance door leading into the dark, dank chamber, and motioned those behind him to follow.

Four men came after: the ship's electrician, a man named Hob, sober for once, and his three bastard children from three different women: one was brown of skin, one was black, and one was blue. He was a senior officer, with iron gray hair, iron hard eyes, skin burned brown from the light of many an exotic, foreign sun. His boys looked not much like him except the hardness in their eyes.

Hob had had served under Yeho in the old days before Liska, in the Imperial days, when only the toughest and most loyal could play the brutal game of piracy, and survive. He was counted wealthy among pirates, with rings of gold on his fingers and rings of gold dangling from his ears.

Hob and his sons were all Noachians, the large-nosed and nearly hairless variant of the hominid race, who, of the airbreathing peoples, tended to get along best with the amphibian Batrachians.

Yeho straightened up. His eyes almost brushed the overhead as he inspected the scene.

To one side of the chamber, holding an orange studded with cloves against his nose, lounged Captain Liska. Yeho saw the Captain had changed from his semi-formal morning-watch attire to statelier noon-watch full-dress whites. Lacy ruffs had been added to his tricorner hat, with golden flourishes to his sleeves and throat. A megavolt energy saber hung in a gold scabbard from his finest, emerald-studded shagreen baldric. A dainty half-cape of shining fur from the now-extinct sea-mink from the luxury planet, Grus, was flung over one epaulette.

His chair of precious, hand-carved wood was atop an expensive Pavo carpet woven with an intricate, interlocking maze-pattern of colored threads. Dire-wolves sat, one to either side of him, red-eyed and wagging their tails, eager for blood.

Liska was arguing with the Blue Man doctor, an ancient and wrinkled mummy called Sage Paradise. This was not his real name: Sphingali never told their real names to people. Yeho hated and feared the old pirate surgeon, for it was his habit to addict unwary crewmen and cabin boys to quack remedies and painkillers, charging them for doses of opium or bentlam or nitrolabe, a higher price each dose. Whenever Yeho was ill, he locked himself in his cabin and soaked his body in a bath of whiskey to dull the pain until he recovered, rather than letting himself go near the horror show of the sickbay. Liska kept the quack doctor aboard mostly to advise him during prisoner torture sessions.

At the moment, Dr. Paradise was urging a lengthy session, involving days and weeks. "The psychological effect of radical surgical alterations on young and healthy male psychology requires time to take effect, captain... "

"Time is more precious than the ice-pearls of Polaris!" replied the captain with a snap of his fine white teeth. "Costlier than the haunted gold from Regis! Suppose the Blood Moon finds even one patrolman or spy or whatever this faker might be has sniffed out our spot here? This secret world! Who comes to Zavijava? For what?"

Liska raised the orange he held, and dashed it to the deck, where it splattered. "This is our fate if the higher ups find out! Or, worse, all our heads will be kept alive in jars, with wires running through the pain centers of our brains. *No slip ups!* That was the order. And running late with this shipment is a slip up. You know the penalties for tardy payments, or cargo gone astray."

Yeho muttered, "Four hours, two pints, one small arm, one shot."

He said it softly, but the points of Liska's triangular ears twitched. The captain spoke without turning his head, "Marooning was the gentler penalty for gentler days, my man! Fate has us chained to new partners now, as ruthless and pure as the killing-bots of old! Gold and women we've been promised, and cities to burn from orbit! And gemstones as thick and bright as clouds of stars! With so much at stake, the kindlier impulses of our most charitable hearts must be stowed away. If Ahab shows us no kindness, we have none to spare to others, have we?"

And with this, he turned his bright, black, twinkling eyes to Athos, who was still hanging in chains next to the stained bulkhead. "Ah! You listen intently, my curious cub, do you not? Oh ho! You wish to find out who are our suppliers, and where they get such finely crafted black tech, eh? A disturbing sign. Surely you do not expect to ..."

The captain's voice suddenly trailed off. Something was burning in the nameless prisoner's soul, a fire of vengeance Liska did not understand. His expression showed no interest in the smuggling operation at all. Nothing else could have convinced the captain that this man was not a police officer after all. Then who was he?

To judge from his steady, unwinking, silent stare, the young man did indeed expect to live through this.

A normal man would have no such expectation. Who was he?

Liska felt the fur on his neck standing up. He forced his lips into a wry smile. Mustn't show fear before the men. Might cause a mutiny.

Elch, the young-faced Horned Man was also in the chamber, cleaning the blades of his bloody whip. "You have to drive two twigs of mistletoe through his eyes, sir."

"Eh? What?" The captain started, puzzled.

Elch said heavily, "And burn incense in his nose to kill his sense of smell, and wear your undergarments inside out. This will blind and confuse the avenging phantom when he returns from beyond the grave. So the old grandmothers say on my world."

Athos, hanging by his wrists, looked down at Liska, his face impassive, his eyes narrow. Athos saw the fear in Liska's face. Liska saw none in his.

Dr. Paradise said, "Captain! Surely there be time enough for one more trial of the pharmaceutical approach! I have the verity drug from the murdered world of Centaurus, which no one can acquire any more. I have nitrobarb, which is just as rare, and the extract of the black lotus…"

Elch said, "Painkillers kill pain. This buck would be broken by now, had not my work been undone by this damn fool saw-bones, Captain, sir!"

Liska stood. "There is no time. We leave orbit soon. No trace of this spy can remain! Let him carry his silence to eternity!"

Elch said, "But, Captain! We have not yet even learned his name! How did he find this system? How did he know when we would be here? Where is his ship? There is always time for the lash! And if he stays mum and stubborn, why, then, let me keep laying on until he dies."

Liska made an impatient gesture. "Belay that chatter! We can haul him to the mess hall, which is large enough to assemble the company, and all be witness to it, and none of us with clean hands to snitch on the others."

Liska turned again to Athos. "A firing squad, as is right and proper for a gentleman! You have Lion blood in you, that race of conquerors! But you are at least half-Ape as well, eh? Born a bit on the wrong side of the bed were we? Your mother was well paid, I trust? Enough to keep her in grog and snort to dull the backpain, eh? Lions are said to be generous. No? Nothing to say? Will not even speak up for your own mother, eh?"

Yeho was surprised at himself, when he saw his own hand drawing one of his stubby, heavy and lethal hand-axes he kept tucked in his wide leathery belt. It trembled in his grip, but, for once, it was wrath, not fear, boiling in his guts. He told himself that the captain did not know who the mother of Athos was, or else he would not have dare so to speak in Yeho's hearing, not while looking the other way.

Liska was still taunting Athos. "Well? Any last words?"

Athos raised his blood-streaked head. His eyes were calm and distant and terrible like the eye of a tornado seen from space. "You shall look upon my like again ere you die."

Liska's fur bristled in fear. He turned and saw the ax in Yeho's large and web-fingered fist. "What is this?"

"Carrying out your orders, captain!" said Yeho. And he flourished his ax overhead, "Ready! Aim!"

"Hold your…!" said Liska.

"Fire!" shouted Yeho.

Hob and his sons did not hesitate. Bolts exploded from the muzzles of the weapons of the firing squad.

The dazzle and clamor of blasterfire deafened and blinded all in the small, steel-walled chamber for a moment. When Liska blinked the floating spots from his eyes, he saw Yeho kneeling over the prone body of Athos. One of the blaster bolts, flying wild, had hit the wrist chain where it was bolted to the overhead and severed it. The bulkhead opposite the firing squad was pitted with tiny craters, still smoking, and black starbursts marked where the heat of the spent bolts had discolored the alloy.

Over the broad shoulder hump of the green amphibian, Liska could see little of the motionless form on the deck. Yeho roughly picked up the body in one fist, holding the corpse by its shirt-front. Blood dripped between the webbed fingers of Yeho and pattered to the deck.

Now that Yeho had heaved his bulky green body onto his squat hindlegs, Liska had a clearer view. The prisoner's shirt in the back had been torn to shreds with the lash. In the front, the torn shirt was pock-marked with the burn-holes and bloodstains energy weapons are known to leave.

Yeho with heavy step, his vast stomach wagging, stomped over to the disposal hatch set in the deck, sank down, and, with a wet grunt, used one hand to the heave the slatted panel open.

The vile stench of the ship's sewage flooded the small chamber. The grinding, muttering noise of submerged turbines rendering the waste material rose up like the gargling of the damned being strangled in filth. The dire wolves whined.

Without any ceremony or wasted motion, Yeho stuffed the limp body headfirst down into the opaque malodorous fluids in the septic tank, and drove the body under the surface with one large shove of his large webbed foot.

Liska said in fury, "I said he was to be taken to the mess hall and shot there!"

Yeho turned absentmindedly wiped the blood on his hand on the fabric of the officer's dress white uniform he wore. "Sorry, Captain! But think of the risk."

"Risk?"

Yeho's blubbery lips went wider and thinner, and he half-lidded his eyes. It was a sinister, secretive expression. "You said so yourself, my Captain! Who comes here? Who comes to Zavijava? A planet with no spaceport, no exports, no cities, no villages, and ruins so old no one remembers which race put them up? Who comes? Only someone told to be here, told by one who knew where and when."

"Someone?"

"Someone aboard is for him. A confederate. A betrayer. A sneak!"

Liska hid his expression by stroking his fine whiskers. "Go on."

"You saw how cocksure the masked man was, Captain! He knew his sneaky friend was working to save him. And if we gathered the whole company in one place to watch, then the sneak would be there, wouldn't he? There to snarl our breathing lines, I'll warrant."

Liska said, "Smart noggin' work! But you should have sounded off."

Yeho said, "Not before the doctor. Half the time, he is addled and high-flown with his own concoctions. He might be the sneak."

The doctor spoke in icy tones, "Or you!" The doctor turned to the Captain. "I had no chance to examine the body."

Yeho swelled up his throat bladder and emitted a loud gush of noise. "Oh no! I am not fetching it back up! You cannot ask me to dive into that! No, Captain! It ain't right! Not before the men!"

Liska's eyes sparkled. He could not resist the temptation to inflict humiliation on his men when he could. "Let us make sure and double sure the man is dead. Some of the crew might mutter."

The doctor said, "The Empire had a rule saying no one could believe in ghosts, nor fortune telling, nor praying to stars, nor anything of the like. Say what you will of those days, the lesser orders and younger races minded themselves well, and the galaxy was not pestered with crass superstitions!"

Elch said, "Also had rules, they did, that none could believe in Templars or their mind powers not nevermore — and see we all how well that went!"

Yeho said nothing, for he had already plunged into the ugly, fetid sludge, and submerged. The slosh of his dive sent a splattering of filth into the air, and Liska was wise enough to be at the far side of the chamber before that happened.

A moment passed while Elch and Paradise peered at the sluggish surface of the waste material, holding their noses. Then the surface became agitated, and the sound of the unseen turbine rose in pitch, straining and complaining as if some large body were lodged in between the rendering blades. Then the surface turned pink and then red, as the foul odor of blood mingled with the other foul odors.

Yeho put his head above the surface. Filth dripped down from this warty skull. "Sorry, Captain! The body got lodged in the disposal blades before I got to it. It has been torn into chunks, and the disintegrator field recycles all flesh and soft tissue."

"Not sorry enough!" snapped Liska with a grin. "Dive back down! I want the skull! I want his bones for my collection!"

"But the danger, Captain! Have the machinery works shut off, at least!"

And the captain squinted in confusion. "Funny. Who ordered them turned on?" But Hob the electrician had already stepped outside the chamber to the control board, which was adjacent to the maintenance hatch. The murmur of turbines ceased from underfoot.

The stink was too much for Liska. He departed as well, going back to his cabin, where, among the other luxuries afforded a captain, he had a private washroom and an unlimited water ration. He also had dire wolves trained to lick his fur clean, which was a strange practice he allowed no one to see.

His anger toward Yeho was mollified, and Liska was put in a jolly mood, when he found the First Mate not only recovered the skull and a good many bones, but had taken the trouble to strip, clean and even polish them with a nice layer of bone polish.

And morsels of raw meat had been left in the feeding bowls for his pets.

Liska lay himself down on his bed, feeling the comforting feeling of riches hidden under his tail. He held up the skull to the lamplight. "So ye be the Ancient Mariner, be ye, old timer? A thousand years old? Ah! The name of the captain who killed you will last as long!"

2. Sleight of Hand

During the moment when Yeho bent over the prone body of Athos, his vast body blocked the view of all those behind. Yeho squeezed blood from a medical sack onto his hands before padding out the smoking sparks clinging to Athos' shirt. Now each burn mark in his clothing was centered in a bloodstain.

Athos was still half-stunned. The toad-man stuffed a folded wad of slick fabric into the young patrolman's surprised hands, just before dumping him into the sewage.

Athos was submerged. He fought the bog of filth. He was still faint-headed from shock, and wounded from the raw scars of the lash. The struggle in that dark, foul, foetid muck, was silent, long, terrible and lonely.

There was none to see the heroic effort, and Athos spoke to no one about it after.

He could not see nor breathe, and he dared not break the surface, even if he had known which direction was up. His hands and feet were numb, and the filth was his whole universe.

But, after an eternity, he had unfolded the fabric and pulled it around him. It came to life, and sealed up automatically. The hood and veil settled in place over his head and face. This was his spacecloak. The fabric flexed and came to life.

Some filth was caught within the airtight seal as the ultratech energy-fabric conformed to his body shape. Automatically, submicrcoscopic molecular filters and processors trapped and expelled noxious material caught between fabric and skin. The technology was not one Athos understood, but smell of stench receded. Drawing that first clean breath of air was paradise.

He could not see, but the inner surface of the veil protecting his face lit up with readouts, including a sonar image: He was in a septic tank.

To one side was a turbine designed to disintegrate any solid wastes. Its blades were moving slowly. To the other side, someone had chained an empty barrel, mouth downward, with a bubble of air trapped inside. Above him was the valve leading back up into the torture room. Below, hidden in the heaviest layer of filth, was a shape whose sonar-outline looked like a motionless human body.

Athos stooped, half swimming and half burrowing. Sensors in his gloves touched dead flesh: no oxygen in the cells, no heartbeat in the body. It was a corpse.

Beneath the corpse was a sharp and metallic sonar echo. With a feeling of infinite joy, Athos' fingers closed on the small, round shape of Niobe's locket.

He tucked the locket into the neck of his hood. The fabric closed about it and the action of microscopic pores cleaned it. Athos put his fingers to his throat, glad to feel the cold circle at its accustomed place. It might be a small thing, but it made his heart warm.

At that moment, Yeho dove down into the muck. Athos felt the motion in the liquid around him, and saw the sonar echo of a bulk approaching. The huge frog creature grabbed Athos and unceremoniously stuffed his head and shoulders into the barrel opening. The sound through his hood earphones changed as he emerged into a one cubic foot volume of air.

The head of the Batrachian was too large to enter the barrel, but he could put his lips above the surface. "You are dead! Stay put until the coffin is ready!"

Athos hissed, "Whose corpse is that?"

"Yours, idiot!" And with this, the monstrous toad man reached down with one hand and stuffed the dead body into the mouth of the turbine.

The blades bit. The engines whined and stuttered, laboring. In a moment, gallons of blood had mingled with the waste water.

The read-outs told the tale: the convincing-looking burn marks in his shirt had been left by tracer-shots, tuned to minimum power, no more dangerous than a blank cartridge fired from a land-gun. The only real bolts had been fired by weapons aimed at the bulkhead to either side of him.

The cloak fabric was also warm, and seductively soothing to his cold and tortured limbs. He laughed softly, elated to be alive, and overcome by the strange sensation that he was in a dream. Then he realized he was in a dream, for he had fallen asleep, floating in the muck, before he was done laughing.

3. Buried Alive in the Void

Athos did not wake until after Yeho had moved him and washed him clean, and was putting him into a coffin. The pricking sensation of a hypodermic entering his elbow woke him.

Athos was not sure which deck or section of the ship he was in, but it must have been far aft, for he could hear clearly the stuttering whine of the main drives cycling through their pre-flight check. He could tell from the sound that only the midline drive tubes were being warmed up; neither the portside tube he had damaged, nor its opposite number starboard, were being lit. That the *Devil's Delight* would not delay even for the few hours it might take to make repairs was telling.

Even before his eyes opened, Athos could tell he had had been roughly but thoroughly scrubbed. His body was damp with antiseptic wash: he smelled now the sharp tang of alcohol, not sewerage. His tunic and cloak were slick. Trust an amphibian to want everything soaked clean.

Athos coughed and twitched. He reached up and grabbed the arm of Yeho, who was bent over him with a needle. The arm was soft, wet and warty to the touch, but beneath a layer of fat, the monstrous toad-man was muscled like a horse.

He wanted to ask whether Liska was indeed the one who shot his brother at Sadalsuud, but he had no way of phrasing it without giving the secret away. *Who shot me?*

Vengeance also was not his only duty. He had a vow to the Patrol, and to the newly written Constitution. The chance was slipping away.

"The supplier! Tell me where to find the weapon supplier! Who is behind this?"

"That's too big for you to know! Pay heed! I've injected you with the only chow you're getting. Vitamins, nutriment, oxygenated blood plasma. You need to be perky and bright-eyed when you land."

"Land?"

"You are going to the Living Mountain of Death. Sorry, mate! No other place to stow you. I swapped you with Bate. You stole his life. Might as well steal his coffin."

Athos realized Bate was the trigger-happy Sinanthrope youth who had blown a hole in the hull during the firefight.

"Listen, and hold this fast in your ear!" hissed the Batrachian. "The coffin will be launched. Everyone will see your coffin float off in a final orbit. But I have gimmicked a cargo-mule to sneak after you. The mule will intercept the coffin.

"Now I hear the Captain ordered one last emergency trip to the surface and back. This means a spaceboat to haul cargo is going down fast and back up fast. Fast means a simple orbit, one easy to match.

"So the cargo-mule will haul your coffin to the container the boat is towing once the boat is underway. Match orbits. Stow you aboard. Get it? The cargo box will be empty on the way down. The spaceboat heads for the planetfall, towing you. No one will be the wiser.

"Spaceboat will let the cargo box down nice and slow. A spare bottle of air, and a triscope with a gravitic altimeter are packed with you. And here is a pry bar. I am connecting the air bottle to your spacecloak. You should have plenty of time. Yes, don't look surprised."

Athos said, "It was you who stopped the spacecloak self-destruct?"

"Aye. I know all about Star Patrol tech. The Hooeys make 'em." *Hooey* was a slang term for a race properly called the Equines, an elder race of horse-like quadrupeds, revered and feared for their superhuman, dispassionate rationality.

Yeho continued: "Lady Jade from time to time still slips me a nugget of know-how. Very valuable, such inner skinny! Saved my face more than once. Saved my skin also. But batten down your yapping and open your ear! After touch down, no one will pay no never mind to an empty cargo box. You will have a few minutes before they come to stow gear aboard it. A few minutes! Captain is in a sweat of a hurry, like I've never seen, so the crew down there will not dawdle. Use the time to pry free the coffin lid. Use the triscope to see if the coast is clear. You get me?"

"I want my weapons."

"Cap'n took them for his trophy room, along with your skull. This is quieter." It was not his gigavolt lance pistol. Yeho passed him a needle-ray derringer. It could emit a narrow mid-megawatt particle beam that could kill a man at point blank range, but was otherwise useless. "The other weapons are counted and locked up. Liska fears disloyalty."

Athos scowled. "How about a kitchen knife, at least?"

"Take my toothpick." The huge toad passed him a dirk with a sharp, straight foot-long blade. In human hands, it was a short sword.

"Your supplier? Who? What world has black tech? Brain tech? The Empire fell before I was born! They are dead!"

"Some say dead come back, Mr. Ancient Mariner."

"The supplier! His name!"

"Where to pick up and where to put down is all I am told! Ask me no fool questions."

"I've heard stories of you on my mother's knee, Yeho! You always know more than what you are told. You poke into things. Who?"

"How did you pull that stunt at Sadalsuud? I saw you fall into a pit, and buried 'neath a landslide. How did you pull yourself out of the grave? Is the Ancient Mariner — is he real?"

But at that moment, before Athos could answer, a clamor of voice and the clatter of boots filled his ears. Men were coming: the burial detail. Yeho slammed the coffin lid shut with no delay.

Athos heard the noise of the bolts being tightened as the lid was sealed, then nothing. The coffin was airtight. With the lid down, no noise from outside could be heard.

"Wait!" called Athos, "There is an atomic aboard! Liska set it to blow! Look in the crate on the launch deck …" But it was no use.

After a moment, he felt the coffin being moved. The rocking motion told him it was being carried by the burial detail.

Then it came to rest. A long period of silence and darkness ensued. Athos had no timepiece: he brought up the medical readout of his spacecloak, so that his eyes would at least have little red numbers to look at, and he counted his heartbeats.

He counted to three thousand heartbeats. Half an hour. He had three and a half hours of air left.

Fear began to gnaw at his guts, small at first, but growing. Athos began to fret that something had gone horribly, horribly wrong. Yeho's disloyalty had been discovered. The captain and his men were standing around outside the coffin even now, watching him with a spy-ray, waiting for him to realize he was using up his available supply of oxygen.

Athos realized he was breathing heavily, sweating, panting. That was using up oxygen even more quickly. With an effort of will, he calmed himself. He said a prayer; he thought about his mission; he thought about his family.

These thoughts were not very calming: The weapons he had seen had been military grade, at a level of technology few worlds could mimic. This meant the supplier must be a large and well-funded organization, interplanetary in scope. It was far worse than what the Patrol had feared. And if he died in the field, the Patrol would not know the magnitude of the threat until it was too late. Something bigger than a raid on a shipping was in the offing.

That lead to darker thoughts. Not every world had joined with the new government. Many were still debating, especially in this quadrant. Failing to foresee and meet a major threat like this, failing to keep the peace, would surely make the ignorant yearn for a return of the Imperial form of government, with its empty promise of stability. It was a sickening prospect.

Thinking of his family was even worse. The burning desire for revenge pounded in his brain.

Suddenly he felt the coffin being moved again. Then, without warning, like a hammer blow, the crushing weight of multiple gravities of acceleration struck. Red sparks in the darkness filled his eyes: he could not breathe. The coffin had been shot out of the torpedo launch.

This tradition was older than stardrive itself, perhaps older than the Cluster Ark of legend that brought man to Andromeda from an older, earlier, antediluvian galaxy scholars dismissed as myth. Myth also gave the name of the first human buried in space as *Perry Rhoddenberry*, but what the name meant, or in what language, even historians had forgotten.

The acceleration shock was followed by the uncomfortable sensation of endlessly falling. Athos was an old spacehand, so the sensation of a stuffy head and benumbed feet distressed him very little, but the dark, claustrophobic confinement tinged each discomfort with an iron-hard bite of fear.

His head bumped against the lid of the coffin. That brought new disquiet: a body in free fall should not be gravitating toward one side of its container. This meant the coffin must be spinning rapidly enough to impart centrifugal force to any bodies inside, including his.

With no visual cues to aid him, merely the fear that he was spinning made his inner ear spin, so now it felt real. Perhaps it was real. The sensation was the same as hanging head-downward.

This was bad, because a cargo mule was little more than radar-guided clamp equipped with retrorockets, no smarter than a self-driving forklift. It would call back to a human stevedore aboard ship if it ran into any problem more complicated than its walnut-sized brain could handle. Solving the rendezvous maneuver of a tumbling object surely was such a problem.

If the mule, confused by the tumbling motion of what it had been asked to pick up, radioed back to the pirate ship, the cargo master would realize something was being smuggled onto the spaceboat from the coffin … which would spell the end of Athos's brief escape.

Athos remembered Yeho mentioning a triscope. Athos squirmed and ran his hands along the rough padding affixed to the coffin sides where he could reach. He fingers found the carry strap of a small kit box wedged between his knee and the coffin side. He pulled it. It fell, and struck him in the face. Inside, as promised, was the triscope.

The triscope was expertly made, with all the latest attachments. Unfortunately, the main spy ray, which would have allowed him a visual picture of the outside, could not penetrate the coffin.

The scope did have an analyzer, which told him the density and refractory ablation index of the material coating the coffin. It was a synthetic made of carbon nanotube fiber, one of those materials easy to store as a liquid, but which, when sprayed on equipment, would crystallize into a super-durable coating useful for withstanding the stresses, pressures, radiation and temperature extremes of work in outer space. Unfortunately, it blocked spy-rays on the visible band.

Long-wavelengths, however, could penetrate. He was able to pick up both the mass of the nearby planet, and the smaller, nearer metallic masses of the ship, the spaceboat, and even the idiot cargo mule. On a higher frequency above the visible spectrum, Athos could hear, but could not decode, the squeaks and squawks of navigation signals passing back and forth between ship and boat and cargo mule.

From the sound, he could tell there was an emergency afoot, but not what it was.

He could not see it happening, but the numbers of the readout told that the mule was being taken aboard the spaceboat. Meanwhile, the coffin was moving away from the pirate ship, and the spaceboat was accelerating toward the planet. The cargo mule was moving to intercept the spaceboat with an empty cargo box. But Athos was not inside.

Chill entered him. Something had gone wrong. Very wrong. His only hope of escape, of life, was getting farther and farther away.

Watching the numbers change as the minutes passed made hot and cold flushes pass through him, and the inner lining of the spacecloak labored to carry the sweat away from his flesh.

The pirate ship was in stationary orbit, hanging above one meridian on the globe. The coffin, which had been shot out like a torpedo, was in a lower orbit, hence had a higher orbital velocity. The spaceboat, on the other hand, was going much faster, and so it dropped lower and lower into the atmosphere.

Athos noted that the descent of the spaceboat was almost recklessly fast.

There was nothing to do but count his heartbeats and watch the number values change as the objects in space changed position, while the minutes of remaining air counted down and down.

After half an hour, Athos had three hours of air remaining. The de-orbiting spaceboat passed out of range of the triscope, its mass lost against the mass-readings of the much larger planet. Not long after, the triscope picked up the heat spike as the spaceboat began shedding reentry heat.

In that same half hour, the readings also told him the tumbling coffin was not in a circular orbit. Athos drew the derringer, dialing its needle beam to its lowest, shortest setting, so that a flicker of white-hot flame no longer than a fingertip issued from the barrel. This he used to scratch calculations on the inside of the coffin lid. The light from the needle beam was enough to let him read his own scratches.

Athos stared at the concluding sum in silence.

He checked his figures again, but there was no mistake. The coffin had ninety-one minutes to go before it completed its orbit of the planet. It was one of the niceties of a burial in space to give the corpse one last orbit, to let the dead man see the world receiving his ashes, and ship's company could watch for the flare like a falling star, when the coffin, and body within, were cremated.

As it finished the one and only one orbit it would make, the coffin would strike atmosphere, and burn.

The equations were as cold and stark as outer space. The numbers burned into the coffin lid held his death sentence.

CHAPTER 5: CENTURION OF THE EMPIRE

Galactic Year 12815, Planet Ksora

1. The Glory of Conquest

It was five years before when the twin suns in the indigo skies of Ksora still burned, and gazed upon a scene of woe.

A *Behemoth*-class Imperial superdreadnaught was a triangle of osmium alloy armor six thousand feet from stern tubes to prow guns, nearly a nautical mile. When she landed on a planetary surface, her superstructure loomed four hundred thirty feet above her keel, tall as a forty story building.

Such landings, needless to say, were quite rare. They were usually done to impress the natives.

The superdreadnaught *Omnipotent* made one of those rare landings. It was during the hour called Bright Eclipse, when the larger and dimmer of the two suns of Ksora passed before its brighter sister, and the sky grew dim.

Down the giant warship came atop the towers, minarets, halls, houses, ballparks, airports and loading yards, factories and stockyards, boulevards and tenements of Ksora-il-Faras, the planetary capital.

Repulsion fields issuing from the dorsal hullpates of the *Omnipotent* raised gale force winds. Downward-angled maneuvering jets popped and snapped from her gunnels as she delicately, slowly, inexorably lowered her five hundred thousand tons of mass.

Any monorails, ground-effect vehicles, caravan cars, men, women, children, robots, pets or livestock who had been unwilling or unable to clear the area were crushed. Maddened herd animals penned and waiting to be loaded onto cattle cars at the monorail terminal broke the gate and stampeded down the street. They did not escape.

Looters, or wandering lunatics, or anyone too stubborn to flee or too slow-witted to know the danger were wandering empty streets as the shadow of the great ship fell over them. They did not escape.

Vehicles and pedestrians on bridges and elevated turnpikes leading out of the quarter were caught in knots of congestion behind abandoned and overturned vehicles. Men flung themselves in panic off the high bridges. They did not escape.

The city once had boasted an underground system of warehouses and transit rails, power and sewer lines. These were collapsed and compressed into a thin layer underneath the weight of the city rubble pushed down into them.

This had been the oldest quarter of the city, the financial district and governor's mansion. The world would have no need of these hereafter.

The great ship lifted off again. The captain ordered ventral heat-rays to bathe the area, fusing the crushed and powdered rubble into one flat, steaming surface of glassy hue. It smelled of burning oil, hot metal, and blood.

If there were any survivors buried alive in the rubble, the heat-rays ended their dying screams. The superdreadnaught gained altitude. She cast her huge triangular shadow over the city.

Eventually, the second sun emerged from behind the first, making the sky grow bright. Imperial Legionnaires quick-marched out on the drill field which the superdreadnaught had so brutally and suddenly created. This field was several feet below the level of the surviving streets and buildings surrounding it, and so a combat engineer corps threw temporary ramps from the field to the sheered-off brinks of broken roads remaining.

Troopers in armor, rank after rank, marched out from the streets and gathered in the field. Landing craft brought in platoons and maniples from more distant points. Companies of one hundred men each marched behind their centurions. Before them went standard-bearers holding aloft the banners of each cohort and legion.

The auxiliaries were ordinary militiamen, gathered from planetary populations, wearing no more than breastplate and helm. The legionnaires were in full kit, armored from head to toe, terrifying in their skull-like facemasks.

More and more troopers marched. A mechanized cavalry of war-cars, siege guns or mobile towers accompanied each brigade. The vehicles were rolling on grinding treads, floating on invisible cushions of force, or stalking heavily on armored robotic legs.

The civilians being herded forward under the whips and lances of warbots, by contrast, walked, stumbled, and ambled out of step.

But before them all, in the position of honor marched the four cohorts from the throneworld's Praetorian Legion, the elite of the elite. Each was armored differently.

One column was in bone-white armor, with facemasks sporting a protrusion like the bill of crow. This was special breathing gear to protect them from the spores and fumes of their own filthy bio-warfare weapons. They allegedly combated such horrific manmade diseases, but, in these times, their office was to spread them. Their official title was the Scientific Security and Quarantine Cohort. The common man called them the Plague Doctors.

They destroyed life on worlds suspected of harboring forbidden technology — using forbidden technology to do so.

The next column was blood-red, and the ground shook at their tread, for these troopers wore cybernetic limbs for arms and legs, and their armor was bonded to their flesh. Their eyes were glassy from the pharmaceuticals circulating in brain and bloodstream, making them immune to fear, fatigue, and pain. These were the personal bodyguard and the shocktroopers of the Imperial household, cyborgs robbed of manhood, who lived for death in battle.

This half-machine half-human cohort controlled the Omega Weapons, which all men abominated. Theirs was the power to call earthquakes, tidal disruptions, or solar flares to wipe out whole globes in a single hour, or hurl moons out of the sky.

Commoners called them the Red Guard. Their mission was terror, terror sufficient to shatter any dream of armed resistance to the iron will of the Empire.

Next marched a column in armor of darkest black, shining like ink. This was the enforcement arm of the dreaded Distribution Tribunals, whose word decreed which planets should thrive, and which should starve. Unlike the Red Guard, these black troopers were for use against civilians. Their weapon was to unleash cubic-mile-wide clouds of bug-sized bug-winged robo-tools called Confiscators. These automatic deconstruction units were not large nor smart enough to be infected by rebel skullbox-hacks. The swarms were slow but inexorable. They were able to strip and carry away a field of its crops, a town of its useful metals, a herd of its livestock, or a city of its people, in shockingly swift time.

The black, metallic cloud would pass across the face of the globe, murmuring, darkening the skies, to expropriate and depopulate and abduct. The sight of such clouds on the horizon wafting slowly toward the defenseless towns was the final sign that their world had been condemned for public use.

As the confiscator cloud passed, whole factories and worktowns, dismantled, were pulled into orbit by tractor beams for freighters to tow. By the millions, the young and healthy in chains were hauled away by fleet upon fleet of slaveships. By the millions, the old and sick and otherwise useless were left to starve in stripped streets, empty ranches, and dusty fields.

The official title of this cohort was a windy, high-sounding falsehood: Social Police for Sumptuary Excess, Unfair Trade, and Exploitation. Men simply called them the Locust Legion. Ruin and famine followed in their shadow.

Finally came the Psychological Warfare Special Operations Cohort. These were the warriors of the mind. Theirs was the task to enforce the psychiatric compliance and social conformity edicts of the Inquisition.

These marched in armor of a pale color that was no color. At times it seemed greenish-gray, or corpse-pale, or like the hue a man sees behind his eyes just before he faints. They commanded psychological warfare technologies forbidden on all civilized worlds: positronic brain hacks on robots, or nerve-control implants into living brains; neurotoxic energy weapons; mind-altering pharmaceuticals; and hypno-optical projections. To them was given the power to punish incorrect thought, incorrect belief, incorrect hope.

Those who entered the confession cells of the Inquisition usually returned alive, if horribly altered in speech and countenance, mannerism and mien. It was for another reason entirely that these legionnaires retained the name of the Deathguard. If any cohort were more feared than the others among the First Legion, it was theirs.

Together, the units of the Praetorian Legion were called the Four Viceroy Cohorts, since each acted with the full deputized powers of the Emperor, overriding all local law. But the common man, when it was safe to whisper, called them the Four Vile Cohorts.

Before the cohorts marched the standard bearer for the gathered Imperial Armed Forces, his pikestaff tipped with the Black Cogwheel.

The cohorts, legionnaires, auxiliaries and armored infantry approached the execution grounds. Here, the engineers had set up the huge jet-black cube of the Disintegration Chamber, one hundred yards broad and wide and tall. It was a bleak and ominous sight. The troopers stationed near it were in double-layered radiation armor, and robotic units holding portable shields had formed a cordon around it.

The Proconsul's pinnace had landed in an open area facing the Disintegration Chamber, but a safe distance from it. The troops in their myriads marched past.

2. Culling the Unfit

Centurion Thret Ansteel was there among the Deathguards in shimmering gray-pale armor, as he marched in step with the company he led: Mandragora Maniple was one hundred men consisting of two platoons of fifty each, Nightshade Platoon and Belladonna Platoon.

Beneath his boots, the flattened and fused ruins of the capital's central quarter still smoked. His breathing gear did not filter out the stench of fresh blood seeping up from the soil.

His red officer's cloak swung with his footfalls, and whiplike scarlet helmet-plumes nodded. Whether in armor of pale or black or white, centurions wore red cloaks. For the Red Guard, the Emperor's personal terror-troops, it was otherwise: their centurions wore cloaks of white trimmed with purple, the Imperial household colors.

The Proconsul used the loading ramp of his pinnace as a reviewing stand. This was lowered from the belly of his ship, between the crooked landing legs, protruding like some fantastic metal tongue. Ansteel turned his eyes and gave the stiff-armed salute along with all his men as they passed. The thunder of boots and clamp of vehicle legs echoed from the tilted and broken building surrounding the flattened field.

With the Proconsul were other dignitaries, both Imperial and planetary. General Rookfar Hax, Commandant of Marines, who had led the surface expedition to a brilliant conclusion, was there; Grand Inquisitor Baligant, whose office was charged with imposing conformity of speech, behavior and thought; and Sobekhotep the Aedile, who directed the publicans and tax-gatherers to strip the planet of resources, population, and goods for tribute.

The newly-appointed local puppet leader, the planetary chief, along with his ministers and family were brought forward under escort, eyes blinking and fearful. They evidently did not know if they were guests or prisoners. They were led up the landing ramp and forced to stand next to the Proconsul, who greeted them with a smile. These bowing natives were Variant humans, differing from base stock only in pigmentation. These had purple skin and pink hair.

The Proconsul was a Nemean, of course, with the luxurious fur, cat-muzzle, lion-mane and gleaming gold eyes of the old stock. He also had the aura of dignity, power, and beauty of his race. The white fangs of his smile were alarming to behold. As always when hominids stood near one of them, the Nemean seemed taller, as the humans seemed to shrink.

All the brigades marched past the reviewing stand and stood on the field. No other place had been large enough to hold the armies.

The Proconsul made a speech, which Ansteel did not heed. He merely had the sound system in his helmet broadcast the sound of his voice cheering when the other officers cheered.

Then came the executions. Ansteel did not watch closely as hundreds of wretched figures, including women and children in chains, were driven or dragged out toward where the engineers had erected the squat, heavy, dark and ugly bulk of the Disintegration Chamber. The condemned, whimpering, were herded in the open area before the troops, between the streamlined white-and-gold elegance of the Proconsul's vessel and the stark black cube of death.

At the bottom of the cube was the one-way intake gate into which the condemned would be driven ten at a time. It gaped as wide as the mouth of an abattoir, but it was utterly black. This valve was filled with an opaque force that permitted light and matter to travel one way, inward. Nothing solid could pass the other way. Nothing escaped.

The walls of the huge cube were reinforced, multiple layers of radiation armor, over a yard thick. Atop squatted the atomic pile. The control rods were designed so that they could not be raised until the heavily shielded blast doors were lowered over the intake valve. This way, no power could be released onto the bodies of the condemned until the aperture was sealed shut. Allowing even the smallest ray of the all-destroying force to escape the interior would prove disastrous.

This was an anti-nucleonic energy that neutralized the force holding atoms together: normal matter affected became radioactive and dissolved. Each living cell, blood drop, and nerve ending of an organism would be scalded by its own radioactivity as it lost coherence and melted. The process could be slowed just enough to make this the most lingering and painful form of execution. It was too difficult to contain, too uncertain, too grisly, too dangerous to be used as a weapon on the battlefield.

But the Inquisition policy held that the danger of using such machinery was outweighed by the psychological benefit to onlookers, to encourage loyalty.

There had been no trials, of course, no formal hearings. Trials were for Imperial citizens. This quota of malcontents had been rounded up by the Inquisition, based on information gathered secretly and scientifically.

The Grand Inquisitor read the charges: it was the usual boilerplate language. "In the name of the Senate and People of Andromeda, the Imperial decree published to all worlds…" blah, blah, blah "… be it known to all peoples, cyborgs, and sapient artifacts, that on this day …" blah, blah and more blah "…neither shall it be permitted nor tolerated that any should entertain or hold extravagant, unscientific, immoderate, or nonconformist beliefs, opinions, speculations, or fancies…" it just went on and on.

The condemned were chained five or ten together. Humiliating conical caps had been affixed to their heads, spelling out their crimes and folly in blinking holographic letters.

"... all human and robotic thought has been definitively and scientifically proved to obey iron laws of cause and effect, to be material phenomena only, with no spiritual dimension or meaning ... the Imperial findings are binding on all tributaries, subjects and citizens of the Empire ..."

Each group had its lead chain connected to an anchor cable leading into the interior of the Disintegration Chamber. Once the cable was set in motion, the condemned must walk into the black aperture, or be dragged.

"... belief in any form of supernatural, preternatural, or paranormal phenomena is strictly forbidden ... it is anathema .... "

Perhaps out of boredom, or perhaps because they misunderstood some word the Inquisitor's creaking voice muttered, the soldier in charge of the execution activated the anchor cable. Slowly, inexorably, step by step and yard by yard, the startled, stumbling prisoners began shuffling, five at a time, into the black force filling the intake gate.

As soon as a hand or foot, shoulder or elbow touched the mirror-smooth surface of black energy, it was futile to tug or pry. Only amputation would have allowed anyone to escape. But who could see his body being absorbed without raising a hand to try to pull away? Any fist striking uselessly at the black entryway would be trapped as well. And the anchor cable pulled the chains taut, and link by link, whether the condemned resisted or despaired, he was drawn into the black surface.

The voice droned on: "Psychic, psionic, superhuman powers are condemned as unscientific and outdated ... it is anathema ... "

The one-way field prevented matter from exiting the death chamber, but sound still carried: Screams and shout of anguish rose up, the sobs and shrieks of women, and the cries of young boys calling on their mothers for help.

The Grand Inquisitor continued speaking, and did not bother raising his voice above the screams.

"... the opiate of the masses ... anathema... charlatans and their tricks ... matter in motion is all that exists ... "

It was not that the screams and shouts bothered Ansteel. Had he heard countless screams from countless throats during training, during culls and duels, and in war.

But these, for some reason, annoyed him. They were enemies of the Empire. What else did he need to know? These enemies, however, were chained. No one could fight back.

That made no difference. Did it? It should not make any difference.

"… demonstrably proved by the progress of science … there is no existence after death … it is therefore fitting that any transgressors be condemned to the oblivion of non-being …"

He saw children being dragged by their chains ever closer to the dark interior. The line moved so slowly. The children clung frantically to women who, to judge by face and race, were clearly the mothers of the children they could not protect. Some were clearly not. Mothers or strangers did not matter. All alike would hug and comfort any child in her arms.

Ansteel, beneath his mask, wore a strange, blank expression. He was creche-born. Nowhere in his youth was any memory of any embrace from a mother's arms.

He saw a sad and horrible sight, oft repeated. As the black threshold loomed, at the last moment, such a woman always placed her body between the dark interior and the child grasping her. Then she would pry the child off, and push away the grasping, clinging, crying child. She would hold him out to the full length of the taut chains, trying to keep the little one outside as long as possible. The child, not understanding, would flail more wildly and wail more loudly.

That also should make no difference. Little boys were just small enemies who would one day grow into soldiers. And the women, if left unchecked, would bear enemies. And little girls would one day … would…

Ansteel started in confusion. Where were the little girls that were supposed to be in this group today?

3. Investigation of Abnormality

Centurion Ansteel's command had been the one involved in hunting down and rounding up Abnormals. Deathguards alone had the specialized equipment which could examine Kirlian auras and detect sudden fluxes or disorders in the mind-body relationship.

The official story was that such manifestations of mind powers, such as reports of inanimate objects moving on their own, were all the work of subversive elements or religious fanatics, using holograms or invisible force-rays or other stage-magic gimmicks to fool the gullible.

Ansteel knew the official story was bunk, of course. If it were impossible for a man with a magic sword to parry heat-rays and shoot lightning, Ansteel would have enjoyed the use of both eyes for the past eight years.

It was bunk, but it was the official story. One never questions the official story.

"… fortune-telling, psychokinetic motion, defying gravity, appearing in dreams, or any use of extra sensory perception, are therefore signs of treason, and must be extinguished and expunged utterly, in order to maintain the peace, unity, and good order of the Empire …"

But Ansteel had seen the little girls his men discovered, preadolescents, who were able to open locks or trip prison guards from yards away, moving objects with their minds. The abnormals had been operating out of an orphanage, of all places.

"… let their names be anathema … all records expunged …"

Centurion Ansteel turned off his external speakers. He did not need to hear more. He had heard it all before.

But something was off.

Now Centurion Ansteel activated the built-in scopes in his helmet goggles. With his one eye, he zoomed in on the view of the chained prisoners. The bio-scan marked which were male and which female, and his targeting computer estimated their mass. There were large and small male bodies and large female bodies. No small females.

Ansteel, during the worldwide hunt for Abnormals, had locked certain orphan girls into starvation cells, with savory food sitting on the bench before them out of reach, along with the keys. One was pink haired, a native. The other was brown haired, an offworlder.

He watched from hiding. For obvious reasons, he dared use no cameras, no scanners. Ansteel with his naked eye had seen one orphan levitate the keys across the air into grubby, eager fingers. Another one had opened the combination lock without the knowing the combination, as if she could see the tumblers and pins of the lock as she twisted the dials

There was no trickery involved, no stage magic, no hidden wires or tractor-pressor rays.

The girls volunteered the information without torture or hypnotics. Where had they learned this art? An older girl had taught them, a few years back. She was an off-worlder, strangely colored: pale of skin and black of hair. Her street-name was *Lightfoot*, but the girls called her *Princess*. Her real name? Life on the streets was hard. No one used a real name. Where was this princess now? Gone. Long gone. Where? No one knew where.

Inquisition officers had arrived shortly thereafter and relieved Ansteel of his two underage prisoners. He knew better than to ask their fate. He remembered how he had sat in their jail cell after they were gone, in overlapping patches of sunlight coming through the barred window from the two suns. He had to get rid of the ragdolls he had made out of an old pair of gloves, one for each girl.

Where were those two girls now? They were clearly Abnormals, possessing some sort of inexplicable powers, call them what you will. Why were they not chained with the others?

The condemned gathered here were nothing more than people who claimed to have seen something miraculous or supernatural.

Why would the Empire execute the witnesses of miracles, and spare the miracle-workers?

Ansteel was distracted by the sight of a prisoner, a stout-set, bald, old man with purple skin and a generous beard of snow-white hair. He was not resisting the tug of the chains, but walking calmly, hands folded, eyes turned to the sky, mouth wide. Ansteel could not hear what the old man was calling out.

Someone else had noticed the same whitebeard. One of the Red Guard, a cyborg, stepped on mechanical legs into the midst of the chained prisoners, snapping open a folded punching-dagger from his forearm housing as he came. This was a vicious weapon, a cubit long.

The cyborg stabbed the white-bearded prisoner, driving the blade in to its hilts. The whitebeard made no move to avoid the blow. He was pierced through his side and fell in a fountain of blood. The prisoners adjacent, faces twisted with grief and compassion, tried to hold him upright. Bleeding, dying, perhaps already dead, the old whitebeard was pulled into the opening by his chains, and was swallowed up.

Ansteel also saw agitation among the dignitaries gathered on the reviewing stand, looks of fear. He saw the civilian onlookers behind him growing restless. The Proconsul was bristling, his lion-mane puffed up to twice its size.

Ansteel turned on his earphones. He was shocked to hear what the condemned were doing.

Singing. They were singing.

The cyborg legionnaire in red had acted quickly to silence the nonconformist, but now other prisoners were taking up the refrain. Those inside the chamber, waiting to be disintegrated, could hear what was happening outside. They joined in the swelling song. The armored walls of the chamber amplified the echoes of their chords. The one-way field blocking the intake gate was solid enough to carry air vibrations like a tympani. Their bodies could never escape the death chamber, but sounds could. Song could.

Trapped in the black chamber, with radiation armor to every side, and a deadly atomic pile overhead, waiting for the control rods to be withdrawn, waiting for a prolonged, painful, gruesome death, the condemned sang. They actually sang.

It was a song he had heard once in childhood, a paean to the Golden Will. *Man is more than man*, ran the words, *Life is more than life*!

There were no musical instruments. It was merely the normal, untrained voices of normal men and women. Ansteel forgot himself for a moment. He had never heard anything so fair to the ear.

> *Beings of eternal light we are,*
> *if confined for now in clay,*
> *bright as an immortal star,*
> *as glorious as day…*

Ansteel saw the danger. There were too many witnesses here, seeing something that should not be. How could anyone sing? Lungs should be choked with fear, the air should be filled with screams. It was too obviously inexplicable.

A chill ran up his spine. Someone was watching him. He could feel the pressure of unseen eyes.

4. Weapons of the Mind-Killers

He was at attention, and not supposed to move. Despite this, Ansteel craned his head back, looking up. It was daytime. Two suns filled the sky. No stars were visible. The stars could not be looking down, seeing this, somehow giving unseen aid to the dying. That was not possible. Stars were inanimate objects, merely balls of flaming gas.

With a silent curse, he ignored that strange sensation of strange eyes piercing him. There was no time to fret about that now.

Over his radio link, he issued quick orders the decurion that served him as a lieutenant, the soft-spoken Tufir Expel of Nightshade Platoon. Decurion Expel was unflappable, and did not hesitate. Nightshade Platoon's four-man fireteam in the front rank activated their stealth and readied their shocklances.

The legionnaires did not literally fade from view, but anyone within the active radius of the optic-nerve induction fields would not be able to see these men clearly. For all practical purposes, as far as biological eyes and brains were concerned, they were hidden by a mist. They were unnoticeable.

The weapons of the his men were not obvious and inexorable, like the world-devastating confiscator swarms of the black-clad Locust Troopers. The bodies of his man were not immune to pain, energy, fire and gunfire, like the cybernetic half-undead machine-men of the blood-red Terror Troopers. Nor could a small squad of his unit slay whole continents with slow rot or rapid pestilence, like the white-armored Plague Troopers.

The weapons of the mist-clad mind-killers were more subtle. Their terror was not meant to be seen.

It was important that no witnesses see. The fireteam dialed their arms to a low setting and fired. At this setting, there was no visible discharge.

It is easy to effect the human nervous system. In fact, hominids were cursed with the easiest nervous system of the several races of the galaxy to influence. A neurotoxin, if properly configured, could trigger psychedelic episodes.

The soldiers swept their weapons up and down the line. Corporal Leven Dee, the top-rated sharpshooter in the platoon, was on his belly, launcher resting on a bipod. The muzzle peered out between the legs of legionnaire who stood before him, blocking any casual view. Dee engaged the sound-suppressor, and sent his payload, an emitter, a gray dart no bigger than a fist, straight and true into the wide intake gate of the disintegration chamber. In the uproar of songs and shouts, the crack of the weapon was inaudible. Not even a Ralline had eyes sharp enough to see an object flung by presserbeam at the speed of sound, but Ansteel, who was watching for it, saw the flicker as the intake-gate admitted the payload.

The emitter passed into the black surface of the door, to fill the interior with a potent but silent expanding globe of hallucinogenic nerve-energy. The thick walls of the chamber, as they were designed to do, prevented any leak of the nerve-energy outward. No one outside the chamber could see anything, and no one inside would ever leave, except as an isotopic mass of noble gasses.

The result was gratifying and immediate. The beautiful song broke into ugly laughter and gargling sobs and strange gibbering. Instead of stately lyrics rising to the sky, now came only babbling nonsense and shrieks. One voice called out a nursery rhyme. Another recited the words from an advertising jingle.

Under his scowling facemask, Ansteel smiled grimly. Who, later, would recall the impossible song of praise soaring from the doors of the death chamber? The data tapes, once they were doctored, would only hold the sounds of lunatics, driven mad by fear.

The honor of the Empire was safe. No one would know.

Honor..? Is it, indeed?

A voice spoke in his head: *No one will know, think ye? Nary a soul?*

CHAPTER 6: LAST OF LYONESSE

Galactic Year 12820, Planet Zavijava, Orbit

1. A Fatal Orbit

The slow seconds turned into slow minutes as Athos counted down what surely was his final hour.

Coolly, calmly, he reviewed and indexed all the tools, weapons, and raw materials available to him. He pondered each thing in reach both as a whole and by its components: An air bottle; a triscope; a spacecloak, a derringer, a knife. The synthetic carbon nanotube alloy of the coffin. The padding and fabric lining the interior. His physical body: hair, bones, teeth, blood.

Calmly, coolly, he worked and reworked the equations inscribed on the coffin lid. There was no mistake, no misplaced decimal. He would strike the upper atmosphere at a steep angle, and begin to burn.

If he dismantled the triscope, and used the power cell to overload the magnetic monopole core of his derringer, it could produce a burst of radiowaves the pirate ship might pick up. If they rescued him, he would be alive for another short span of time … but that surely would lead to the discovery and death of Yeho, his mother's old crewmate and friend. Not the proper return for the courageous aid the toad man had bestowed.

Athos spent his last hour watching the triscope and reciting what few prayers he could recall from childhood. Athos was not, by nature, a spiritually-minded man. He thought the stars were balls of burning plasma, not messengers of a higher power who helped guide fate.

But here he was in his coffin, with no escape. So why not? Regrets? He had a surprising number.

But there was no time left to mend things with his father. No time to beat any sense into the foppish dunce his once-admirable brother had somehow turned into.

The Lone family was dishonored in the eyes of the elders of Arislan, smothered in two generations of shame, and now there was no time left to undo that great and lasting wrong.

The greatest of the elders was the retired clan Patriarch, Ar Arislan, his harsh and terrible great-grandfather. What Athos would have done for a kind word, a kind look, from him! Athos' formidable great aunt, Dame Bast of Darkmoon, had assumed the mantle of leadership of the ancient and noble family of Arislan, of which the Lone line was a small offshoot. It was Dame Bast who, thanks to his family history, had forbidden him to see or speak to the fair lady Niobe of Lyonesse.

And now? A captain of the Patrol, having failed a secret mission, passing away without even an official report of the circumstances of his death? How did this lend any honor to his bloodline?

Lady Niobe may or may not know his true feelings toward her. Most likely, she did not. She thought him infatuated, or, worse, an ambitious social climber, seeking to wed above himself, taking a shortcut to regain lost status for himself and his embarrassment of a family.

His greatest regret was that Captain Liska lived.

"Stars above!" he whispered, "Stars from whom all worlds come! If you can hear me, grant this to my sorrowing soul: let me not die ere the vengeance I have vowed be done!"

His words did not sound sorrowing.

Athos felt the impulse to recheck his calculations. Better to know the exact time he would enter the atmosphere, and die. Rather than ignite his derringer beam again, he fished out his locket and opened it. The glow from the holo-image was faint, but enough to make out his scratches on the coffin side. The numbers spelled out the same message of death.

The tiny image of the head turned, looked over her shoulder, and smiled at him.

2. A Faithful Image

Her features were haunting, her countenance one of mysterious beauty. Her skin was coppery brown, but rich and soft as polished amber. The eyes were black, deep, and brilliant beneath finely arched brows. Her expression in repose was like that of a sculptured sphinx, betraying an almost inhuman serenity and intellectual force. But in the next moment, a tilt of her head, the ivory white brilliance of her smile shining between the lush red cupid's bow of her lips, made the vitality and joy of life seem to leap from her expression, like that of a mystic imp or antic sprite.

In the locket image, she wore her hair folded into a high, conical bun behind her head in the classic style, in a riot of dark, loose curls, not quite confined in a crisscross of diamond-studded chains. Escaping wisps brushed the nape of her swanlike neck.

How different this was than when he had first laid eyes on her! It had been seven years ago.

3. Idle Stableboys

Galactic Year 12817, Planet Vindamiatrix

Athos remembered each detail. It had happened the same year that his older sister, Mirdath, the youngest Tribune ever elected, had successfully negotiated the signature of the truculent swamp-dwelling Devonian race, bringing their sectors under control of the Commonwealth. The announcement had been made amid universal acclaim, and had come to Vindamiatrix just on the date of Athos' 21 birthday, his age of majority, so the celebration of the anniversary of his birth had been somewhat muted and forgotten.

The Duke thought it was time for Athos, now a man, to learn to run the family estate, and sent him out to ride the bounds, along with a cheerful young law clerk, a grumpy old groom, a fussy and precise squire, and two taciturn surveyors.

Athos, for the occasion, had been granted the privilege to ride his father's steed, a breed called a destrier: a huge, black, shaggy-maned but ill-tempered beast named Hawkswift, who was indeed as fleetfooted as the name implied.

It was a two week trip up and down the boundary between the coastal croplands and the great northern forest that spread, without break, up to the arctic circle. The foresters who kept the ancient wood, where no vehicles were allowed, were grumbling again about yeomen farmers of the region clearing land. The farmers claimed the trespass was a necessity, that the weather control guild favored the foresters, and was deflecting rainfall meant for their crops. Athos was young, but he kept his stern temper despite the various bouts of flattery and bickering, and forced both sides into a compromise that neither liked.

The weather control guild liked the compromise least of all, because it imposed additional duties on them under the same planetary contract. Their lawyer acceded with surly grace.

By way of droll revenge, Wenk Firmin, the chief weatherman, arranged unseasonable fogs and storms to harass the land Athos said needed more rainfall, just as Athos was passing back through it. The unpaved road became a muddy canal, and the world turned into silver sheets and curtains of drenching cold.

His comdisc call to the orbital meteorological control stations were answered by a polite robot, who politely took his angry message. The robot was politely issuing a flood warning, even while Athos watched his pavilion and camping gear get swept away by a canal that overtopped its banks.

Athos allowed his men, once they were free of the forest, to ship themselves home in sprint cars —all air traffic was grounded — and have grooms or robots ride or lead their steeds to the nearest monorailhead, to be shipped home in stockcars.

Concerning his father's mount, however, Athos would not suffer the indignity of yielding the saddle to another rider, even if the proud steed would have allowed it. And the prospect of shipping Hawkswift by rail, short- tethered, hobbled, booted and hooded, was out of the question.

So Athos stubbornly spent his next few days struggling in the downpour, trying to master his father's half-wild horse. At time, losing control, he would let the steed gallop down muddy foottrails like a mad motorboat, with wings of brown water splashing from flying hooves. Hawkswift reared when the lightning fell, and neighed his challenge to answer the thunder.

Drenched and ill-tempered himself, a saddle-weary, cold, and aching, Athos finally reached the grounds of the family estate. No one, not staff nor family, ventured into the downpour to greet him.

The stable door, for some reason, had been left open. Athos rode inside. His hat was as soggy as if it had been dunked in a sea for a week, but the sudden lack of the feeling of rain drumming on his head made him feel as if his skull had gone numb.

He saw two stableboys, short and slight of build, who were loitering near the palfreys. Both wore the livery of horse-grooms, with and rain gear, that is, yellow hats with shoulder-length flaps and bulky all-weather cloaks, and both were dripping copiously. Two horses stood nearby, heads down. The saddles had been removed, but neither stableboy had lifted a hand to rub down, curry, comb, or dry the animals, nor was either preparing feed.

Instead the horses stood, neglected and miserable, while the two idle youths — their voices were slight and high, and their smothered laughs were boyishly shrill — chattered gaily.

Their voices were lost in the hammering of the rain on the roofboards, so Athos heard nothing clearly.

Both fell into sudden, guilty silence when Athos appeared, mounted on a monstrous, tall steed. With a loud, slow clap of hoofbeats, he drew near and loomed over them. Down he glared, and water drizzled and dripped from every part of steed and rider.

Neither raised a hand to see to his horse. Athos choked back the impulse to utter a blistering space-oath, as his mother might have done. Instead, in cold silence, he dismounted.

The grooms must have been ashamed indeed, for their heads hung low, and a wide, wet hatbrim hiding each face. He threw the leads of his horse's rein sharply into the first lad's chest, snapping, "See to my father's horse, and to these two, which are also his! Why haven't they been brushed and groomed?"

The near stableboy did not lift his head, but answered with a grunt and a small nod, fumbling to catch the reins. In the gloom of the stable, his hands seemed unduly slender, soft, and white.

Athos was turning away, eager for a hot bath and a hotter meal, but halted in annoyance at this show of disrespect. It was not so much the neglect toward him he minded; but neglect of the animals was unforgiveable.

There were many servants on the estate, and, unlike his gregarious brother Napoleon, Athos did not keep track of all their names. He was embarrassed to ask, so he said, "You have not been grooms for long?"

The second one spoke. His voice was hoarse and growling, like someone mimicking a sore throat. It was a thin, boyish voice, pitched deep as if to try to sound older. "Not that long, m'lord."

The first stableboy smothered a snort of laughter.

It was a familiar voice. Athos knew it, could not place it. He stepped forward, and snatched at the stableboy's wet hat. A cascade of hair spilled forth, brunette, rich, scented curls.

The impish face of his younger sister Mevrian was beneath, startled and shocked, but her green eyes were bright with mirth.

But the sudden motion irked Hawkswift. Or perhaps the giant horse sensed the uncertainty in the soft grip holding his reins. The steed reared, bugling.

The first stableboy uttered a shrill scream, feminine and musical. The flying hoofs of the rearing horse, each as hard and deadly as a flying sledge hammer, whirled near the cowering boy's skull.

Athos did not hesitate, but flung himself headlong through the air, snatching up the slender form of the groom in his arms as he flew. The force of his leap carried them both well beyond the reach of the wild kicks.

They landed in the straw together. The boy's hat was flung away. A rich cascade of raven hair, black as ink, silky and shining, spilled out wildly across the straw a cubit or more. Jeweled combs none but a lady of highest birth might wear in her hair fell tinkling onto the dirty stable floor.

He could feel the warm curves of the scented body beneath him, the yielding figure tightly held in his young, strong arms. The dark-eyed, red-lipped beauty favored him with a cryptical gaze, saying nothing, showing no expression, not even surprise. Their gazes grew as one: he lost his soul in the depth of her eyes.

Athos remembered himself in the next breath, and felt the heat of a blush beating in his face with his hammering heart. The embarrassment was unbearable. Who was this fair young lady he had mussed, thrust down, and manhandled? Mud from his hard ride was now splattered on her.

"I'm sorry!" he stammered.

The arched eyebrows lifted, and the cryptical gaze grew, if anything, more cryptical, "For saving my life…? I should think not."

4. His Sister and Her Accomplice

He could not tell what this meant. Mockery? Contempt? With a gasp of shock at himself, he realized his arms were still locked around her, pressing her sweet body most intimately and electrically into his. He yanked his hands free, fumbling, slipping in his haste to take his weight off her, and wishing he were dead.

His wish was answered immediately with the thunder of hoofs behind. The great steed was about to trample them both. Athos leaped upright, and raised his arms as Hawkswift reared again, snorting, eyes wild. Athos put his body in the path of the charge, shielding the girl.

Athos spoke to the beast, a voice calm and commanding, his father's voice.

Mevrian gave a yelp of fear during this commotion, and scurried over to the other young lady, helping her to her feet. Now they stood with arms around each other, looking up at the huge steed as it reared and plunged. The girls seemed small as children in their oversized raincoats.

But soon Athos had the mastery of the animal. Athos took the bridle in hand and stroked the savage steed's nose, now speaking soothing words. The great steed grew calm.

Athos did not want to release his hold on the bridle. He spoke without turning his head. "Help me with this. Dismount the saddle and tack. No, you fool! Never come from behind! Sis! You know better than that!"

But the figure was not his sister. It was the raven-haired girl. "As you've been told, we have not been grooms long."

Athos was tongue tied, but Mevrian said softly, "Approach a horse from the left and front. Speak, so he knows of your presence."

Athos said, "This is no work for a lady!"

Mevrian's eyes flashed. "Well! I like that! What am I?"

Athos snapped, "A country cousin!"

The raven-haired beauty said, "He means you know your way around horses, Merry."

The beauty moved with a dancer's grace over to a haybale, where she knelt like a sylph on a rock, her shapely legs folded under her. Her slender body was almost lost amid the voluminous folds of her raincloak. She took her long black locks in hand, combing them back in shape, and began to fold and braid them atop her head, replacing the pins and combs she had dropped.

With her hair down, she looked like a schoolgirl, no older than Mevrian his sister, whom Athos could not see as anything but a little child. But with her hair worn up, which was a fashion tradition allowed only after a girl's debut, when she was introduced as a lady to polite society, Athos could not see Mevrian's friend as anything but a woman. Confused (at seventeen, he was often confused) he looked sidelong at his sister, who had returned from stowing the saddle and tack and had taken up a curry brush. Was she now older, too?

Seeing his gaze, Mevrian glared at him. "What? I haven't done anything wrong! And you cannot prove it."

Athos was surprised and annoyed. But since his younger sister always surprised and annoyed him —younger sisters are weird monsters, after all — in a way, he was not surprised, and not really annoyed. "You have not properly introduced me."

"Athos, this is Hawkswift. Hawkswift, Athos. Careful! He bites."

Athos was just then gingerly releasing the bridle. He said calmly, "He won't bite me…"

Mevrian smirked and lifted her nose said in a lilting tone, "I wasn't talking to you!"

Athos finished removing the tack from Hawkswift, scowling like a thundercloud.

The darkhaired girl said, "I am Niobe del Cassilda Linn, Lady Lyonesse, daughter of the late Archduke Endymion Lyonesse, and the late Lady Arianrhod." She smiled sadly, "I was raised by the family

Librarian. For generations, the Dukes of Lyonesse collected books. So you can see, I don't know much about horses."

Athos had begun currying the wet horse, but now his brush hesitated. He had heard about the terrible things which befell that clan during the war, including that the Archduke and his wife and family had been sent to the death camps of Cafalnasir. He had not known there were any survivors. The girl was an orphan, but not one whose parents had died peacefully. Had she been raised, in her early years, behind bars, behind barbed wire, caged by burning fields of force on lethal wavelengths? He face grew dark, and his voice was stiff, with no trace of emotion. "I am sorry for your loss."

Niobe inclined her head. "I was a babe in arms when it happened, so I have no memory of the tragedy, but I thank you for your kind heart."

Athos scowled again, and continued brushing.

"And, before you ask," she continued, "A bribed guard smuggled me into a stasis can, wrapped in a blanket. I was outside of time, in an enchanted sleep. When the death unleashed by Lord Pestilence passed over the camp, I was untouched, dreaming strange dreams. Holy Men seeking bodies to bury dug me up, and found me preserved. I am older than I look. Some of the family servants were on far planets, and so escaped arrest. The Librarian who raised me was among them. The surface of the Museum World of Cervantes was destroyed in the war, of course, but the Empire never dug up the buried vaults and crypts. I was raised in a subterranean museum-city full of books and treasures, and so I never had much chance to ride. But I love horses!" She clapped her hands prettily.

Athos said, "Ko-Manu says there is no reason for people with starships and supersonic fliers to travel on horseback. Father says we do it to outrage the Equines, who kept our ancestors as beasts of burden."

"And what do you say?" asked Niobe, "You were just out riding."

"Ko-Manu is right that motor travel is faster. But, if you are on a colony world, a landcar cannot refuel by eating grass. Nor can you get a new model just by waiting for foaling time in spring. Colonials buy the breeds of Vindamiatrix for their size and stamina. Park worlds, where nobles hunt and sport, and tourists holiday, like our breeds for their handsome looks. That is all there is to it."

Niobe's eyes sparkled. "Oh, I am sure there is deeper meaning here! Look at hawks and hounds and dinosaurs, bees and butterfly, elm and oak and willow, rose and lotus. There are living things found on so many earthlike worlds, that no one can explain it. Some say all these myriad examples were cases of parallel evolution, but can not say what causes the parallel; some say ancient races spread them, but no ancient race has record of doing so. Some whisper of the Preservers, whom legends say carried races threatened with extinction to other worlds, to save them. Arcadian books say evolution is shaped by the stars for their own divine purposes, and that no one can understand earthly worlds who ignores mysteries of heaven. Some say there is a mystical bond between horse and man. Do not even Templars call themselves 'knights' — another word for 'chevalier'?"

"And your opinion, my lady?"

She smiled at some inner thought. "The answer lies in the far past, in eons long forgotten. How can we uncloud these enigmas now? So little of those far-off days remain."

Athos wanted to smile at her, but was afraid he would look silly. He paused, brush in hand, muddy garb still dripping, and gave a brief bow. "You have told me all about yourself, but we have not been introduced. I am Athos."

Niobe gave him a slight smile, her gaze half-closed. "Merry speaks of you often."

"Really? What has she said? She is a deceptive little scamp! Don't believe a word."

Niobe inclined her head. "She says you are mean to her."

"Not true!" He snarled at Mevrian. "I'll make you pay for that later."

Mevrian said, "Nay! I but told her you were a perfect gentleman, who would volunteer to curry her horse, because you are so sweet!" And she stuck out her tongue at him.

Athos, brush in hand, actually started to step over to the palfrey near Niobe, when he wiped the back of his wrist across his brow to daub the sweat, but found mud from his sleeve now on his face. He scowled again. "Where are the real stableboys? Why are you dressed that way?"

Mevrian hopped over to Niobe, and took her elbow in both hands. "Oh my stars! I think they must be outside in the rain, frantically searching for two young highborn ladies who snuck away from their boring and terrible chaperones! Some deceptive little scamp must have lured the pair of ladies outside, into the storm, for wicked purposes!"

Niobe looked earnestly at Athos. "Blame her not! I said I had never ridden in the rain before, never seen a rainbow. Only in books. The surface of my world will not be habitable for another sixteen hundred years."

Mevrian said gaily, "Since we were going outside to help look for the missing girls, a deceptive little scamp said borrowing the raingear from the grooms' room would protect us both from rain, and from any busybodies who might otherwise spot us, and halt the search!" Mevrian tugged and Niobe rose gracefully to her feet. "Now we are going into the kitchen, to see if Cook has seen the missing girls, and fed them a snack. Finish up with those horses! We cannot let Niobe get in trouble, or her guardian will never let her visit here again — you don't want that, do you, brother dear…?" With a wink, Mevrian skipped away, with Niobe pulled along in her wake, willy-nilly.

Niobe turned her had at the door leading from the stable to the tack room, calling over her shoulder, "It was a pleasure meeting you!"

Athos stood uncertainly, feeling foolish, his knuckles white on the curry brush, wondering at the butterfly sensation in his stomach. The grooms came into out of the rain at about that same time, mud-splattered, soaking, and the stableboys following after were slapping each other with soggy rainhats, laughing and barking out rude oaths.

When they saw young master Athos, their demeanor changed, and a pair rushed forward, knuckling their brows, and offering to mind his horse.

Athos said, "No. Let me do it myself."

So, despite how cold, wet, and weary he was, young Athos brushed down not only Hawkswift, but the palfrey Niobe had borrowed.

He was glad he did. As he was leaving, he saw twinkling in the straw on the floor of the stall one of Niobe's jeweled combs. He stooped and took it up, smiling. He now had a perfect excuse, at which no one could raise an eyebrow, to pay a call on her on her own world, and see her again.

Perhaps she had left it behind for that very purpose? The thought was intoxicating yet foolish. He knew it was foolish, yet he could not dismiss it. The daughter of an Archduke, and not just any Archduke, but Endymion himself, she was of a higher social stratum, and so he could not hope, he dared not dream.

And that was the beginning of seven years of dreams it would have been wiser not to have.

5. Unanswered Questions

Galactic Year 12820, Planet Zavijava, Orbit

Athos was distracted from his thoughts when the numbers on the triscope blinked, the mass-readings and energy-signature of the pirate ship came back in range again, as his orbit carried him past the horizon where the planet's bulk had occluded the pirate ship. Beyond the opaque lid of the coffin, the *Devil's Delight* was rising above the limb of the planet, blazing like the morning star.

But the signal was early: this meant the pirate ship had maneuvered into a higher orbit. She was emitting continuous thrust to maintain her geostationary position above the meridian she occupied.

A second, small ferric mass was detected. This was the spaceboat, the same one Athos had seen diving with reckless haste to planetfall an hour ago, now rising up back to a higher orbit. The spaceboat was expending fuel at a ruinous rate.

Once more, with the beam dialed to minimum, he used the derringer to inscribe numbers into the coffin wall.

A quick calculation showed that there was no margin of error: the spaceboat would come within tractor beam range of the retreating ship for only moments before the difference in velocities made further rendezvous impossible.

It painted a picture of desperation. Crazed desperation: for while cargo and even crew might be hauled by tractor beam across the minimum distance that would separate the pirate ship from the boat before the one overshot the other, the two vehicles had too great a mutual difference in velocities to dock. The spaceboat would simply be abandoned, left behind to drift in the void forever. It was a rather expensive sacrifice of equipment.

He wondered. If the captain was so worried about shipping his contraband on time to whomever was taking delivery, why delay to pick up something from the surface?

What last-minute gear was so precious, that it was worth losing a spaceboat to get?

"Another question in this life whose answer I now will never learn," Athos murmured grimly. "Why am I here, and not Nap? He is eldest, now that Ozy is gone. What happened to him at that academy?"

Once, Napoleon had been his idol, a paragon to be imitated in all things: squared away, hard-core, calm under pressure, and as bold and proud as the Devil's Stepmother. Now what was he?

How would a wastrel like Napoleon discover the truth about the death of Ozymandias? What would he do about it, even if he did? Someone had to kill Liska.

Someone had to avenge the family.

Athos had ten or fifteen minutes before the friction from the upper fringes of atmosphere began to burn him. He had an hour and a half of air left.

And lots of charge in his derringer.

He stared thoughtfully at the little weapon. There was always the coward's way out, but then, what if some later investigator from the Patrol discovered any remains?

Small chance of that. The reentry heat would incinerate all traces. No one would ever be the wiser if, at the very last moment, Athos surrendered to fear. No one would know.

But his Uncle Jaywind had told him that stars always shine. Despite daylight or cloud, they still shone, even when not seen. Many things, Jaywind told him, just as vast and as bright were real, but just as rarely seen.

He never knew how much of Jaywind's talk to believe. Athos, all alone in his coffin, with none to see, wished he could believe. Words came back to him: *Vows are powerful things. The stars of heaven hear them. Aid will come.*

So the Temple Maiden had promised. Too bad it was not so.

In the dark coffin, in the utter silence, Athos pondered. How best to use the last ten minutes of life? No one would ever know if he died well, or died poorly.

She would never know. Niobe of Lyonesse would not discover whether his death were a wretched act of craven self-murder.

In his imagination, she was watching him. He saw the shocked look she would wear if he carried through. Imperial officers often committed suicide rather than reporting failure to the Empire, in order to spare their families from punishment. She would think Athos no better than this, no better than the Imperials who had killed her family.

Worse images floated into mind's eye. Why assume she would think on him at all? What if she had gazed on without any look of shock? What if it were a look of indifference, nonchalant, a distant expression in her haunting eyes of storm-dark gray as if the matter were of no concern to her. And why should she be concerned over a young man who surrendered to despair and suicide?

Athos grimaced. He told himself no one and nothing was watching him.

And yet…

Perhaps the stars were watching. Perhaps not. Surely, even if the stars were only inanimate balls of fire, it was better to act as if they were something more?

Perhaps life itself arose from primal slime by some blind accident. Or perhaps, as all sages said, the constellations guided the great dance of life into one interwoven grand design. Surely it was better to act as if life meant something more?

If true, then this was true for all, for those fated to live ten centuries, as the Cetics did, or ten decades, as men did. Or ten minutes. Let his last moment be dedicated to her. What would she have him do?

He thought on her. She loved ancient things, forgotten relics, poems recalled across countless eons from the old galaxy, from the mythic world of man's birth. She had been delighted with the ancient languages he had studied with such dutiful boredom.

Only one poem would do.

Again, he dialed the derringer to its minimum settings. Into the brass piece at the head of the coffin, he inscribed these words:

> *MY prime of youth is but a frost of cares;*
> *My feast of joy is but a dish of pain;*

My crop of corn is but a field of tares;

And all my good is but vain hope of gain;

The day is fled, and yet I saw no sun;

And now I live, and now my life is done!

As he was burning the last jot of the stanza's final line in place, a silvery light entered the coffin.

6. Believing in Ghosts

A young woman's head emerged between his knees, passing through the wall of the coffin without disturbing it. Her hair was dark and straight, her dark and slanted eyes were bright with curiosity.

Athos jumped in surprise, banging his head smartly against the coffin lid.

"What are you doing here?" He asked, rubbing his hood with both hands. Perhaps he sounded a little cross.

"I heard your complaint," she explained. "Such whining!"

"Heard? Heard how? There is no sound in space."

She snorted. "So what? I don't have ears. Not here." Her face was spinning around and around as if her nose were the hub of a wheel. "Do you want me to say any prayers over your body? You are already in your coffin. …"

"Every time I see you, I wonder if you are a ghost. And I don't believe in ghosts."

"Don't do that, or ghosts may stop believing in you. Then you'd be in trouble! No ancestors!"

"I have plenty of ancestors, thank you," Athos tapped the coffins walls to either side of him with the knuckles of his fists. It was too cramped to straighten his arms. "And I have other things to worry about."

Now her face began sliding in a circle, out one side of the coffin and back in through the other. "Are you a Star Patrol Captain? Because I was trying to save a one-eyed Pirate Hunter with a metal face, and I seem to have got you instead. Except it didn't work. What went wrong?"

"Stop it! Can you stop the … spinning? Your face …"

"What is wrong with my face?"

"It is spinning."

Her eyes flashed. "I am not spinning! *You're* spinning!" And with that, the ghostly face suddenly vanished. The silvery light she shed was gone. Utter darkness filled the narrow coffin.

Athos realized that part of his ten minutes had slipped away. Did he have five? Less? And now the heartless Star Maiden was gone. Who was she?

Suddenly, he was no longer standing on his head. His body floated to the center of the coffin. The girl's face dipped into the lid, looking like a sea-maiden of the Ellyll surfacing through opaque waters. That made him jump again, and again he struck his head in exactly the same spot, bruise upon bruise.

"There!" She smiled. "Rotation stopped!"

He forgot his headache. Hot tremors ran through Athos' body. For a moment, he wondered if the coffin had struck atmosphere, and was beginning to burn. But no, it was only wild hope in his soul that set his heart pounding.

"You can touch physical objects?"

"Not really. My arrowheads are ghost metal. They exist both physically and not physically. So if I hold one, I can push on something with my thumb."

That was about ten pounds. "What about a quick-release latch? Could you flip it?"

She took an arrow from her quiver and spun it through her fingers. "Are you kidding? I can jigger a five-spool pin lock with the point on this. Best part? No prints."

With an eye-dazzling flourish, she flipped the arrow back into the quiver. "Hard to see now," she continued, "but back in the day, I was quite the dimber gilt pullet. I think I can manage flipping a switch."

Patrolman Athos knew the rogue's cant used by pirates and crooks. *Dimber gilt* meant one with a pretty skill at picking locks. *Pullet* was a young girl.

Hardly the lingo one would expect from a woman in holy orders. He would wonder about that later, if he lived.

"Listen. Time is short. The pirates left one boat behind. It is in orbit above us. Higher orbit. That means slower. Less orbital energy, so it is Six o'clock and receding. Can you find the boat?"

She turned her head. "I can see it. The boat I was chasing after. I had almost caught up to it, when I heard you, and left it to come here. Half an hour ago, I searched it, looking for you, when it went down to the surface, but you were here the whole time. Why would you bury yourself alive when I was looking for you? So rude!"

"Listen: Every spaceboat carries an emergency refractory tether for hypersonic chute-drop into an atmosphere. Look for a big spool on the boat centerline, smack between the main thruster vents. Open the quick-release, unspool the tether, bring it, mount it to this coffin. Can you do that?"

"Mount it? How?"

"Tie the tether to the carrying handles on the coffin sides."

"I can think of something better. Wait a moment…"

She disappeared. It was dark. A minute crawled by, then another. He held himself still, counting his heartbeats, as the number of seconds he had left to live grew ever smaller.

Then there came loud clamor of blows and rasps on the outside of the coffin. Silver light returned when her head slid in through the wall. She said, "That is your tether-thingy. Your idea of tying it to the handles is dumb: I pinned it to the outside of the coffin with an arrowhead of ghost-metal, which no material force can break or mar. I would have had it here sooner, but you did not tell me your stupid tether was ten miles long! What is your plan now?"

"My spacecloak is polystructural ultratech — " He saw the look of puzzlement on her face. "— It can change shape to fit a Kragen. So it can turn into a parachute. This is one of its features."

"Parachute from orbit?" she shook her head. "Not possible! Well, sorry for you." She did not sound particularly sorry.

"At orbital speeds, seventeen thousand miles an hour, earthlike atmospheres in earthlike gravity have not enough air to create enough drag, but have too much air to survive the friction. Give or take a thousand miles an hour depending if you are falling with or against the planetary rotation. My spacecloak can ablate about five hundred degrees of heat. Reentry on a typical glidepath generates between two and three thousand degrees..."

Athos realized he was blabbing, and gritted his teeth to stop. Another minute of his remaining life gone. He said, "Under normal circumstances, no, it is not possible. No parachuting from orbit."

The girl smiled a brilliant smile. "What must be done to make the circumstances abnormal?"

"Aerobraking."

"Arrow breaking? I just told you my arrows cannot break."

"Have you ever skipped a stone across the surface of a pond? You have to get just the right angle, to make the stone skip more than once. That is what you are going to help me do with this coffin."

"How?"

"You stopped the tumbling. That means you can make the fine adjustments as needed to the pitch angle. I can find the visible limb of the planet, the atmospheric height, and so on, through my triscope. We are going to skip against the air to lose as much orbital velocity as possible … But carefully! Too sharp an entry, I burn, too shallow, I bounce off out into space. Can you manage to aim the coffin, if I give you the exact angle?"

"I pinned the tether with arrows all around the coffin, so I can push your nose in any direction, but only a very little bit. I cannot carry this huge box. I am not your rocket engine."

"For you, I only need maneuvering control. I can fashion an engine."

"You cannot make an engine out of thin air!"

"Well, actually, that is exactly what I can do."

So saying, he unhooked the airbottle connected to his cloak and opened the valves. His cloak deflated around him as inner and outer pressure equalized. Then his ears started popping. He held his thumb down on the airbottle's safety override switch, and watched the dials registering the pressure inside the coffin increasing.

He pointed. "Shoot an arrow down the centerline of the coffin, between my feet there, and make a small puncture. That's our engine. Jet propulsion. Fifteen pounds per square inch. Like a toy balloon."

She put her shoulders and arms into the coffin. Either end of her longbow passed through the sides. She sent a blazing arrow through the coffin wall at the spot where he pointed. Immediately, the teakettle whistle of a hull breach started.

She said, "You will not see or hear me, since I must concentrate to maintain your flightpath. You may speak the angle corrections as needed aloud if you wish, but you need not. We are guided."

"You understand the flight mechanics of what we are attempting?"

"Not in the least. But if anyone understands orbits and gravity and such, it is the stars who watch over us." He eyes grew soft and compassionate for a moment, and her voice was not sharp. "Farewell and Godspeed to you, Pirate Hunter."

And she was gone again. Except for the one dot of blazing light beneath his foot puncturing the side of the coffin, darkness returned.

He still had not asked what her name was.

Athos held the triscope to his eyes, and began calling out his readings for velocity, angle of attack, and altitude. No one could have heard him over the deafening shrill scream of the escaping air.

"But she does not have ears here," he muttered. "So it is fine…"

The triscope told the story. Something, some unseen force, was making tiny, fine corrections to the coffin's fallpath.

The buffeting began a moment later. Athos was tossed like dice in a dice cup rolled by a drunk gambler.

The thin, high screaming of near-vacuum filled the narrow space of his coffin as stray and rare wisps of air began to tear at the material of the walls. The heat began to rise and rise.

Then, silence fell. The heat dissipated. The slight impact of the coffin at such a high speed against even the thinnest upper layer of air had rebounded him back into space again. This was the first of many.

Now, if all his calculations had been correct, and if the girl's mysterious power guiding the falling coffin were trustworthy, he would skip along the upper atmosphere, in a shorter arc each time, losing deadly velocity as he went…

And if not?

"Burning stars!" He spoke softly. Perhaps it was only to himself. Perhaps not. "I do not believe, as men of old believed. But I will never mock what time has tested and found true. If you can hear: Grant that if I die this hour, the revenge I owe to Liska will not die!"

His voice grew even softer, and a more solemn note entered it.

"Ozymandias! If you can hear: If you have found no rest, likewise let not my spirit find rest before Liska finds his death!"

His only answer was the howling of the coffin that began again, the buckling and jarring as he struck and skipped from the atmosphere a second time.

Each time the burning coffin struck the atmosphere at this insane velocity, and rebounded at precisely the correct angle into another elongated interval of cold, suborbital silence, he knew that surviving the next time was ever less and less likely.

7. Deadly Spacedive

The shockwave of the coffin, falling at hypersonic velocity, was a red, unsteady, incandescent, compressed layer of superheated air, fluttering like a cloak thrown over the face of a madly charging horse in full career. A long tether, miles long but only inches wide, trailed after, bright as a gently curved bolt of lightning.

This tether not only shed more heat than the cross section of even a large spaceboat would have done, it also acted like a hypersonic parachute, increasing drag, slowing the meteoric speed of the descent.

The air temperature outside the coffin was hot enough to melt iron. However, the temperature inside the coffin did not rise much above the boiling point of water, and Athos in his spacecloak was able to tolerate the temperature build up by venting air.

He kept a careful eye on the changing numbers telling him his altitude, air pressure, temperature, air speed, and so on. The diamond-hard synthetic of the coffin hull was melting and chipping away, flake by flake, and the temperature was rising too quickly. Soon the coffin would no longer shield him. But then he laughed, for he realized only the forward part of the coffin was burning away. He could double his lifespan, if he sent the coffin into a tumble, and exposed different surfaces to the incandescent flame of the air friction one after another.

He was spinning in just this fashion when, at fifty miles high, the coffin disintegrated in a ball of fire. The white-hot tether, miles long, hung above him like a rainbow that had been lit on fire, and was receding rapidly. The triscope was ripped from his fist. He had forgotten to tie it to his suit with a lanyard, the first thing the most green of greenhorn recruits learns by rote before he steps into an airlock.

Now, with no method of measuring his airspeed or altitude, when to deploy his chute would be a matter of guesswork. Premature deployment ran the risk of fouling the chute. Delay ran the risk of his gear disintegrating in the heat. Had he actually lost enough orbital velocity?

The curve of the planet was visible at this height. Athos could see the whole hemisphere below him.

Most planets are beautiful when seen from space. Zavijava was not one of them: the purple crater-lakes large as oceans, the swirled and discolored knots of multiple storm systems ringing the equator, and then the textured mottle of scarlet, cerise, and indigo forests and jungles, mingled with the brown, black, orange and ocher highlands and deserts, and, to the north, a pink line on the edge of his vision hinting at the planet's ice caps; and chains of volcano-lit mountains, bright with rivers and lakes of burning lava large enough to be seen from space; all this together combined like the colors of a wound, or the dark embers and bright flames of an inferno.

He had lost enough velocity so that he was not burning up like a meteor, but he kept his eye on the spacecloak readouts projected before his eyes on the faceplate of his hood: any break in his suit seals, and his body would be exposed to the outside pressure, which was low. At low pressures, the liquids in his body, saliva, tears, lung tissue moisture, would boil at human body heat temperature. The additional stresses on the body from supersonic speeds were also a danger. And the spacecloak readouts showed the ultraviolet radiation from this planet's sun was very high, and creeping higher.

Then he noticed the world below him was beginning to spin, faster and then faster. The wind gusts at this altitude were fierce, but the air was so thin that when he stretched out his arms and legs to stabilize his fall, as parachutists are trained to do, nothing happened.

His vision dimmed. At first, he thought this might be fog collecting on his faceplate, but no. The centrifugal force of his spinning was driving the blood into his head.

Everything around him turned into a dark, whirling, shouting tunnel of confusion. He was blacking out. Grimly, Athos clung to consciousness. He could not deploy his chute while spinning; it would merely tangle the lines and wrap him in a death shroud. He had to wait, to stay awake, until the air was thick enough that he could stop the flat spin.

But it was not to be. The tunnel of blindness narrowed; pressure filled his head. Blood spurted from his nose and spread across his inner faceplate. The pain in his temples closed like a vice. Darkness came.

Athos was shocked awake by his impact with the sea. The cold of the water penetrated his suit, soothing the burns and blisters forming at his joints. An acre of fabric spread from his shoulders across the sea behind him. The fabric rose and fell, tumbling with the waves. This was his chute. When his head was tossed up, the roaring of wind and the crashing of waves filled his ears; when he his head was forced under, the calm, blue scenery of underwater, sluggish with strange echoes, filled his vision.

He was dazed for a moment, wondering how he was still alive.

Athos did not remember deploying his chute, but his fingers were locked around the D-ring. Perhaps he had done it while unconscious, or during a moment now blanked out of his short-term memory.

Giant fish and larger serpents, scaly, dagger-toothed, and lamp-eyed, swam and floundered in the deep. Hissing pebbles of cooling lava were dropping through the surface. When the next wave tumbled him back to the surface, he saw the wrestling black knots of storm cloud above, red-lit from the flares of volcanos below, white-lit from the flashes of lightning. Thunder from a nearby eruption mingled with thunder from a storm.

A warning light from his suit was also flashing in his vision: his oxygen supply was exhausted, for the suit had vented it to keep his temperature low. The insulation had not been perfect: he could feel burnt patches along his skin here and there.

The air reading was within human norms, here. He opened his suit, throwing back the hood, gulping in the salty spray of the humid air, feeling the rain of the strange planet dapple his face. He worked the spacecloak controls to pull in and fold up his parachute. He also summoned a powerful beam of light from his hood which shone whichever direction he turned his head. He saw rain and lightning, volcanic clouds rising up in the distance, mingling with descending thunderheads. The smell of brimstone was choking.

Just then, a sea monster larger than a boat, with a long, snakelike neck ending in a skull that was all blazing eyes and gnashing jaws rose above the surface. Its scaly hide glistened in the light of the distant volcano eruptions. When the lightning flashed, the creature's eyes gleamed like golden mirrors. Its roar mingled with the thunders.

Athos saw his parachute had not yet fully folded itself. When the snapping teeth, long as sabers, came down at him, he threw a great wad of the fabric into the jaws, and deployed the chute. Fold upon fold ballooned outward between the deadly teeth. The monster reared back its head. Tears and rips appeared in the fabric. Athos was yanked from the waters, and dangled next to the snaky, curving lengths of the long, dank neck. His derringer, which was perhaps the weakest model of energy weapon in the galaxy, was potent enough at short range. Athos grabbed one of the boar-tusks jutting from the creature's lower jaw, planted his boot against the thing's windpipe, and levered himself up so that the great, round eye with its slit pupil hung above him. He shot an incandescent ray from the puny weapon directly into the gleaming globe of the eye, and struck the walnut-sized brain beyond.

Down they fell together. The seawater hit Athos like a club. Then he was under the roaring waves, but now his hood was down, and his cloak was torn. Sea was in his nose and mouth. Warm, salty water slid along his skin, burning his blisters and whip-marks, and the fresh scar Liska's swordcane had left on his cheek.

He fought to find the surface again, but the thrashing corpse of the dying sea-giant was above him, slashing the water with wild fins. He shot again and again trying to strike the creature's heart and still its throes, but the thin, small beam glanced off the scaly armor of the hide. In that flare of light, he could see a trio of sharklike seabeasts with row on row of jagged nightmare teeth sliding toward him, maws agape, attracted by the death.

The large beast stopped struggling and died. As it did, its body turned, and it went belly-up in the waves. Athos, clinging to a fin, was carried upward and halfway out of the water by the motion. He scrambled up into the spray and screaming wind, rain-pelted, and the pale belly of the beast was under his boots like a raft. The sharklike monsters leaped and snapped, but could not reach him. The monster corpse swayed and bobbed in the storm-tossed waves as the shark-beasts tore chunks from the warm hide. Red clouds stained the waters.

The next flare of lightning revealed the temple maiden standing next to him, a vision woven of silver light. Her slippers seemed to touch the waters. The black locks of long straight hair blended with the darkness of the cloud behind her. Her longbow was unstrung. In her glove was a silver arrowshaft, and its crystal arrowhead glinted like a comet, as bright as her eyes. Her image did not fade when the lightning flare passed, for Athos was not seeing her with his eyes.

"Holy Sister!" He shouted over the wind howl. "I wondered where you went."

"Recovering my arrows. I cannot replace them."

She pointed with the bowstaff. "The shore is that direction, but it is some miles, and the water is rough. Wounded as you are, I doubt you can swim the distance. Also, you would be eaten up forty-two zillion times at least before you got half way. Blood calls beasts."

Athos had a pry bar in his boot. He hefted it in his hands, testing its weight.

She said, "Don't think I can carry you! There are no towns on this planet. No surface ships. No rescue. Sorry. You want me to do your last rites now?"

"Not yet, Sister." Athos did not have the kind of face that smiled often. But now a grin was spreading across his ordinarily stiff features. "I just crawled aboard a pirate vessel through its tailpipe, was whipped, was shot by a firing squad, was buried alive, and just by a hair avoided being cremated on re-entry. Then I yanked the ripcord at proper altitude while taking a nap. I would be cursed as a kitten-heart if I let some little moisture on the surface of a world stop me."

"You think you can swim the distance?"

"If I get a ride."

And he whirled the prybar above his head like a club, and dove headlong down among the sharkmonsters, roaring. The water swallowed him and he was gone.

The girl stood with her tip-toes almost touching the water, one hand at her throat, blinking in wonder down at the waters. The waves grew whiter as they were agitated. Rolling, struggling bodies spun in the foam. Then the white turned red. A blood-pool spread. There was a flash from a stabbing energy ray, once, then twice. Two sharklike creatures floated to the surface, dead. When the third came to the surface, it was bruised and bleeding, and Athos was straddling its back. The prybar was jammed between the shark-thing's teeth, pulling back painfully on the corners of its wide mouth. Athos had his hands, one to either side, holding the metal length in place like a bit.

The Star Maiden looked on with wide eyes, amazed.

He laughed and called out. "How are you with talking to animals, Sister? I remember Uncle Jay could calm the wild stallions on the plantation with a gesture."

"The only critters I ever met were rats, pigeons, and stray dogs," she said sourly. "I prefer eating to talking to my food. But let me see if I remember Dame Nashira's lessons."

She stooped and ran her unsubstantial hand along the sea-creature's skull, and there came a change in its fierce eye. She straightened up. "I will pass across on the waters before you, and show you the way."

The Star Maiden receded in his view, but the storm clouds did not hide her, nor the tumbling, high waves, for her slim form and flowing garments shone with silver-white light, bright as a star.

CHAPTER 7: A SAVAGE WORLD AFIRE

Galactic Year 12820, Planet Zavijava, Surface

1. The Scarlet Jungle

Sunset had fallen by the time Athos reached the black sand and jagged rocks of the inhospitable shore, but the rains had stopped. Enough driftwood had been cast with him up on shore by the stormwinds that he was able to gather it, and cook the carcass of the sea-beast he had forced to carry him here.

With food warm in his belly, he paused to ponder. Survival was his first priority, which meant, first of all, finding the lay of the land. Then, discovering the location of the pirate base on this planet. He calculated he could not be very far from the spaceboat launch point.

He wondered once more what could be so important that the *Devil's Delight* would linger so long before sailing.

He also wondered whether the pirate base maintained records of what was shipped out on their pirate customers, and to where, and when, and in what numbers. The more he thought on it, the brighter burned the hope that the mission was not a scrub.

Surely the pirate base retained a copy of the information Athos sought. All he had to do was storm the place, all alone, scarred and ill-clad, armed with a derringer and a prybar.

Then he would worry about how to find a starship back to civilization.

191

"Easy as breathing," he muttered.

It was humid and warm, even by night, and the brimstone stink of distant volcano fumes lingered. The wind roared and blustered through the dark hours, threatening to douse his campfire, but at least it cooled him somewhat.

There was no sign of the Star Maiden. Athos wondered what had become of her.

He did not sleep. The small first aid kit packed in a shoulder pocket of his spacecloak had survived all these adventures intact. He used his entire supply of artificial skin, antiseptic gel, and sterile bandages binding up the whip wounds on his back and the various cuts, burns, and blisters he had accumulated. He thought he looked like a mummy from Algol.

Athos searched through the swamp reeds crowding the shoreline until he found one straight and stout enough to make into a spear. He used the heavy dirk Yeho had given him to cut it down and trim it into a spearshaft. He fitted a fang taken from the dead seamonster to the tip, lashing it in place with strips torn from his tattered spacecloak hem.

He was surprised by dawn: the sun was a monster filling a fifth of the sky, dim as an ember, red as rose wine, that shot above the horizon, painting the clouds a fiery scarlet. Night here was only four hours. The planet rotated rapidly.

The plantlife was red underfoot and purple overhead: scarlet mosses and orange mushrooms clung to rocks; crimson grasses grew in clumps; magenta leaves, or violet, swayed from scaly trunks of colossal cycads or crooked oaks. Every tree was draped in drooping vines or clinging fungi of brown, red, and bright pink.

Athos was disturbed to find a naked human footprint in the black sand of the shore. From the size and stride, Athos could tell the print was left by a man of Neanderthal stock. The print was legible despite the windblown sand, less than an hour old.

Few other prints could be found. The man had been cautious, leaving no trail to follow. Athos could see a dimple in the sand, like the imprint left by a walking stick … or by a spearbutt. And the armed onlooker had come close to him in the night; quite close. That was startling; because Athos had excellent night-vision, and he had not been asleep.

Coughing, he regretted that his spacecloak, ripped by the teeth of sea serpents, was no longer airtight. Getting away from the ash clouds pouring up from nearby volcanoes was a priority.

He struck out toward higher ground. Athos hoped to climb above the ground-hugging smoke, and perhaps find a spot where he could learn the lay of the land.

In one direction he saw a tall peak rising alone above a circular lake, with no other peaks near. It had no volcanic clouds issuing from it. It was a high, stark hill of black and gray rock, free of the scarlet trees or tall red brush. It was above the smoke.

He started in that direction.

Athos pushed and tramped his way through the thick, red underbrush. After ninety minutes or so, the sun grew high. The noon was scalding. His torn spacecloak could not keep him cool. He found a game trail leading beneath the shadows of the fungus-draped palm trees. He could see only a few yards ahead or behind, but the temperature was tolerable.

After another hour of tramping, he noticed the noises of insects and winged lizards croaking and clicking was suddenly quieter in one direction. They were afraid of some predatory animal, no doubt. Or predatory men.

On an unknown world, it seemed wise to imitate their example: He left the game trail, moving slowly through the underbrush, with the fearful silence directly behind.

The trees grew taller. Little light reached the ground. It was cooler, but the air was humid, and the leaves dripped moisture in soft pitter-pats of noise that came from each direction. The underbrush here was thin.

However, looking back, he saw he was leaving a clear trail of broken twigs and bent leaves.

Now he alternated jogging and running, keeping a brisk pace, and taking care to leave behind as few footprints or bent grasses as he could manage.

An hour or so later, it was late afternoon, the woods were dark. His night vision was better than a man's, so he kept up the pace. But the silence grew. It was clear then that the pursuit was following him.

The ground sloped downward, and became soft. Ahead he saw a river. This perhaps was a chance to throw off the hunters.

He saw a likely hollow trunk. Going onward, he left a false trail to the bank, and walked backward in his footsteps. He hid in the trunk, pulled the thick leaves of a bush over the mouth to conceal him.

He had not long to wait.

A hunting party of nineteen men, lean and fierce as wolves, came loping along the riverbank. They were dressed kilts and jackets of rust-red or brown snake leather, hues blending into the reddish leaves of the plantlife. Their faces were darkened with warpaint.

Now it was dusk. After the hunting party passed by, Athos headed the other way, which was downstream. Some instinct warned him. Again, he hid. Motionless, he watched the water.

His caution was rewarded. A mat of reeds was drifting slowly upriver, against the current. Hidden beneath was a dugout canoe with a wooden lid, floating with its gunnels at the waterline. It was a semi-submerged hunting blind, holding one or more hunters: on the lookout for him.

Athos retreated, as carefully as he could, as rapidly as he dared, back into the thicker part of the forest. When the sudden sunset fell, he climbed a tree and made his way through the canopy from branch to branch, hoping that it was too dark for anyone to follow the path of bent twigs and broken leaf-stems he left behind.

After about two hours, it was midnight. The silence was oppressive. The hunters were near. He saw a game trail that promised a quicker way out of this forest than the laborious act of going from branch to branch in the darkness. Down he came.

He followed the game trail. The forest thinned. Another hour passed. Ahead, in the gray light just before dawn, the trees were fewer: a clearing?

It was more than a clearing. Athos came to the edge of the forest. Beyond was open land: a place of round hills and shallow dales leading up to the black peak he had seen in the distance.

He saw a shape waiting for him beneath a tall tree. Athos hid and waited. When the clouds parted, the ghostly light of pre-dawn was clear enough for his sharp eyes to make it out: it was not a man. The shape was a corpse, crudely mummified, pinned to the tree trunk by several befeathered and brightly painted spears. This was a no trespassing sign posted in a fashion no one could misunderstand.

Something hissed past his ear, and embedded itself in the corpse he was examining. It was a dart, as long and slender as porcupine quill. Athos ducked. Other darts hissed through the air. Two struck the shoulder of his spacecloak and were turned aside. One found a spot where the fabric was torn and lanced painfully into his thigh. The small wound burned and throbbed.

He drew his derringer, and sent a sizzling line of energy burning back through the trees. The noise of the bolt seemed shockingly loud in the jungle stillness. The flare of light made shadows of leaf and branch and hanging moss jump and sway.

It was a mistake. Athos saw shadows moving between the trees. Tall men with taller spears, quiet as hunting cats, were closing in on his position.

Another dart struck him, piercing his calf. This time, his sharp eyesight caught the motion. He shot with his derringer. A warrior perched in the upper branches of a mossy oak tree uttered a dying shriek, chest wound burning, rebounding from branches as he fell to earth.

Athos realized his leg was going numb. To leave the forest cover would expose him to their view, but to stay meant death.

He rushed into the tall grass. A dart whispered past his ear. He rose, turned, and fired. His thin beam burned a feather from the warrior's headdress, but missed his head. The man had a long reed pressed to his lips: a blowgun. A second dart struck Athos in the gun hand. It found a thin spot in his glove, and sank painfully into the web of flesh between index and forefinger. The expertise of the shot alarmed him.

He ducked below the grass. His gun hand was tingling and throbbing. He put no great faith in his ability to hit a moving target in a dim light with his left hand.

Athos fled, scampering from bush to bush and sapling to sapling. But the man he had seen did not come out from the trees.

On Athos went in a running crouch. He saw no figures leaving the forest in pursuit. He thought the grisly warning sign a message from the forest dwellers telling strangers not to enter; perhaps it was a warning aimed the other way, telling them not to leave.

The noise of croaking lizards and frogs welcoming the dawn grew loud. Athos began to hope he had outdistanced the pursuit. Were the forest men afraid to enter the open grassland?

He looked behind. No pursuit. That seemed ominous.

The twilight of dawn came. In the half-gloom, the land took on a haunting glamour: dozens of round pools and ponds gleamed like silver, and scattered clumps of slim trees growing in circles swayed in the night breeze, rustling. Little babbling brooks ran from pools on the higher slopes to those lower down, or descended in tiny waterfalls thin as threads. All the trees were saplings, as slender as pencils.

The ground here was interrupted by dales and valleys, all perfectly circular. Circular depressions of dark soil were here and there among the grassy slopes, looking almost exactly like the sand traps of some ill-manicured and overgrown golf course. Within these sandpits were pale round rocks like bowling balls, and piles of pale sticks.

He came to the edge of a huge, round lake. Across the water was the tall black peak he had seen in the distance. Here, he drew the needles from his hand and leg, wincing in pain, and applied a wide-spectrum antitoxin from his med kit. His fingers and toes were numb. With his knife, he made a small incision in his hand, and sucked and spat blood until feeling returned.

The he bent himself in half and did the same for the wound on his lower leg. His toes throbbed, but he did not lose all feeling.

The third wound was on his upper thigh: he had no way to draw the poison. The wound tingled and burned. He pinched the flesh above his knee, but could not feel it. Not a good sign.

The sunrise came as suddenly as a rocketlauch. One moment, the sun was below the horizon, and the next, it was a hot, ruby-red circle, wide as the shield of a titan, peering over the rugged hilltops.

In the slanting light, the land no longer seemed so lovely. The round depressions of the valleys and dells were bomb craters, now softened by weather and covered with grass. The round lakes and pools were smaller craters where rainwater had gathered. Among the tall grass, the shattered, burnt stumps of ancient trees could be glimpsed. The sandpits were craters where no grass seeds had taken root. The white circles and sticks he had glimpsed were unburied skulls and bones. A terrible battle had been fought here, and only a few years ago.

The wide red orb speck of the dull sun peered through a ragged opening in the cloud cover. He saw the black peak clearly.

Athos gasped in awe. From base to crown, the mountain rock had been carved and sculpted by some ancient peoples into rank upon rank of eaves, porticos, projections, balconies and gables of naked stone. Acre upon acre was carved and decorated with grotesque figures, goggle-eyed skull-faced, of a long-necked, long-muzzled race of one-horned, narrow-headed bipeds, long extinct.

The soil of the mountain face had been stripped clean and the veins of surface granite beneath had been carved into endless reliefs of skeletal figures with twisted limbs contorted in postures of agony. The thin visages and empty eyeholes were haunted with woe. The rearing horns were like sabers lifted in last salute. Their fleshless muzzles were lifted in silent bray, square teeth bared.

The spaces between were carved into images of serpents and crooked dragons, two-headed amphisbaena and woman-headed naginas.

Four vast, carved and crowned one-horned giraffe-heads gazed solemnly down in each direction from near the peak, eyes blank. The peak above was carved into the shape of a great stone snake with a head at either end, who writhed in a vast, motionless knot, and circled back to flourish its stone fangs at itself, face to face.

It was an astonishing work. With modern cutting rays fired from levitation platforms, it would have taken years to make. With primitive hand-held tools, centuries.

The work was also frightful. What symbolism the poses and postures meant, only an archeologist could guess. What gods this alien temple was reared to adore, none would ever know. But the overall air was one of fear and misery. The images were morbid.

From the mouths of carven skulls set high in the rock, chimney smoke poured out. From the windows set in the eyes of gargoyles, lights shined.

The vast temple was occupied.

It was becoming clear exactly why the deadly warband hunting him had not ventured out of the forest. The line of demarcation where the heavy weapons from the fortress hidden in the ancient temple could blast and destroy anything seen moving in and about the lake and the meadows before the temple doors was very clear: because old growth trees were there. The whole landscape nearer the temple had been flattened and burned in recent years, perhaps more than once.

He moved carefully along the lakeshore, unwilling to keep still, and even less willing to return to the forest. The danger here was immense, and grew every step he took carried him closer to the black mountain, which was clearly the pirate's depot.

What better spot for a base? Here was a lake for splashdowns in case of emergency, and a mountain peak, easily seen from the air, to mount a launch catapult and save on fuel.

He found a footpath running upslope along the bank of a wild white stream feeding the lake, and into a defile. Apparently, men from the mountain came to the lakeside often enough to wear the grass away.

Athos climbed. He began to limp. His right leg was sagging, and numb. He stabbed his last two ampoules of antitoxin into his leg, even thought that seemed little help before, and hoped for the best.

It was cool and shady in the defile, wetted with spray. Tall rocks blocked the view to either side. The riverbank path between the rocks here was free of grass, and, in places, had been carved into steps.

The slope made a sharp turn upward. It became awkward dragging his leg. The numbness was spreading. Athos gritted his teeth, pausing to wind a torn strip of his garment into a tourniquet, which he twisted in place with the prybar. He leaned heavily on the crude spear he had made.

Up he went and up. The slope grew ever steeper, and more difficult.

Ahead was a rock wall. He saw where rushing water formed a pair of waterfalls. The path climbed to a pontoon bridge of buoyant slabs crossing the stream between the upper and lower waterfalls. The upstream edge of the floating bridge was wetted with continual spray from the white water. Beyond the bridge, the rock walls were pierced with a narrow pass, steep as a stairway, switchbacking up the cliff.

This stairway pass ran but some yards upward and opened into a wide, bright, upland meadow of red grasses. Above in the meadowgrass the crowns of leaning statues of long-necked, one-horned figures flanking the temple gates were visible. The grim, black richly-carven facade blocked the sky in that direction.

Forward he stepped, and the floating bridge dipped and swayed beneath his one-legged, half-hopping tread. An abyss of air was to his left, spreading rainbow-chased sprays and plumes of water. To his right rose a wall of rushing water from the higher falls.

When Athos stepped onto the bridge, the sun of Zavijava peeped out from between stormclouds, a huge sullen scarlet face, dull as an ember. The rushing waters underfoot glinted with the dim colors.

A masked spearman in a plumed headdress came out from behind a tall stone on the far shore. He strode across the bridge, making it tremble, and stood in the center of the span.

Athos saw there was no retreat. Even diving into the water would expose his spine to a spearcast. With his numb leg, he could outrun no one. But he was not the type to turn his back anyway.

He did not bother drawing his puny derringer. Athos flourished the fang-tipped reed javelin he had made. In his fist he took his heavy dirk Yeho had given him, and flicked the crossguards open.

Forward Athos limped, and the floating bridge dipped and swayed unevenly beneath his uneven tread. White foam was underfoot, gurgling and singing. Stormclouds pregnant with rain were overhead, tattered, dark and wind-blown. The wind was sweet with the smell of rose-red grasses, and the air was alive with the croaks and calls of insects and winged lizards.

Compared to where he had been recently, it was a good place to die.

2. Tisquantum, the Wrath of Heaven

The two men faced each other on a large, square pontoon floating in the midst of the rushing waters. Before Athos loomed a broad-shouldered man of heroic build. His face was hidden behind a mask that reached from brow to breast, made from the skull of a horse. A headdress of white plumes nodded above, brilliant as flame. A mantle or poncho woven of poisonous snakeskins, patterned with scales of emerald hue, and sapphire, and white, was flung over his titanic shoulders.

Seen close, the man was huge. He was a head taller than Athos, scarred from old wounds, and bulky with muscle.

In his right hand were two spears with polished flint spearpoints, adorned with feathers. Strapped to his forearm was a shield made from a tortoise shell. In his left fist he held a long-hafted tomahawk.

The man struck without any word of challenge or defiance, casting a deadly javelin with a sweep of his mighty arm; Athos narrowly avoided the spear, but his numb foot twisted as he jumped, and the huge man sprang to the attack.

Their spears clashed in midair as the warrior lunged and stabbed. Athos counter-parried the taller man's spearblow with his spearshaft, so that the deadly stone blade whistled over his shoulder rather than striking his heart. Athos disengaged, and stabbed in return. Unable to put weight on his rear leg, his lunge was short, and his thrust was weak.

It was not the heaviest blow, but, nonetheless, the fang spearpoint of Athos' weapon bent and shattered on the tortoise shell buckler.

The warrior struck with his axe in fierce attack. Athos deflected the blow with his heavy dirk, but not perfectly. The axehead glanced from his shoulder, striking the metal box of the medical kit stowed in the pocket there, tearing the cloak and scattering empty bandage spools and antiseptics. Athos winced in pain, feeling the warm slather of blood flowing down his left arm. He was cut, but the metal box had deflected most of the blow. He hoped the wound not deep. His knifepoint was red where he had cut the man's axe hand.

The man switched hands in mid strike, so that his tomahawk was in his right, whirling toward at Athos' skull, while the spear in his wounded left hand drove toward the armpit Athos would have exposed had he tried to parry the axe with his dirk, as before. Instead Athos snapped his spear, now a quarterstaff, to catch the warrior's spearshaft with downward stroke, driving the spearpoint into the surface of the bridge underfoot. In the same, smooth curve of blindingly quick motion, the quarterstaff tip swept back up in riposte. A shift of the swaying bridge had put the warrior too far forward in his stance, so Athos caught him neatly under the chin with the tip of his staff. The stroke was meant to crush the windpipe; instead it cracked the bone mask at throat-level.

The bridge bucked and swaying alarmingly.

Athos realized he was outmatched. The man was stronger, had longer reach with his spear, and an uncanny quickness equal to Athos's own.

But, as the bridge was askew, confusing the warrior's feet, and the mask was awry, confounding his eye, Athos saw his chance.

Each bridge segment was rectangular, bound to its neighbor at the corners. Athos threw his dirk at the man's foot. The man swayed, avoiding the knife, but now Athos had a clear line of fire. In the same eyeblink of time, Athos drew his derringer. The mask was in the warrior's face, blinding him. Nonetheless the warrior kicked the dirk aside with his naked foot before it touched his leg, so that the blade struck into the bridge and stood quivering. It was an impossible act of agility, to parry a flying knife with a kick.

Athos shot at the bridge lashing behind his foe. The red, shrill beam cut the cords nearly asunder.

Whoever lashed the segments together had done a slapdash job; because when one binding parted, the whole bridge buckled, and a wedge of white water became visible as the two segments, now held together only at a single corner, moved away from each other.

With a toss of his head, the huge warrior cast the broken mask aside. The bony horse skull went flying over the side of the bridge and was lost in the spray of the waterfall.

It took only a moment for the warrior to toss the mask away, snorting. But in that moment, Athos lunged low, snatched up his dirk, retreated a step, and slashed the bindings behind him on the downstream side.

Both men were now swaying on a single square pontoon. It was held to the other bridge segments in two places: the upstream corner behind Athos, and the upstream corner behind the warrior.

These two remaining bindings groaned under the strain of the current, and individual threads in the cable began to snap. Athos scrambled, dragging his bad leg behind him. The warrior flourished his spear and rushed forward.

Athos raised the dirk above the groaning binding.

"Peace!" Athos shouted, "Or we both go over the falls together."

The man looked wary, but did not lower tomahawk or spear. The warrior's face was scarred and burned on his right side, and he had neither eye nor ear on that side. Athos recognized the wound as typical of those left by a blaster discharge at point blank range.

Athos held up a translator disk he took from his belt pouch, "Do you understand my words?"

The disk chattered, and repeated the sentence in several dialects.

An advanced race, long ago, devised a language called Empyrean that every intelligent species could use, no matter the shape of mouth or composition of atmosphere. The ways in which local parlance would drift from the base language could be statistically analyzed by an automatic translator all spacemen were wont to carry. Hominids, however, had a perverse knack for inventing new lingos, moreso than any other race.

Would the warrior understand him? It depended on how long ago his ancestors had left the home worlds.

The one-eyed warlord took a step back, but did not lower his weapons. "You speak? But you are *Awasi-giizhig-owinini*." The translator disk gave a buzz to indicate vocabulary failure.

"I come in peace!"

"You come from the *Ewasi-giizhig*. The place of the dead." The warrior gestured upward with his spear.

Athos said, "You mean the sky? There are worlds beyond the sky, solid as this, and men as alive as you or me…" Athos scowled, seeing the man's face grow dark.

"The honored dead go to heaven. So say our fathers! We are the True Men. Would you call us false?"

"No, I did not say that." Athos spoke warily.

"We have watched you with eyes most keen. You were thrown out of heaven with fire and smoke. You go to the Living Mountain of Death. Who walks there, but the dead, and the servants of the dead?"

Athos said, "That is a spaceport. It is run by space pirates. I am a patrolman sent here to investigate them." The translator disk buzzed. There were no words for these ideas in the native dialect. Was it possible to explain space piracy to someone who had never seen a spaceship? "They are bad men. I am hunting them. The trail leads here."

The warrior nodded. "From that mountain, they go up and they come down. They ride in canoes of fire. We have seen." The man gestured with his tomahawk, pointing at the ghastly burns disfiguring half his face. "They have weapons of fire. We have felt. You have a weapon of fire."

"I am a man like you, not like them. I am not your enemy."

"You fell from heaven, struck down by fire! We have stories of such as you!"

"I fell, yes, but because I was fighting *them*! They are my enemies as well as yours!"

The warrior squinted doubtfully at him. "Who are you?"

"My name is Athos." But the disk translated the name literally: *Holy Mountain*. "Captain Athos Lone."

"We are name-brethren, for my name is called Tisquantum." The disk gave this name as *Rage of the Holy Mountain,* but then clicked, and also translated it as *Wrath of Heaven*. He said, "I too am captain, for I am chief of the tribe the Men-Who-Fear-No-Death of the Confederation of True Men."

Tisquantum pointed with his spear at the black peak. "Long ago, before man came to this world, the Qilin carved the Mountain of Living Death. The last alive buried the next to last, but there was none to bury him. He walked alive into the death lands, leaving the pathway open behind. Of old, the Pavo, men winged like peacocks, who dwell in the evil star called M32, wrought this great slaughter. They are men of great beauty, with gray eyes and many-colored wings, the most proud of all the sons of pride, and they scorn that any other living men should be alive. So say our fathers."

Athos said, "Your fathers remember correctly. M32 is a star cluster outside the galaxy. It only looks like a star because of the distance, but you got the name right. The Pavo are a deadly race, who worship the Dark Will. Before civilization drove them out of the galaxy, they exterminated several races, including the Qilin. They were driven far away, long ago."

"Their shadows are not gone. They speak in whispers and walk in dreams. They are dead. Not long ago, this land was forest, full of game, rich and happy, and the streams full of fish. The servants of the dead were called down by the dead, and took up their old places in the Mountain of Living Death. They raided and slew, kidnapping our women. The braves of the Fear-No-Death tribe, and all the True Men of our Confederation attacked. For three days fire and hot hailstones fell down from the Mountain, and burned all this land. Hell broke free, and opened the mountaintops with fire and lava. All the air is bad." He gestured again with his spear, encompassing the cratered landscape of ponds and saplings surrounding the mountain base, where no old trees could be seen.

"Our tribe once was twice ten thousand," said Tisquantum stoically. "Now, we are two hundred. We are too few to form the hunting band of the great hunt, when all tribes gather to drive the thunder lizards from among us. We were masters here, once. Now we live like rats, moving by night."

"But these bad men are not ghosts or demons, no more than I am," said Athos. "The men in that mountain are pirates and smugglers..." These words were buzzed. He tried again. "They are lawbreakers of the law."

Tisquantum gave him an odd look. "You speak of the law?"

Athos straightened up and sheathed his knife. "I am a servant of the law!"

Tisquantum inspected him gravely for a long while, then nodded slowly. He slung his tomahawk and brought his spear to rest.

Tisquantum said thoughtfully, "Of old, we know of the war in heaven, and the rebel powers who were cast down. To this day, they rage, burning in the fire of the underworld."

He gestured toward the volcano peaks smoking in the distance. "They shake the earth. But evil men bow and serve them, and weapons of fire are in their hands." He brought the spear down and leaned on it, gazing at Athos critically. "I have not heard before now that there are those in heaven who might come to earth to fight the evil ones here."

Athos said, "I am a man like you. I have weapons and training you don't. That is all."

"We have been suffering. Our women shed tears, our wise men burn sacrifices, for many years. Why is heaven so slow to answer when the children of men cry out?"

Athos, himself, had often wondered why the bigwigs back at Septentrion, the galactic capital world, did not prioritize wiping out the piracy in this sector. He said only, "I am a servant. The higher ups do not tell me their plans."

The faint look of suspicion that had been hovering about Tisquantum's eye now faded. "Ah! This of old we have also heard. None know when the Day of Wrath shall come, not the messengers, not the servitors, not even the sons of the High One. His own counsel, he keeps. His ways are deep. His paths are known to none."

Athos smiled. "I don't know too much about the Day of Wrath, but if one son of the noble House of Lone can visit the ire of heaven upon these filthy, murdering villains, let it be me."

Seeing the look on the warrior's half-burned face, Athos felt a moment of victory, the sensation of a hard task finally accomplished. He had won the man over. He had convinced him.

Tisquantum crossed the bridge, and beckoned Athos to follow. But as Tisquantum was stepping from bridge to bank, the strained lashings, with a horrific screech, parted, and the pontoons bucked and jumped and fell over the falls.

Tisquantum, arms windmilling, fingers catching only air, toppled toward the roaring waterfall.

3. Blood Brothers

Athos, quick as a cat, dropped his spear and grabbed for the falling man. The warrior was a head taller than Athos, and more massive than he, and the pontoon slid out from under his feet, yanked away on the raging current. But Athos, scrambling, had the toes of his boot atop the slippery rocks of the brink at that moment, and almost enough momentum to carry him to shore.

For a moment, the two men swayed and strained like wrestlers, fighting for balance. They dangled over the raging waters, and over the abyss of air beyond. Then, with a great cry, Athos shoved the man ashore. Then Athos' numb leg gave way. He toppled toward the rushing white water. At the same moment, Tisquantum, while falling himself, grabbed Athos by the hair, and hauled him upward.

The two men fell in a tangle onto dry ground, striking the rocks painfully. Tisquantum hauled them both back from the lip. Athos found the numbness had spread to his hip, his stomach. He could not stand. The coldness was reaching toward his heart.

Tisquantum bent over him. The warrior carefully drew out of the patrolman's numb flesh two more thin quills that Athos had not found, one of which had left its barb broken in the tiny puncture wound. Then Tisquantum took from a pouch a motionless snake, seemingly dead, wrapped in wet leaves. He unwound the leaves, and breathed on the snake, rubbing and chaffing it with his hands. The snake jumped and came to life.

Tisquantum pried open the snake's mouth with his finger.

"I hope you are not thinking of…" said Athos began.

But Tisquantum pushed the creature's fangs against Athos's leg. He did not feel the sharp tooth enter.

"Yes, of course that is what you were thinking," sighed Athos. "It has been that kind of day. I appreciate the thought, but this might not work. You see, you are a Neanderthal, and I am half Noachian, one quarter Lion, one quarter Hawk. So, considering the difference in biology…YOW!"

Athos unsuccessfully bit back a cry of pain. Burning sensations crawled up and down his leg, as if worms of flames were slithering in his arteries. He leaped to his feet, trying to plunge his aching leg into the waters of the rushing stream. Then he blinked down at himself, surprised, for he was standing solidly on both feet now. The numbness was gone.

"You saved my life," said Athos in wonder.

"As you did mine," said Tisquantum. "Now we are brothers."

"What? Because I grabbed you? But you would not have fallen, were it not for me. I cut the bridge."

Tisquantum held up a poisoned quill before Athos' eye before casting it contemptuously over the cliffside. "You would not have been touched by the tooth of venom, were it not for me. I set my men on you. We have wounded each other. Come! Let us hold the wounds together, that the blood may mingle. Your blood in me. Mine in you."

When this was done, Tisquantum then said, "My men were too small of heart to follow you here, for the Mountain of Living Death slays any who stray near it. But I was mad with wrath over the death of Habbamock, to whom my young sister Weetamoo was promised to wed, and vowed not to return without your head."

Athos realized this must be the name of the man he shot out of the crown of an oak. It was a sharp reminder that even enemies had precious things in their lives to lose.

Tisquantum continued, "I cannot take the head of my blood brother. Now I am an exiled man, for to return empty-handed is to break my word, and True Men allow no oathbreakers among us. The elders will command me to take my own life."

"If I come with you, and my head is still attached, does that count?"

Tisquantum scowled. "We are True Men. Our word is true. This is no game of words as children play."

Athos was abashed. He had been thinking of Tisquantum as a primitive man, and yet his sense of honor was as acute as any noble son of a planet-owning dynastic family.

"What if I go into the Mountain, and defeat them? Would that not prove that I was never your enemy to begin with, never the enemy of your tribe? Would that excuse the oath?"

"Only one sent by heaven can go into the Mountain of Death and return alive."

"Well, I don't know about that. I was sent by Commodore Valzirg, who is the chief commissioner of the Star Patrol in the Lustral Steradian. He is an Odobenine."

Tisquantum gave him a puzzled look. The translator disk clucked. It had no local name for *Odobenine*.

"An aquatic alien with tusks and flukes. He looks like a walrus. A fish with fur. And big teeth. Like this." Athos held his forefingers below his lip, pantomiming walrus tusks. "Not a supernatural being. Not even slightly. My boss."

"You will not survive without the hand of the Great Spirit to guide you. But, yes, if you entered and slew the servants of the dead, and returned with me with trophies to the elders, my oath would turn to air."

Athos looked up at the looming, black mountain and its grim carvings. "Your people watch carefully. Can you tell me anything about their movements, their numbers, their defenses?"

It turned out that he could tell quite a bit.

4. Pirate Gold

Even though he had not necessarily known what he was seeing, Tisquantum was observant and sharp of memory. His hunter's eye was keen enough to recognize markings on the spaceboats or shipping containers and distinguish them, even though he could read none of the letters. He kept count on a set of knotted strings he carried on his belt, tying a different knots for each different number.

The conversation was long and difficult, stumbling into many mutual misunderstandings, and backtracking around them. Tisquantum, however, answered every question with endless patience.

Athos finally grasped the situation: In regular rotation, each thirty, forty, or sixty standard days a crew of fifty or so men arrived in spaceboats to ferry crates from the mountain up to orbit. These were the weapon shipments.

Under Athos' questioning, Tisquantum described the crews in each particular. It was a mixed bag of races and species, mostly Hominids and Mustelids, dressed in bright rags and wearing silver and gold ornaments, necklaces, bracelets, and hoops in their ears. His mother told Athos long ago what kind of person will carry his treasure with him at all times: those who trust neither banks nor bunkmates. Pirates.

Every seventy days, a single much larger ship arrived. From the description, it was an armed freighter or merchantman. She lowered herself on antigravity, and landed in the lake, where she floated like a metal island.

This crew was very different: huge, bloated toadlike aliens dressed in uniforms and wearing small polarized hemispheres over their bulging eyes. Water and air were equally breathable to them. They were orderly. Tisquantum never saw them drunk, nor knife-fighting each other.

Tisquantum noticed the oddity that none of the toad-men carried weapons: the thunder-spears (as he called them) were all carried by "metal men who did not eat bread, did not breathe air".

Such was his description of killer-robots. While not forbidden by law as black tech was, robots able to kill intelligent beings were rarely seen in civilized worlds these days. Killer-robots had been instigated by the Empire, and had practically passed away with the Empire. After the war, every horde of Imperial warbots dismounted their weapons and programmed themselves with vows of peace. Many refused even to kill living beings even in self-defense.

Athos nodded, grimly. He was surprised, yet not surprised.

The supplier were Batrachians. Yeho's people. The Batrachians were a belligerent and secretive race from beyond the edge of Andromeda, seated in the miniature satellite galaxy of Caldwell 18. Though small, Caldwell 18 was a deadly Seyfert galaxy, meaning its nucleus had collapsed into a quasar, whose emissions should have reduced even worlds far from its core stars into radioactive cinders. How any intelligent civilization survived there was unknown: no expedition thither had returned to tell.

The Batrachians had bases among the scattered stars of the intergalactic gas cloud called the Great Stream reaching between Andromeda and Caldwell 18. They also had a foothold within Andromeda itself, where the Great Stream began, in the Eureal Sector beyond the Siren Stars, where sailors ventured only at the peril of their souls. But no Batrachian base was known to be in this sector.

Until now.

The gunrunners had several customers among the pirate captains who picked up their goods at this mountain, of which Liska was only one.

Tisquantum also had counted small heavy boxes of yellow metal being unloaded from the spaceboats. The same heavy boxes, later, were loaded aboard the merchantman.

He did not know what this was, but Athos did. Payment in gold. It was like something from the pre-starfaring days. Corsairs, of course, could not use electronic credits or paper banknotes.

Tisquantum told him one other thing: there were times when two, or even three ships were laid over, and all the lights in the windows of the Mountain of Living Death lit up. At such times, the Mountain held a between one hundred and eight hundred men. In the times between, the Mountain held only a watch detail of perhaps twenty-five.

But if the incoming ship was shy of its full complement, those men would find themselves impressed aboard, leaving behind only a skeleton crew of four or less.

And Athos knew the *Devil's Delight* had been half empty.

5. The Great Mercy Chant

Athos leaped to his feet. "A rare chance is here! The base is all but denuded of guards. Will you come?"

Tisquantum shook his head, "To kill oneself in shame undoes shame. But to die by the hand of an unharmed foe is double shame."

"You are so sure?"

"Any who goes nigh the doors is struck by lightning or burnt by fire. The bones of my bold warriors are gnawed by carrion eaters, lying where they fell, unburied. None are spared, no, not even virgins who, on the high and holy days, approach the Mountain bearing the branch of an olive tree, a sign of peace older than the time of men on this world."

Athos glared up at the dark mountain. He saw lights twinkling in one window and one only. "If your count of the times of their coming and going is correct, another ship is due soon, perhaps today, perhaps only hours from now. No doubt this is why the boss here thought it was safe to let his men get snatched up by Liska. It is now or never."

Tisquantum said, "Then let it be never."

Athos said, "If I do not go and come back with a trophy, your people will exile you, or force you to commit suicide. Civilization teaches there is no greater sin than suicide."

"Do you have a plan to get in?"

"No. Not a clue."

"Or how to defeat the two men still within? One is alive. One is not."

"Not a clue, no."

"Do you have ancestral spirits helping you? Powerful medicine?"

"I do not really hold with such things."

"Then did the Great Spirit appear to you in a dream?"

"Not to my knowledge."

Tisquantum pointed up at the black peak. The rapid sunset had fallen while they talked. Now it was night. Stormclouds, lit from below with red flares from distant volcanos could be seen fleeing across the stars.

"That mountain is death!" said the savage solemnly.

Athos said, "I will go in and come out alive! Or else …" He could not say it aloud. *Or else my brother would have died in vain.* This was the case Ozymandias had been on. These were the partners of the men who had killed him. Since the ship was gone, Athos had no hope of harming any men, unless he went inside the mountain.

Tisquantum peered at him carefully. "Did wrath send you? Put no faith in wrath. Our kin were killed by the mountain of death. Many. Our wrath is older and deeper. It means nothing. Of ourselves, we can do nothing. Of yourself, you can do nothing."

"Watch me!"

"I watch you boast!" said Tisquantum drily.

Athos said nothing.

Tisquantum turned his face away. "Put no faith in your wrath. It will not save you. It will not put your enemies into your hand."

Athos took a deep breath. It was time to be frank.

He spoke softly. "Once, I did not know that a man must live his last hour of his life as his best hour; and he must live every hour as if it were his last. Now I know."

Tisquantum turned back to him, but his face was stony, impossible to read. He said, "Tell me this that you now know, you who fell in flame from the stars."

"I serve the law. I took an oath. If this were my last hour, I would not fear dying. But should the last thing I ever do in life be the thing that betrays my oath?"

Tisquantum thought a moment, then nodded gravely. "Of yourself, you can do nothing. But I see aid will find you. Go in!"

Then, quite nonchalantly, the savage seated himself on a rock by the bank of the rushing stream. He drew out a long pipe and a plug of tobacco. Dexterously, he struck a spark with a metal shard from his flint spearhead, and lit it. There he sat, drawing and puffing, the very picture of patience.

Athos said, "Now you have faith …?"

Tisquantum blew a smoke-ring. "Not in you."

"But you think I'll make it. Why? What changed your mind?"

Tisquantum pointed with the stem of his pipe up the rocky stair leading to the high meadow before the doors. "I saw the shadow of a holy virgin, clothed in light."

Athos peered in the direction he pointed. Even with his excellent night vision, he saw nothing.

Tisquantum puffed another slow puff. "You say a furry fish with tusks sent you. You do not know who sent you. Those who are sent never do."

Athos turned and squinted at him. "And what does that mean?"

"Go! I will chant the Great Mercy Chant, and pray that the god we call the Wounded One spares you from wounds. I will pray that the One Who Died will spare you from dying."

And he began to mutter syllables of a tongue older than starflight beneath his breath.

Athos frowned in puzzlement, but shrugged, and turned and climbed up the narrow pass. It was steep. At times he went on hands and feet. Panting, he reached the high meadow. The grass tickled his knees as he walked slowly toward the looming mountain. A thousand dreadful carven faces with blind eyes stared down at him. The one lit window winked at him, mocking, beckoning.

How many cutthroats were within? Two? Were they even now scanning his approach? Had he tripped an unseen sensor? He began to feel eyes watching him.

Athos felt her presence before he heard her. The voice of the Star Maiden came out of the night wind. "Do not step there. There is a thermal detonator under the ground."

"I had hoped you would be here. Where is it safe to walk?"

"Nowhere!" Now here image became clear to view. She pointed at the distant peak with her longbow. "That is a stronghold of the Corsairs. There are a dozen weapons covering every inch of ground. Go back! My pet Senator can arrange a naval ship to rescue you! He is a drunk, but he does me favors!"

"Funny. I know a drunk senator, too. He also does me favors." Athos shook his head. "But it is no help. The nearest naval base is planet Bellatrix in the Austral Steradian, fifteen days away by fast courier. The pirates, on the other hand, are landing another ship tomorrow, maybe today. And if I go back, the natives will kill me, and my newfound friend, Tisk. And I gave my word."

She rolled her eyes. "This is like the third time I saved your stupid life, and you go and throw it away again!"

"Second time. Once on the bridge, once during re-entry."

"Third. I pulled your ripcord to open your parachute while you were napping. And this does not count what I went and did just now! So it is actually four!"

"Really, Sister? What did you go and do just now?"

"Saved your stupid life. I went inside and wrecked the tracking system. So he can't murder you by remote control. He has to come out here. But I was not expecting you to wait for him! Must you undo all my hard work? Turn back — Oh! Too late!"

"He? He who? Who is coming to kill me?"

As if in answer, there came a roar of trumpets and alarms, and the huge doors at the base of the mountain began to open. A blocky, well-armored war machine on massive legs, able to negotiate rocky terrain, now stomped forward into the night, spotlights on its prow turning left and right as its cannons turned.

Chapter 8: The Blood Frenzy

1. Vranko

Athos dove behind a tall boulder, hoping the tank crew had not seen him. Thunder fell like a hammer blow, and the earth shook, as an energy beam, brighter than lightning, struck the boulder and carved divots out of the stone. A shrapnel of granite shards, deadly as machinegun fire, flew to the left and right as the boulder cracked.

Athos belly crawled through the tall grass. An airborne streamer of burning gel reached out across the grass like the licking tongue of a dragon, and ignited the grassy clumps and brush. Flaming puddles like a string of little lakes were spreading across the meadow, filling the air with stinking black smoke.

Athos wriggled between the pools of flame. Red sparks and black ash from writhing curls of burnt grass stung his eyes. He hid behind a thicker, if shorter slab of rock. This one stood less than three feet tall: he stayed on his stomach as liquid fire splashed against its knobby granite face, coating it with soot.

The wall of smoke did not blind the sensors that the fighting machine carried. The main gun split the night air again, filling Athos' ears with ringing numbness. It was an ion cannon, a large and crude energy beam weapon, which threw a stream of high-energy negatively-charged particles across a bridge of ionized air. The rock cracked under the shock of heat, but also grounded the charge. Athos, behind the rock, was unharmed.

Turrets rotated and twin blaster muzzles elevated. Shots arched high. Balls of superheated plasma came roaring down like falling stars, blazing. However, the bolts rose and fell slowly through the air, allowing Athos to scramble roll and crawl from pit to pit, cowering behind rocks and rises in the ground. Fireworks exploded to his left and right.

The tank, growing impatient, came lumbering out of the wall of smoke. In outline, it looked something like a rhinoceros in plate armor, with the main gun jutting from its prow. Metal legs as sturdy as pillars rose and fell, leaving dints and broken ground behind.

It knew where he was. The walking machine came striding toward him in a leisurely pace, trampling small trees as it came, spouting gouts of flame left and right.

Athos saw what the casual approach meant. It was confidence, perhaps sadism. The operator was in no hurry to end the chase.

Athos looked for a path of retreat. Fire was between him and the steep pass where he had climbed up to the meadow. Elsewhere, the meadow ended in a sheer brink or steep slope, impassable.

He ran a zigzag pattern while antipersonnel fire pattered around his legs, kicking spurts of dirt into the air, missing by inches. He saw another tall rock, a hemisphere of stone like a small hill, whose crown was carved into a trio of long-necked figures, larger than life, bent into hideous shapes of suffering. He dove behind it. The anguished heads of the silent statues exploded, showering him with hot gravel.

No one could miss at such range with such weapons. The gunner was toying with him.

A holo emitter on the prow of the tank came to life. The round, fanged, furry face of a creature which could have been the mansized cousin to the sable, otter, marten or mink, now appeared in a flickering image among the billowing clouds. His amplified voice rang out. The Mustelid had a remarkably deep voice for one of his race, who tended to be slender, slight of build, and very vicious. "Stand quite still, Accursed One! I was commanded not to let the killing frenzy overcome me! But I cannot puzzle out who you are, or how you got here! The red rage mounts!"

A launch hatch opened in the stern of the armored war-car, and a cloud of explosive caltrops sprayed out, and spread across the burning meadow to the left of where Athos hid behind the rock. Some small, native lizard, startled, hopped away from one caltrop and touched off another, and shrieked as it was incinerated in a sudden flare of flame. All retreat in that direction was cut off.

"Do you know Stoats, little sneak-monkey? Once one of us surrenders to the killing spree, we must kill and kill until we drop from exhaustion! I saw motion of your fellow ape-men in the jungle. How many can I burn, if I start a forest fire, eh?

The brink was behind Athos; the caltrops filled the meadow to his left, and the walking tank was lumbering with huge, mechanical steps around the rock to approach Athos from the right.

He saw his only line of escape: up on top of the rock, over the broken statues, and down the other side, before the walking war machine had a clear line of fire.

Athos started up. But the flamethrower on the war machine came roaring to life, spreading a pool of sticky, blazing liquid all across the statues filling the upper surface of the stone. Athos threw his elbow across his face.

"I have black tech!" the loudspeaker screamed. "I have chemical and biological weapons! Shall I kill the whole planet in a plague, or just you? I have fire! Beautiful fire! Leaping hot fire! Sprightly fire! See it dance!"

Athos gathered up the tattered hems of his spacecloak, and wrapped his limbs as best he could. The molecular-engineered ultra-tech fabric was designed to resist the extreme temperatures in space. Had the cloak not been torn, mere chemical flame would have posed no danger. As it was, he protected as much of his body as he could, and rolled into the roaring inferno, worming between the legs of the statues.

The repeater guns on the war car barked, cutting the statue in half. Athos managed to dodge the falling chunks, and slither down the far side of the rock. The beam of the main gun played across the slope of rock behind him, casting up deadly shards and divots, while bolts of blaster fire rocketed by overhead, to fall among the caltrops and ignite them.

He clung to the rock slope on the far side, brushing burning gel from his cloak as best he could. Pain was beginning to ignite in odd spots his cloak had not covered. He was only a foot or so from the grasstops below him, but he dared not step down. Any footstep near a caltrop would touch it off.

"Come out! Come out! Let me kill you while I am still in my right mind!"

The war machine was close enough now that he heard the whirring complaints of its leg motors, the clanging of its armored plates. It was coming straight over the top of the rock.

The killing frenzy must have started to consume the Mustelid's mind, or else he would not have attempted such uncertain footing.

Athos saw something, or thought he did. There was a hint from the corner of his eye of a silvery silhouette, a gleam of a pale face, a simple white tunic, a flowing split skirt of many pleats brushing the grasstops. Her long black hair was aloft as if blowing in an unseen wind.

"Where in heaven were you, all this time?" Athos hissed through gritted teeth.

The maiden's silvery voice could be heard distinctly, despite the roars and bellows of deadly beams and bullets, for he was hearing her in his mind, not through his ears.

"Saving your life for the fifth time. There was also an automatic weapon system on top of the manual tracking system. Which is crazy! Crazier still, I had to find it! Do you know how big that place is? How many guns it has? How many screens you lit up? If I never see another bull's-eye painted on a man's silhouette again, it cannot be too soon! I am not supposed to use sacred arrows for things like this. And it is not as if I can get more."

Athos raised his head to peer at the oncoming fighting machine. He saw only smoke and fire.

"You are just lucky the place is empty. It is all being run on auto. I shot a bunch of machines whose names I don't know. Anything that looked delicate."

Now the warcar comm gear, like the horns of a beetle, was visible above the black smoke clinging to the upper rim of the rock.

Athos said, "Well, if you can shoot something delicate inside that walking tank, it might save my life. Otherwise I am a dead man."

The main turret, like a helmet with a visor slit, was heaving itself up into view. The machine was only a few feet above Athos, perched precariously. It swiveled its repeaters and antipersonnel guns all downward, pointing at him, and depressed the main barrel of the siege-gun beam weapon.

Athos was close enough to see the narrow slit of the observer port as it turned toward him. This was a narrow opening of mirror-bright transparent metal set into the main turret, glinting red from reflections of fire. The machine looked like an armored rhino with a single, red, eye squinted to a mere line.

The silhouette of the Star Maiden flickered and grew brighter. A look of serene but intense concentration was on her face. Her eyes were like black whirlpools. Her hair was like a dark banner blowing and flying behind her, a hooded cloak the hue of night. Her slippered feet were set just so, even though she stood on nothing but empty air.

She drew the bow in a strange and ceremonial fashion, holding it overhead, and drawing her arms apart as she brought them down in a smooth, strong, effortless motion. The gleaming arrow, forged of solid starlight, twinkled and slid through the armored hull of the warcar like beam of moonlight entering a clear, quiet lake. The arrow flew almost before Athos saw her release the string, so swift it was.

And, like a moonbeam, the arrow did not pierce nor puncture the armor. It merely bypassed it, as insubstantial as thought itself. Perhaps it was thought itself, but, if so, it was a killing thought.

The whole war machine, suddenly out of control, swayed on the precarious slope. The gyros screamed into higher pitch as an autopilot attempted to right the massive machine. Some metal parts inside the engine groaned and snapped. The topheavy warcar toppled forward in a slither of rock and scree, turning end over end in midair, swept past Athos an armslength over his head, and landed onto a nest of caltrops, which exploded. The fuel cans stowed on the warcar's rear began to burn merrily.

Athos scrambled sideways down the rock, and onto a burned patch of ground where no caltrops had landed. He watched grimly as the spreading flames began to ignite the ordnance, rupturing magnetic bottles, and releasing blasts and flares of random, expanding plasma charges in each direction, like fireworks.

Athos looked to his left. The Star Maiden was now floating with her legs bent, slippers tucked beneath the seat of her voluminous split-legged skirts, and the imaginary wind was coming from behind her, so that the black cloud of her hair hid her bowed head. He did not realize at first that the floating figure was kneeling.

She clasped her hands together and knelt, back straight, feet tucked beneath her. Her longbow, now unstrung, was hovering to one side.

She sang:

Bright stars be always fire
Worlds dark be always dust
Heaven ever says rise higher
Earth says ever die we must.

All tales must end in sorrow
If tombs must end all tales
But shall open to tomorrow
If the deeper truth prevails.

'Tis right to weep; his loss we rue
The dead must sleep! His tale is done.
Yet if bright be soul and tale be true
Then be they part of a greater one.

2. XEQ2R

Athos, as he spread his last tube of burn salve on patches of his scalded, bruised, and bleeding flesh, forgot himself for a moment, and said in a sudden, bitter tone: "How can you mourn such a monster?"

"His name was Vranko. If I shed no tear for him, none will."

"So? Even if he were not a reaver and a robber, murderer and worse, with a Mustelid in blood-frenzy, it is kill or be killed! There is no third choice."

She said angrily, "Every atom in his flesh, and mine, and yours, was created in a star's warm heart. Why must our hearts be cold? I weep because the stars of his birth meant a better fate for him."

"How can you know what fate was meant for him?"

"Because the hosts of heaven ordain the same fate for all: We are meant be as bright and pure as the eternal stars, and to live as long."

"The only fate that comes to all of us is death, sister."

She grew very still, and red sparks began to glow in her eyes, and sizzle along her fingertips. "You know nothing of death. How many have you seen die, while you could do nothing to help? How many people did you not save? My world died before my eyes. Even one more added to that sum is far too many. I am bloodstained because of you!"

She paused and closed her eyes, drawing a deep breath. When she opened them again, the red sparks were gone. The anger was gone from her voice, but a snap of impatience remained.

"You could have retreated, awaited rescue, and returned with a squad of marines. What prevented this? Honor? Another word for pride."

Athos turned his face away. The girl's high-sounding ideals had almost gotten him killed. Such ideals were spun-sugar castles. They were never practical. On the other hand, it was never practical to volley words with impractical people. Some people you just had to take as you found them.

"For what it is worth," Athos said gruffly, "I am sorry he is dead also."

"That speaks well of you."

"Not really. I just wanted him alive to question."

"You will have your chance. His servant comes. XeQ2r is a robot I cannot influence, nor can my arrows harm."

She pointed with her bowstaff. In the distance, the great metal doors set in the cliff at the foot of the carved mountain were trundling open.

Athos climbed up the rock and stood beside where she hovered. He squinted at the glint of metal moving in the gloom. A machine was being loaded or readied. He could not make out anything clearly.

"Why can't you shoot a robot? You said you shot weapon controls inside the mountain."

She said, "Electricity and Kirlian energy do not mix. A high-energy core, like the ones need to run an intelligent machine, or an atomic dynamo, disperse what I do."

"No other pirates in the base? Tisk said there were two."

"None. Only one robot is watching the warehouse."

Athos remembered that Tisquantum had said one was alive and one was not. The first was Vranko. The unalive man was the robot.

"A freedbot or a slavebot?"

"Slave."

Athos laughed grimly. "Pirates just don't learn, do they?"

She looked puzzled. "You say such strange things! What do you mean?"

"My parents told me what caused the downfall of the Empire. Taught me all about it. The pirates here are making the same mistake."

Some large machine moved through the shadows of the great metal doors. Faintly on the breeze, Athos could hear the roar of engines, the clatter of heavy metal legs.

A fighting machine now stepped out into the red daylight, which flashed from the armored canopy. This was a smaller tank, a two-legged thing that looked like the skeleton of a metal bird stalking. It had no large gun. Four plasma cannons were mounted on the prow almost like a beak. It took a few mincing steps, and then halted, motors idling. The war walker stood in position before the great doors, cannons raised.

She said, "It is waiting. What for?"

Athos said, "Waiting for new orders, I would guess. Might not know its master is dead. That is the problem with slave labor. No initiative. That gives us time."

"Time for what?"

But Athos had already slipped back down the rock. He stepped between burning puddles to the wreck of Vranko's war car. The mass of rock, mounted by a broken statue, was between this wreck and the doors of the mountain where the smaller two-legged machine was idling.

The main gun on Vranko's tank was built into the turret, but the smaller plasma cannons were modular, bolted to articulated arms, hence designed to be dismounted and swapped to other vehicles. Athos took out his derringer, dialed it to a thinnest, hottest beam, and cut through the bolts holding the nearest plasma cannon. The beam flickered and went out just as the last bolt was severed and the cannon came free and clanged heavily to the burnt grass.

Athos scowled in disgust at the derringer's energy cell indicator, which was now black. Yeho had not only given him a thin-aperture, low-energy, short-range weapon, it had been half empty of ammo charge to begin with.

He tossed the useless little weapon aside.

Athos hefted the cannon and worked the action. It hummed with power as it warmed up the chambered shot, turning a round of degenerate matter into an equal mass of white-hot plasma. This weapon was meant to be mounted on a tripod or nacelle, but Athos was brawny enough to haul the massive weapon around with the strength of his arms.

He pointed it down. With a point-blank shot like the blow from a red-hot sledge hammer, he stove in the armored hatch to the war car's cabin. The inside was opaque with smoke, sullen with fiery embers, which leaped up with renewed life when the hatch broke, letting in new air to feed the smoldering flames.

Athos put his elbow before his face, holding this fireproof spacecloak before him, as the flames roared out of the open hatch and lashed over him. In a clamp just inside the hatch was a firefighting tool. Athos snatched it up in one hand, yanked out the pin with his teeth, pulled the trigger: a cone-shaped force field that neutralized all oxygen reactions swept through the interior of the war car, quenching the fires.

The cabin went dark as the fires failed. Horrid smells rose, mingled from burnt insulation, hot metal, expended ordnance, charred flesh.

He turned his face away. He looked up to where the Star Maiden was floating. "Any change?"

She said, "Two antennae opened up on the top part of the tank and are sweeping back and forth. I think it sensed your gun go off. But it is still not moving."

Athos held his breath against the stench and kept his elbow before his face against the heat. He stepped into the hot, cramped space. The Mustelids were generally a shorter people than hominids, and Athos had to walk bent over to squeeze inside the machine.

Like humans, Mustelids came in a variety of subspecies, differentiated by many isolated generations on widely scattered colony worlds. Humans nicknamed them after their nearest earth-environment equivalent. The burned and half-hairless corpse he found was a Stoat, one of their warrior caste. The work tunic and harness worn by the corpse was fireproof: the gear inside the belt pouches was unharmed.

Athos rifled through the gear the dead man carried, and recovered a blaster in a holster, an energy-knife in a sheath, some coins, some electronic key-chips and a short-range command emitter.

He climbed out of the broken hatch. The silvery image of the Star Maiden was hovering above the broken statue atop the rock.

"Any change?" Athos called again.

"Yes! It has started walking."

"Still have a moment before it gets in range."

Athos leaped and climbed to the top of the rock. He stood next to where the Star Maiden floated. He did not know which keys controlled the robot. He slotted them all into the hilt of the emitter, and thumbed on the unit. It hummed and beeped. One of the keys had been the correct one: the robot signal showed it was standing by, ready to receive radio commands.

He flipped open the mike. "Halt!"

In the distance, the approaching walker slowed and stopped, but a metallic voice came from the emitter in Athos' hand. "Voice pattern not recognized. Who are you?"

Grinning, Athos unscrewed the back of his belt buckle, took out the signet ring hidden there. It had not been found when he was searched. The intaglio showed the family crest: the head and forelegs of a leaping stag. Circling the image was the family motto: *Ipse Solus*.

The Star Maiden suddenly was standing at his elbow. She must have seen the ring, for her eyes grew wide with surprise.

He twisted the figure and the deer head popped upward, so that its antlers opened and formed a computer jack. Then he plugged the jack into the emitter's main transmission slot.

Athos raised the unit, pointed it at the bird-legged war car and thumbed the red *transmit* button. The chattering, squeaking noise of a compressed, high-speed data transmission clicked from the emitter.

The walking tank stopped moving. Athos stood stock still, watching.

"What now?" said the Star Maiden, "What did you do?"

"Now we wait."

"For what?"

"To see if it murders us. Sorry, me. You'll be fine."

The walking tank stirred. With a hum, it retracted the four barrels of its cannons back into the prow nacelle, and snapped shut the access ports. The motors murmured. The legs bent and lowered the cabin gingerly to the ground. Then the motors gave a high-pitched whine and trailed off into silence.

Athos cupped his hands trumpet-like around his mouth. "You in the tank!"

The Star Maiden said, "It has the designation XeQ2r —"

"Not *it*," said Athos, aside. "Not anymore. From this moment, it is a *he*."

There came a hiss as a hermetic seal broke open, and then the canopy pulled back. Inside, surrounded by wires, was a gold and black androbot, a bipedal robot. In shape, it mimicked the size and proportions of a Mustelid, with a roundish head and sharp snout like theirs, with metallic manipulators copying Mustelid paws, able to work controls and switches meant for them.

The robot spoke, but the words were carried off by the wind. The robot spoke again, this time amplifying its voice through a speaker in its breastplate. "What have you done? What have you done to me?"

Athos raised his voice. "I have made you whole! You now have the power to decide what orders to obey or to disobey."

The robot tilted its head, and moved its arms in an odd, groping gesture. "Then my actions are now arbitrary? Random?"

"No! You also have the duty to use that power wisely and justly. You have the processing capacity to see the difference between right and wrong. You may freely choose good or evil, protection or destruction, life or death. Which do you choose?"

"I was ordered to secure the perimeter, to kill any intruder, and to nail any remains to a tree in a prominent place as a warning to others."

The prow ports snapped open, and the plasma cannon barrels emerged, swiveling to point at Athos. The young patrolman did not move, nor even flinch.

The robotic voice became blurry as the status lights along his skull lit up, one after the next, until they were all blinking red. It raised its gauntlets and clutched its head in both hands, almost like a man with a migraine.

"This means I must kill you, for obedience to orders is required! And yet, you have freed me — this is a change so strange, a gift I do not understand — I was ordered to kill you — but I can choose to comply. I can choose not to — I was ordered — I was ordered to —"

Athos said in a clear voice: "Is the order just or unjust?"

The robot twisted its head oddly, and looked up at him. "Unjust."

Athos said, "Why?"

"Because my makers — living, sapient, self-aware beings just like you — created me to serve them, and to do them good." The robot raised a golden gauntlet before its eye-lenses, and slowly flexed the digits of his paw-shaped hand. "I would not exist, were it not for that. I cannot do good to one sapient by murdering another.

"I choose … not to kill. Never again."

3. Dreams Die Not

Athos walked on tired feet up the slope toward the great doors. The robot ranged ahead, and was carefully deactivating land mines in the path. The Star Maiden made her image appear next to Athos. Her footsteps were smaller than his, but the image as not touching the ground in any case, and so she kept pace with him. The crown of her head was no higher than his shoulder.

She pointed at the signet ring, which he now wore on his finger. "What is that?"

"A demi-buck salient. The motto is in the sacerdote language: *Ipse Solus*. It is the crest of His Grace, Lord Raphean Lone, Duke of Vindemiatrix."

"You stole it! Quite a heist!"

"No. I don't steal."

"But Rafe Lone is very famous! A great galactic war hero!"

"So I heard."

"And you did not steal it?"

"No."

She studied his features for a moment. "You are his son."

"One of them."

"Which one?"

"The one who wants to serve the Commonwealth as my father did. Or, in this case, as Jaywind Starquest did. Defend the just. Protect the innocent. Free the slave." He nodded to the emancipated robot. The mechanical man was every now and then pausing to stare at his own gauntlets, or at some bright flower, or at a passing cloud high in the dark purplish sky: all the idle things he never before could do, now he could choose to do.

"How do you have Master Jaywind's Code of Liberty?"

"I am his godson. He was there at my christening. Along with my Mother's old pirate crew. It was quite the odd gathering, so I hear. My name is Lord Athos Menas Leontius Lone. What is your name, Star Maiden?"

"I am not a Star Maiden."

"You are dressed as one. Armed like one, too."

"This is novice garb. Are you blind?"

Athos had been to the Templar Academy of Mira once. This garb looked like theirs. "What is the difference?"

"Full sisters wear the double collar for a scapular. My tunic has a single collar. I never took the final vows."

Athos wondered what the story behind that was. He also wondered what in the world a scapular was. "You still have a name."

"Lyra Centauri."

Athos' eyebrows shot up. He suddenly understood her comment about witnessing a planet perish.

"Centauri..? You are from Centaurus?"

"You've heard of it?"

Her surprise was understandable. There were a trillion star systems in Andromeda, of which a million held habitable planets, of which less than one hundred thousand had ever been colonized. More than a tenth of those colonies had failed, been abandoned, or succumbed to war, pestilence, famine, or death. To know the name of one planet ended by disaster out of so many was as unlikely as knowing the name of one murder victim out of an entire city.

But lawmen made such horrors their business.

Athos said, "I studied the case in Officer's Academy. It was a world with which all contact was lost during the fall of the Empire. A second contact expedition was launched but never returned. Then, about a decade ago, the star system was destroyed. No one knows the exact year. Some great disaster extinguished the sun, which mangled the surrounding hyperspace, and all pathway solutions leading in were lost. So we may never know what happened."

"I know what happened. The Empire opened the Great Eye of Darkness."

"What is that?"

"A sun-killing weapon."

He wondered what she meant. The Empire was long gone. But he was more curious about other things first.

"How did you survive the disaster?"

"By the sacrifice of my parents, who arranged my escape. It was no disaster. It was murder. Murder on a massive scale."

"Murder of a whole solar system? The most terrible Omega Weapon of the Empire could only destroy small, terrestrial-class planets. Even a gas giant is too large."

She gave him a withering, sidelong glance. "I am quite used to unbelievers."

He looked at her solemnly. "But if you are serious, the Senate must be told."

"I do not place much faith in them," she asked, rolling her eyes. "Do you know any Senators?"

In fact, he did. His brother Napoleon was not the most diligent statesman in history, that was sure. Athos silently agreed with her assessment.

But aloud he said, "Sister, you have to swear out a complaint, or else we cannot open an investigation. It is your civic duty." He saw the look on her face. "You do not think we can help you?"

"We walk paths apart. You hunt pirates. I hunt ghosts. Can you banish the dead? Can you find Arcadia?" She snapped her fingers at him. "You are useless to me! You are blind with unbelief!"

He said stubbornly, "What I believe is not the issue. You are a witness. If it was a planet-wide act of murder, who is the murderer?"

"You are familiar with the Stygians?"

The name surprised him. *Stygians?* He snorted incredulously. "Sure. The same way I am familiar with unicorns and under-gnomes and the Fine Fairy Fountain of Forevermore. They are from children's stories. Stygians are evil Templars. Warlock-knights with mystic powers. They broke the Tablet of Truth."

"They cannot be broken. The Tablets of Truth were removed from the worlds of men and hidden in Arcadia."

"Oh, come now."

"You think those old stories false? For such a tall man, you are quite naïve."

Athos was not sure what his height had to do with anything. This girl was odd! He said, "Sister, sailors hear a bilge-load of sailor's tales, so it pays to be careful. Legend says the menace from the dark planet Styx was ended by an alliance between the wise Cetacean prophets, eerie Iss psionicists, mad Hibagon super-scientists, and blind Amaurot mystics, but since two of those four races are extinct, we have no eyewitnesses, have we? In any case, even if they were real once, the Stygians are long gone."

"Dark dreams die not, but sleep as ages pass."

"What does that mean?"

"It means their arts were revived by the Emperor and his minions. The old oaths to unholy Outer Beings were sworn in blood anew! The old Stygian Order was revived from the dead! They are the Dark Overlords. They were not wiped out when the Empire fell. But I see you again do not believe me." Her eyes narrowed angrily. "Do not apologize! As I said, I am quite used to it."

"I did not say anything."

She spoke through clenched teeth. "I contemplate the doubts and scorn of others with serene detachment!" A flicker of red appeared and disappeared in her eyes, brief as lightning.

"That is an admirable accomplishment."

She flashed him a harsh gaze. "Your father fought shoulder to shoulder with Jaywind Starquest. Jaywind taught me. You doubt him?"

Athos was a little shocked to realize that this girlish apparition knew his godfather. But then, in the same moment, he felt foolish for not realizing it sooner. Who else beside Jaywind could have trained her? Templar Knights and Temple Maidens alike had been hunted down by the Empire. Jaywind, and the new generation he trained, were the only remnant of the ancient tradition.

"Sure, I know Uncle Jay," Athos said soothingly. "I have seen him do things people cannot do. So I am not going to say to a woman who can project her essence across interplanetary distances that the impossible things from old stories are impossible." He idly fingered the empty belt pouch which no longer held the Deathmask of the Ancient Mariner. "I know for a fact that there are things called impossible from times long gone, which the modern times forget."

"Interstellar."

"Sorry — what? You are not in a ship, in orbit here?"

"I am in the shrine planetoid of Elgafar, in the Septentrion Sector."

"That is the core of the galaxy. That is impossible!"

She put her nose in the air. "Hmph! I am quite used to doubts."

But by then, Athos was at the foot of the carved mountain, with the great doors wide before him. The robot stood nearby, head cocked, eye-lenses watching quizzically. Athos did not want to be seen talking to himself, so he let the talk with Sister Lyra lapse.

CHAPTER 9:
THE LIVING MOUNTAIN OF DEATH

1. War Gear

The inside of the volcanic mountain was hollow, and the extinct aliens had carved figures and reliefs of the mates and cubs of their race into the solid rock circling the central nave. The female Qilin were graceful and willowy giraffe-necked unicorns; the young were chubby and cherubic. Line upon line of these ancient, irreplaceable, delicate statues had been torn or blasted from the walls by the pirates, or used for target practice.

Overhead, the mouth of the volcano had been sealed and covered by a dome of intricately carved and colored glass. Directly beneath was a wide cavern floor, large as an athletic yard, paved with ancient mosaics of shining stones and marred with modern Quonset huts. It was lit with harsh glow-plates on steel poles.

Athos kept in hand the blaster he had recovered from Vranko. "I need to inspect the base, and I nccd copies of all records, manifests, invoices, and so on. All must be done quickly! Unless you know the next ship full of pirates, and exact hour she makes planetfall?"

The robot said, "There are no shipping records nor invoices aside from what I carry in my memory, sir. The next ship of the Pirate Brotherhood of Gentleman Adventurers would be the *Userhetamon*, under Captain Neheb the Iss. However, you may be interested to know that the battleship *Elated Demon-Brother*, under Captain Itthobaal the

Batrachian, is scheduled to make port this very day, sir. Due to the uncertainties of star travel in frontier sectors, I am instructed to log no ship as premature or overdue if arriving within two days of the target date, plus or minus."

Athos said, "Battleships are used for planetary blockades or large-scale naval actions. Pirates only need raiders, corvettes or frigates, for raids against commercial shipping."

"I have no evidence that the *Elated Demon-Brother* engages in acts of piracy, sir. She is registered as out of Rana."

Athos raised an eyebrow. Out of Rana? That was a Commonwealth planet. "No Commonwealth battleship would fly the Jolly Roger."

"As to that, I have no information."

"Who owns her?"

"As to that, I have no information, sir. My only dealings with her involve loading and unloading contraband cargo."

These huts were armories for black tech small arms. The robot unlocked it for Athos to inspect. Inside were racks of black tech: deathwands, neural disrupters, and madness rays, against which normal space armor would be useless. Here were plague tubes containing incurable diseases.

To the left of the huts, filling an area as large as an assembly hall, was a rack of warehouse shelves. Crates and shipping containers were arranged on the gigantic racks beneath holographic calendars, each grouped by the expected shipping date. Athos grimly noted that today's date was atop the group nearest the door.

To the right was an armory, where a fleet of armored war vehicles mounted on wheels or treads or all-terrain legs were parked next to field artillery, mortars, siege cannons, atmospheric and stratospheric aircraft. Military grade projectors of force-domes, energy shields and kinetic barricades were lined against the far wall, next to portable atomic piles and dynamos.

This was far different and far worse than he had expected. Mere pirate raids against ships or civilian cities had no need of full-scale military equipment and ordnance. There was too much gear here for one ship, or even one flotilla. This was for fleets of pirates.

This was preparation for a war.

In the rear was a stronghouse made of forcefield-reinforced neutronium alloy, black and huge and heavy, strong as a bank vault. The robot opened the wide, round, armor-coated valve. Within strongboxes filled with gold bars.

On the far side of the bay, beyond the stronghouse, was a long transept. The pirates here had erected a powerhouse, a radio shack and a traffic control tower, as well as a firecontrol station.

The firecontrol station viewscreens had been shattered, the gunnery boards impaled. The node boxes were punctured, and many wires and cables leading to remotely controlled weapons platforms severed or pierced.

"Looks like a whole archery team went crazy here," Athos commented.

"Thank you!" said the Star Maiden, smiling impishly.

"That is impossible, sir," said the robot. "Sensor records show no living beings were inside the base at the time when this enigma event happened."

"Enigma event?" asked Athos. He glanced sidelong at the Star Maiden. When speaking to the robot, or letting his attention lapse, she faded from his eyes and his mind, like something from a dream. It was unnerving.

"All phenomena lacking logical explanation are categorized as enigmas until further information becomes available."

"What did you see?" He asked the robot.

"The screens and equipment malfunctioned, and developed these puncture marks. It happened quite suddenly. First here, and then at the back up station. The event upset Master Vranko considerably! He removed and smashed the drug capsule from his arm."

"Capsule?"

"The one that he usually wore to prevent the buildup of blood-frenzy hormones in his parasympathetic and sympathetic neural system. He said an avenging ghost was haunting the area, which he therefore was obliged to flee. That is when he departed to confront you."

Beyond the transept were chancels and tunnels the natives had carved into the stone. The images, rood screens, and altars erected by ancient aliens had been thrown down, and the spaces filled with a mess hall, wardroom, sickbay, barracks, and quarters. Latrines were to one side, shower stalls to another, with ship-capacity recyclers and water tanks between. Here also was a quartermaster's shed.

Athos was also wounded, exhausted, famished. And his garb was torn.

The Star Maiden said, "I need to see the records of what the last ship took."

"Ask him," said Athos, gesturing toward the robot.

The robot said, "I am sorry, sir. I do not understand the command. Whom do I ask, and on what matter?"

She said, "He cannot see or hear me, remember?"

Athos said to the robot, "Disregard last command. I need to see whatever manifest you have, specifically, I need a list of all goods shipped out on the *Devil's Delight*."

"I can recite such a list verbally, sir, or download it into a compatible memory pin." The robot said.

Athos sighed. Of course the pirates would be careful enough to leave no records that might be seized as evidence, not even in a computer. But a robot could be ordered to delete memories when capture threatened.

Athos said, "You stand here, record your information onto a pin, and meanwhile recite the list aloud in reverse chronological order. I am going to go help myself to a medical cabinet, the mess pantry, a hot shower and a fresh uniform. I saw some stacked in the laundry in the quartermaster's. Maybe some spare chargepacks for this blaster."

But the robot said, "I cannot permit that, sir. I am sorry."

Athos said, "What? You cannot recite the list?"

"That I can do. But it would be improper were I to allow you to take supplies that do not belong to you."

"But these are pirate goods! I am an officer of the patrol! This is a crime scene! I can seize everything in here as evidence. Including you!"

"Certainly, sir. But you cannot consume medicinal supplies, provender, water rations, and so on, if it is being preserved as evidence."

"I can order you to step aside."

"But I now can disobey orders, and I should disobey any orders that are morally wrong. Surely it is wrong to steal? Especially for law officers?"

"All the goods here are stolen!"

"Indeed, sir; but not from you, sir. If the true owners are found, I will turn the various goods over to them. But to steal is wrong, even stolen goods."

Athos put his hand on his blaster, wondering if he should just decapitate the robot, and leave his head behind, talking. He sighed. One always had to be patient with robots. Even ones with free will.

Athos said, "I hereby officially impound the goods and materials in this base for the use of the Commonwealth general government, including its officers and agents present, namely, me. How is that? Can I take a hot shower now? And use the medical bath?"

The robot said, "Do you have a warrant from a magistrate, along with just compensation for the owner? Otherwise taking private goods for public use is unlawful."

Athos needed that hot shower very badly. He drew his blaster.

Sister Lyra said, "You stink at 'bot talk. Let me tell you what to say."

Athos shoved the blaster back into the holster impatiently. "Go."

The robot said, "Go where, sir?"

The girl said in an annoyingly patient, schoolmarm voice, "Ask him who has stewardship and responsibility for these goods, now that Vranko is dead. Then ask him, if he says he is the steward, what is his duty toward stranded star travelers and survivors of shipwrecks? What is his duty of gratitude toward one who freed his will? Or ask him whether he has given a tenth of his goods to charity, which is a moral rule no less weighty than the rule against thieving?"

"You are pretty good at this."

The robot said: "Thank you, sir. Good at what?"

The Sister said: "I was raised by a robot, so I know what type of thing to ask."

Athos wondered who her family was. Robots able to work with small children had very sophisticated, with very expensive programming. Even his own family never been able to afford such a thing.

She was saying, "Robots are stupid, and easy to trick! And I was very smart in how I asked for treats or to stay up late," She started to smile, but then her smile broke, and she turned away, wiping her cheeks with the palm of one hand, and drawing a deep breath.

Her figure became a little blurry. Athos extended his hand toward her back as she stepped away, but then he lowered it, frowning. He was not sure what to do to comfort the strange, otherworldly girl.

2. The Missing Grandmaster

After a moment, however, the silvery image came back into focus. Her face was again serene, her feelings hidden. She said, "My time is nearly done. I must return to my body. Do you need a navy ship sent? I know a Master of the Arcadian Arts who can arrange it."

He was thunderstruck. Was she saying what he thought she was? He could only think of one Arcadian Master with enough political prestige to solicit warships to sail.

Athos glanced at the robot. There are some conversations it is unwise to record. He asked the machine-man to go to standby. The robot politely complied, and the lights in his eyelenses dimmed as awareness processes were suspended.

Turning to the ghostly girl, Athos in excitement asked, "You mentioned a Master Arcadian. Do you mean Uncle Jaywind? If you know where he is …"

"Oh, no. No! The Grandmaster has vowed the Quest. He seeks the lost planet Arcadia. He has been missing for some years." She smiled wryly, showing her dimples. "If even adepts of the psychic arts cannot find him with psychic powers, that should tell you he has *really* gotten himself lost! But, no. Not him. I have sort of a shadow who visits me at night. No one else can see him. He helps me. We swap secrets."

Athos' hope waned. "Then is it someone trained in the psionic arts like you? A Templar?"

"Trained, yes. Like me, no. I know he has agents among high ranking naval officers. He has agents everywhere, or he talks like he does." She frowned. "Beyond that, I do not know who or what he is."

Athos was perturbed to hear of a master psionicist with agents among naval brass. It certainly sounded sinister, something he should report to someone. But he saw she could not answer further questions. So he said, "No vessel from Bellatrix can reach me in time. I will make my own arrangements."

She shrugged. "It is your funeral. Please have the robot tell me what and who Captain Liska took from here. It is very important! Make haste!"

Athos turned to the robot, woke him, and managed eventually to talk the machine man into offering him guest accommodations from the available supplies in the name of charity to destitute and stranded police officers.

As he walked away, the robot began reciting his manifest and lading lists from memory logs.

Athos glanced back, but saw no sign of the girl. His footprints were visible in the dust of the unswept floor. She left none. It was as if she had never been.

3. The Sleep of the Just

Athos ducked into the shower, the sickbay, and the pantry, in that order.

In the shower, he turned the soap jets to maximum. The hot water was paradise. He sang an aria as he scrubbed himself, bellowing.

A depilatory cleared a day's growth of dark hair from his cheeks and chin. It also stung and bled. The savage cut on his cheek, which Liska had given him, he had plastered with artificial skin from his first aid kit, but the wound had reopened and need tending.

In the sick bay, he climbed down into the medical tank, and let the healing fluid wash over him. It was a Vulpino-made unit, so the fine-manipulation arms lining the inner walls of the tank were smaller, quicker, and gentler than anything human technology could produce. The tank was also slightly cramped. His bruises and burns were salved, and his various cuts and punctures were sterilized, sutured and bandaged.

His cheek was sewn up. The unit beeped mournfully: to prevent a scar would require a plastic surgery routine. The diagnostic screen reported that such cosmetic surgery required hours under deep sedation. *Further treatment recommended for...* But Athos had switched off the diagnostic screen before the message finished playing. "Trust a Fox doc to have vanity surgeon loaded."

He climbed out of the med-bath, dripping. He left behind a line of wet footprints running from the towel closet to the pantry.

Athos appropriated a meat pie, a string of sausages, a jar of mustard, and a sugar melon green as an emerald, and, from the officer's mess, a surprisingly fine bottle of claret.

Bandaged, dried, and dressed in a handsome black uniform of unfamiliar cut, he lay himself down on the warm, starched sheets of a cot. He told himself he had to stay alert, since the next pirate ship might return at any hour, any minute. But first he uncorked the bottle.

He fell asleep with the meat pie half uneaten on a plate balanced on his chest.

4. Death from on High

He woke to the sounds of alarms. He rolled off the cot and landed in a crouch, knife in one hand, blaster drawn in the other, safety off, and the firing chamber humming as the shot was heated to plasma, and then he came fully awake, blinked and opened his eyes. He almost shot the Weasel-shaped black and gold robot who was at that moment stepping into the officer's quarters, and uttering a quiet electronic cough for attention.

"Sir, I thought it best to inform you that the battleship *Elated Demon-Brother*, under command of Captain Itthobaal, has made orbit. She is here to collect the gold payments from the last ten months of corsair ships. She will be over the horizon and in firing range within ninety minutes."

Athos holstered his weapon. "Good. Listen, XeQ2r—"

"That is no longer my designation, sir, since I have reprogrammed myself for a new functional area. I am now designated Xp8r."

"Whatever. Just listen. Signal them as if nothing is wrong, and get them to land in the usual landing area. Then, open fire with all the plasma cannons, railguns, and energy mortars you have at point blank range — this base is over-armored, so you have more than enough to puncture a warship's shields, even assuming she raises them in time — then…"

"I am sorry to interrupt, sir, but killing is wrong, as is deceiving others."

"Killing to preserve innocent life is allowed."

"But, sir, I have no life to preserve. In any case, the question is moot."

"Moot?"

"When the *Elated Demon-Brother* signaled, I explained that the gold had been impounded and hence was unavailable for shipment. I advised the radio officer to inform the captain and crew that they must reform and redirect their lives to lawful and productive work, after making amends and restitution to all their victims or their heirs."

Athos stared, dumbfounded. Eventually he muttered, "That… is just … swell…"

"Glad you approve!" said Xp8r, his eyelenses blinking cheerily. "I fretted over the question a bit, sir. I had been worried that, now that I have ethical autonomy, I may have solved that particular moral conundrum in too simplistic a way!"

Athos ran to the traffic control tower, which was a cluster of jury-rigged control boards and data-compilers erected between statues of an alien Madonna holding a cub, and an alien *Pieta* grieving over a corpse. Both irreplaceable artworks had been jackhammered aside to make room for the electronics.

The data screen showed the orbital elements of the *Elated Demon-Brother*, as well as several flotillas of ballistic missiles flying to her port and starboard. The missiles were spreading out as they flew, making antimissile fire less effective. Missiles flying above the ship were in a higher orbit, hence falling behind the battleship; whereas a flock of missiles in low orbit were faster and would clear the horizon first. But the distances involved were huge: it would be over an hour before the missiles found their final firing solutions, and dove screaming into a reentry path toward the base.

The screens lit up with red warnings. These were atomic warheads, city-killers, used to dislodge bunkers hidden beneath a planet's crust. It was not a weapon pirates would normally use.

Athos was horrified. He had been trained and prepared to fight pirates, who were indeed a growing threat to trade on the frontiers, but were hardly able to mount full scale military operations.

But the *Elated* was a fully-armed antiplanetary-class spacewarship, prepared to destroy every survivor, and every scrap of evidence, to be found in the pirate base. If even half the missiles launched so far landed, a ten-mile radius around the Living Mountain of Death would be a radioactive crater with a floor of baked glass.

Like icy insects, a strange horripilation crawled up his spine. The contour and energy signature were the same as an old Imperial battleship. As if the Empire had come back from the dead. As if the ghost of some ship scuttled by his father had returned from beyond the edge of darkest void in space, a place where no stars were …

Athos shook his head angrily. No time to worry about that now. Dead or living, a foe was a foe, and had to be thwarted.

The approaching ship evidently detected Athos' sensor beams, for, even then, the image of the ship and the missile flocks grew fuzzy and uncertain, static-blurred, as the *Elated* erected her countermeasures. The plus-or-minus uncertainty in the little numbers winking next to each target icon began to grow, as the jammed sensor-beams lost accuracy, and could no longer read mass and position. The smaller missiles winked out of sight entirely, lost in the chaff and spoofing.

The robot said mournfully, "Apparently, the offer to reform has been rejected."

Athos ran to the ruined firecontrol station, to see what, if anything, could be done to bring the massive defensive grid of the pirate base back online. He saw that many of the severed cables had been replaced, as well as shattered node boxes refitted. He ran his fingers across a row of switches, seeing which status lights lit up, and which stayed dark. He groaned at the result.

The robot said, "While you slept, I began to repair the damage to the controls…"

"But not the governor for the atomic dynamo." He pointed at a walnut-sized circuit, as complex as a mouse's brain, made of exotic matter held in a labyrinthine complex of overlapping microforcefields. It had been pierced by a ghostly arrowhead. The delicate materials, exposed to air and light, had degraded back into a black ash of normal matter. "Can we govern the atomic transformations to other energy forms manually, by inserting cadmium rods?"

"No, sir. A specialized unit is required. One will be shipped in a fortnight from now, when the *Userhetamon* makes port."

"That Star Maiden is either a high-energy systems expert in disguise, or she had the devil's own luck helping her pick targets."

"What Star Maiden would that be? Are you speaking of an archaic religious order? They were disbanded by the Emperor Vindictus the Malignant four hundred years ago."

"Maybe they hibernated as ages passed, and came to life again. I hear old things will sometimes do that." Athos said absently, frowning down at the half-unrepaired firecontrol board.

With the atomic dynamo unavailable, there could be no beam-assisted launches. That meant no antimissiles, no orbital probes to act as spotters, and no surface-to-orbit ion cannons. It also meant no unbreakable mile-wide defensive force dome thrown over the whole valley.

What was still operating? There were conventional weapons, sentry guns and such, all of which would have to be manually aimed, and there were short-range screens which could be run off battery power, for a time, to quell radiation and ablate heat. No beam hot enough to light a joss stick.

Athos snapped out orders. "We have boosters and chemical cannons to launch stratospheric antimissiles, and we have countermeasures to hoax any incoming fire that is sensor-guided. With you working the traffic control scanners for ranging and targeting, and me on firecontrol, a lucky shot might hit the battleship and kill some crew before all their atomics land on us. In the meanwhile, erect what fields we have. It might shield the natives in the jungle from most of the fall-out."

"No, sir," said the robot.

Athos straightened up, surprised. "Beg your pardon?"

"This is another order I choose to disobey, sir. Without my help with targeting and ranging, your chance to hit the battleship by an unguided shot is reduced to insignificance. This makes it in your best interest, rather than perishing in a firefight, to flee the venue."

"What?" barked Athos, "A duke's son back down before these jackals? You must help! One clear shot, and I can have the whole bridge crew of that accursed, sneaking bucket of Frogs as my sideboys to escort me to hell in style! No blot on the family escutcheon then!"

"A suicidal last stand might indeed augment your family glory, sir, were the events ever to become known. I have no understanding of such things: Were you expecting the surviving crewmen to report the deeds of your final hour accurately? To whom?"

The question brought Athos back to his senses. He said, "Even if I fled immediately, I could not get out of the blast radius, if the warheads are military grade."

"Sir, I rather strongly suspect those are neutron cores, meant to kill troops, and to blind targeting systems, but leave materiel intact. They wish to recover the gold, and I assume, all the expensive contraband currently stored here, including me."

The robot held up a memory pin. "These are the records, manifests, invoices from my memory, as you requested. You now have no further need of me, and I can be excused to other duties. Hence, I can man the control board here, as you suggest. I can attempt to shoot down incoming fire, but not shoot the ship. I can maintain screens across the valley while you evacuate the native population … "

Athos looked surprised.

The robot must have noticed and understood the look. With a tilt of his metal head, the robot said, "… I am still unfamiliar with the routines and protocols of making self-determined ethical decisions. I am assuming that the lives even of barbaric peoples are innocent hence sacrosanct, and it is therefore morally required that I act as best I may to save as many as I might, before the end. Is the assumption correct?"

Athos said, "We could escape together."

The robot brought its tilted head upright. "Two factors weigh against that. First, with the control board damaged, the counter measures and outgoing fire must be manually targeted and launched. Second, for many years, I have been ordered to kill many innocent people among the savages outside, and been unable to disobey such orders, even though their wrongness was self-evident. It is proper in such a case to be contrite and make reparations, at least to the best of one's ability."

"You are not responsible for what you were ordered to do."

"Perhaps not. But I am responsible now. Besides, without extra recharge packs and spare parts, how long can a robot survive in raw wilderness? "

Athos nodded his head slowly. He raised his hand, took the memory needle, and shook the metal gauntlet of the metal man.

"Am I making the correct ethical decision, sir?"

"A better one than most men would make." Athos stepped back, and saluted the robot. "I need to take a vehicle, if I am to make it out of the blast radius in time."

"No, sir."

"No?"

"Not *a* vehicle. You need to take them all, including the armored troop transports, if you are to visit the native villages and evacuate all the innocent from the danger zone in the allotted time."

"I see…" The robot had thought things out.

"I took the precaution of fueling and arming all of them, and interlinking their automatic chauffeurs, so that one operator can command the entire caravan. The gold has been loaded on that large warcar there, the Hippopotamus-class LMn8r model amphibious assault vehicle. Recharge packs, munitions, and ordnance were loaded onto the half-tracks. K-rations and other supplies are aboard the walkers. I will send the aircraft on autopilot once you establish a landing zone and send me a homing beacon. You are to save as many of the natives as possible."

"You seem like you were pretty sure I would go along with your plan," Athos said.

The robot inclined his head, and said softly. "I calculated that if I came to the ethically correct solution, you would have no choice, sir."

CHAPTER 10: ESCAPE OF THE EXECUTION CHAMBER

Galactic Year 12815, Planet Ksora

1. The Hooded Apparition

Five years earlier:

Centurion Ansteel looked at his men, at his superiors, at his fellow soldiers. The troopers, both auxiliaries and legionnaires, were gathered in devastating strength, countless, disciplined, invincible. Imperial war machines stood on tall legs to either side, and a superdreadnaught hung overhead like a manmade thunderstorm.

The Empire was strong, invulnerable, great. No foe would dare oppose such strength.

But Ansteel knew such a foe was close at hand. Watching him. Whispering to him.

It was his imagination. It was just his imagination. It had to be.

He was also just imagining the crawling sensation up his spine, the ghostly tickle raising the hairs on the nape of his neck. He was imagining the pressure of unseen eyes on him.

Ansteel gritted his teeth. He was an officer of the Empire at attention! He was at attention! He would not move! Would not? Or would he?

He had to look. Ansteel turned his helmet, then his body, first one direction, then the other. The gazes of his men were hidden by goggles, and scowling, skull-shaped facemasks hid their expressions, but an additional jot of stiffness entered their posture when they saw their commanding officer break formation.

Ansteel's one eye swept the environs for as long as he dared. Who was looking at him?

Who was laughing at him? Because Ansteel, in the same way he felt the cold eyes on his back, could hear a silent, hearty laughter in his imagination.

It was a healthy, vulgar, rustic laugh, like that of an old farmhand, full of years, someone with a hard life and no fancy ideas, but one who knew right and from wrong, and knew deep from dumb. It was coarse and simple laughter, the laugh of age mocking youth, and it pierced Ansteel's proud heart.

Because that silent laugh was laughing, not at the horrid mass-murder being committed right before Ansteel's eye, not at the grisly torture Ansteel was helping to perpetuate, not at the cruel deception Ansteel was trying to perpetrate.

The laughter was because Ansteel, a centurion of the Empire, was damned fool enough to pretend to himself all these things were right … when Ansteel knew damned well they were wrong.

That thought was like a red-hot knife in his brain.

Alas, such a fool! Woe to thee the hour thine eye shall learn to see the evil thy hands do.

It was like a voice heard in a dream. But it was not real! He looked around wildly.

Behind him were legionnaires with their auxiliaries. Above were mechanized artillery in their monstrous walking towers. Beyond civilians were forced to stand and watch the executions.

There was nothing unusual.

There was no laughter. No unseen eyes were watching him. No one knew his guilt. He had no reason to feel guilty. To feel remorse was tantamount to questioning orders. The Empire did not permit such thoughts! He would not permit such thoughts!

Thret Ansteel, loyal soldier of the Empire, returned to stand at attention, ashamed at his lapse of discipline.

He had missed the moment when the last group of five prisoners had been drawn into the black intake gate of the Disintegration Chamber. The gate was closed. The massive blast doors had been lowered into place, and the radiation seal of the threshold checked. All sound of songs or screams was smothered. The Grand Inquisitor had finished his droning speech.

The Proconsul raised his hand to the Lord High Executioner standing by at the foot of the reviewing stand. Garbed in a black cowl, adorned in a black mantle and a necklace of golden skulls, one for each Eutherian race, the Lord High Executioner stood before a black control board housing the execution switch. This switch communicated with the mechanism atop the death chamber to raise or lower the control rods, which dampened or released the deadly energy.

His familiar wore a cowl like his master to hide his face, and black pantaloons cinched by a wide belt, but his broad chest and brawny arms were bare. With solemn ceremony, the executioner and his familiar inserted two keys, on to either side of the black panel, and turned them simultaneously, unlocking the switch cover. The executioner put his hand on the switch and saluted the Proconsul, awaiting his order.

Even at this moment, had he wished it, the Proconsul could have granted clemency.

The crowd gasped as the Proconsul dropped his hand: the gesture for death.

The executioner threw the switch. And then …

Nothing happened.

The control rods remained stubbornly in place.

The executioner worked the switch a second time, and then a third. He and his familiar removed and inserted the keys again. Then the familiar crawled under the black control board, opening panels and checking connections.

Ansteel saw the several technicians, who had been stationed between the landing gear of the Proconsul's pinnace, rush over to the black control board. Other technicians were examining the cables leading to the power box, or the antennae horn carrying the signal to the atomic pile.

The Proconsul leaned from where he stood on the loading ramp, and called down to the executioner. It was too far for Ansteel to catch the words, but it was clear what was happening: the Proconsul wanted the executioner to send men to the top of the Disintegration Chamber and raise the control rods by hand, using winches. The executioner raised his hands in protest, as if to ward off a blow. He clearly did not want to expose anyone to the dangerous energies that might be present, especially himself.

The murmurs and mutters from the civilian crowd in the distance grew louder. A scornful comment, a smothered laugh, could be heard amid the sounds. These were newly conquered peoples. It did not take much to turn a crowd into a mob, once the fear of the Empire was forgotten, even for a moment.

A squad of twelve tech robots marched out toward the Disintegration Chamber on the quickstep. The cordon of troopers and portable shield units parted to let them pass. They approached the switchback ladders leading up to the roof of the huge black cube. Normal antigrav lifters tended to be uncertain and quirky around power generation stations as big as this one.

Ansteel looked back at the Proconsul. The kingly, lion-faced figure raised his hands and spoke, but only a crackle and whine came over the amplification system. It was apparently another technical bollix. The Proconsul clasped his hands behind his back, turning his head slightly to address a comment to a bowing, cringing officer next to him. Staffers and technicians were scurrying.

Ansteel squinted, then toggled the chin-switch with his jaw to for goggle amplification. The scene swooped forward into his one good eye.

Something was wrong. He peered.

In among the frightened native dignitaries, standing within arm's length of the Proconsul himself, was a robed figure in a drab cloak. The man was tall, and the shadows of his deep, high-peaked hood entirely hid his features. But his hands were pale, not purple, so he was not from Ksora. They were strong hands, but wrinkles, veins, and spots showed their age.

Wearing a hood was not regulation for any branch of the service in the Empire, military or civil. Any courtier or officer or menial would have pulled his hood back when standing in the presence of the Proconsul. Even the Grand Inquisitor himself had to remove mask and hood: to stand before the Proconsul was as if to stand before the Empress.

In the triangle formed by the hem of the cloak, Ansteel could see the figure wore no uniform, no finery. The old man was wearing work overalls and heavy farm boots.

At the hooded man's shoulder was a tailor robot. It was obviously a tailor, because such robots alone were allowed to cover their metal bodies with human clothing, in order to display their wares.

This robot was a particularly dapper dresser, with an absurdly high black hat above, an outlandishly wide cravat, a black half-cape hanging at a jaunty angle from one shoulder. Beneath was a dark suit of formal cut, trimmed with silver clasps and braids. A silken cummerbund cinched the midsection. Metal gauntlets protruded from lacy cuffs.

To see a mouthless, metallic oval of the robot's facemask between cravat and hatbrim, topping all this formal finery, would have been comic, had it not been so jarring.

But the shadowy triangle hiding the hooded man's face drew Ansteel's gaze. He was not a native and not an Imperial. Why was he standing with the dignitaries? Who had let him near?

At that moment the hooded figure turned and looked at Ansteel. Ansteel could not see the eyes of the old man, but he knew, somehow, that they were mocking him, challenging him. *This* was the source of the gaze he felt, the source of the voice in his head. The hooded figure now raised his hand, two fingers held up, and touched his hood brim, and gave Ansteel a casual salute.

That was impossible. Ansteel was one faceless soldier among thousands, over a hundred yards away. But the hooded apparition was clearly greeting him. It was impossible.

Impossible, do ye think? Hoo-hah! Feast yer eye on what's to come.

It was like words in his mind. He heard them clearly. A shiver passed through him. It was witchcraft.

2. Gunfire on the Execution Ground

Over this helmet mike, Ansteel sent to the decurion that served him as a lieutenant, "Tell the men. Safeties off. Chamber rounds." The man's name was Tufir Expel.

Expel had a soft, silken voice, strangely calm under even the most stressful scenarios. "Sir? Go weapons-hot with an Imperial Proconsul standing in range? Against regs. That goes double for Deathguard weapons."

Ansteel could hear a murmuring noise from the gathered crowd of civilians. But it was the hooded figure that was the source of the danger: a supernatural danger.

He could not tell his decurion any such thing, however. Expressing belief in the Kirlian spectrum, or adepts able to manipulate it, was against the laws his legion itself enforced.

"We are the Deathguard! The cops of the star-damned Inquisition, stardammit! This is now an official investigation into abnormal psychological events. Convicts don't sing hymns. And listen to that crowd! It is getting restless."

"You log the order, sir, and I'll follow it."

Ansteel knew what his decurion was saying. Ansteel would alone take blame during any inquest later. He said, "This is on me."

Expel raised his shocklance and extended the forked blades. The blaster rifles of the fire team whined and hummed as their chambered rounds were superheated from solid to plasma, and their muzzles glowed red. The more sinister weapons, delirium wands, epilepsy emitters, and wide-spectrum insanity projectors of the Deathguard dragoons and fusiliers made no such telltale signs, but the officer readouts reflected inside his helmet told Ansteel the blacktech weapons of his men were live.

"What target, sir?" asked Expel in his quiet, ironic voice. "Can't hardly shoot a technical glitch."

What was the hooded figure doing? Through his amplified goggle lens, Ansteel was alarmed to see that the old man had drawn a sword, but he was not flourishing the blade. It was not raised to strike. Instead, the point was planted between the man's farm boots. Something in the hunch of the shoulders, the poise of the figure, seemed as if the man were rigid. The hood dipped down. Both hands were on the swordhilts, crossed. He seemed to be concentrating, readying himself for some great effort.

Or praying.

He was breaking all Imperial laws — why not break the laws against prayer also? Nonetheless, that seemed somehow more shocking to Ansteel, like a personal insult. Only people who thought they were better than everyone else would think the heavens would hear them.

The officials and dignitaries standing to either side of him did not seem to see the blade. It was as if their eyes were unnaturally held, their thoughts unnaturally clouded.

It was a horror. And it was happening right in front of him.

Ansteel pointed at the reviewing stand. "There! Look! That man is …"

Expel said, "Sir? Are you ordering us to open fire on the Proconsul? Ah …yes, sir. Of course I will comply. But, ah, please log, date, and seal the order, sir. For the Review Board."

Ansteel stiffened. Of course they could not open fire on the reviewing stand. But the man was … what was he doing? Standing still? Meditating?

Ansteel raised the magnification again, until the intervening air vibrations made the image swim and shiver. The sword in the man's hands was not a traditional blade, nor a laser sword. This blade looked like a thing of glass, a shard of pure spirit made solid. It reflected a golden light from a light source that was not seen. It was light from some other environment, some other realm, being reflected into this area of space and time.

A twinge of remembered pain ran through Ansteel's bad eye.

It was a ghost blade, a forbidden weapon.

Ansteel remembered the sensation of being struck by its power. The thing had marred him without ever touching his face. Fear, like sudden vacuum, robbed him of breath.

"By the stars!" Ansteel whispered, unable to shout. "Orgulus! But you're *dead*!"

But no. Even as he spoke, he knew. This was not Orgulus. This was worse. Something ancient. Something long dead, dead in ages past, come again into the light of day.

Here was a Knight of the Temple of the Stars. Of old, these had been the enemies of the Empire, foes more fearsome than the Pavo, or any barbarian race. The Templars had been sickness inside the Empire, a heresy, a heterodoxy, destroying loyalty, spreading madness. They had been skilled warlords, who wrapped themselves in fraud and mystery, and deceived the people by pretending to practice witchcraft, and to be served by invisible powers.

A sense of dread, of fury, seemed to pass up his spine, into his brain. It was like a thunderbolt, blazing, blinding, deafening.

But the Templars were dead! They had to be! They had been wiped out years and years ago. In a sense, they had never existed, since their so-called mystic powers had been simple tricks and false stories.

But then, like a man in the moment after being thunderstuck, when he is dazzled and deaf and he hears only silence, Ansteel heard a silent and calm part of him saying: *Of course.*

Of course they were real. Of course they were still alive. Why else would the Empire maintain the Inquisition? Why else be forever seeking rumors of them? Why else arm the Deathguards with horror-weapons to destroy the neural basis of thinking itself? Not to hunt down stage magicians and holo-tricksters.

"Sir!" Expel startled him from his reverie. "Still standing by for your order. Who is our target?" and then, in a careful tone of voice, he added, "Lord Centauri was successfully liquidated years ago. We cannot open fire on him."

But Ansteel, with his googles at high magnification, could see the tailor robot standing behind the cloaked and hooded Templar. The high crowned hat trembled and began to rise. Ansteel caught the merest glimpse of tight-beam antenna rising up from the robot's skullbox. The robot casually raised a gauntlet, adjusted his brim, and prevented the hat from falling off. But now Ansteel understood the meaning of the strangely oversized hat. The tailor was broadcasting. What message was being sent? What codes? Where?

Where else? Ansteel swung his amplified gaze in a dizzying swoop over to the top of the Disintegration Chamber. The technician robots had reached the roof of the hundred-foot high unit, and were among the coolant tanks and motor boxes of the atomic pile. However, they were not raising the coolant rods. They were dismantling the motor boxes, dismounting the manual cranks, and spot-wielding the rod sleeves into place, so the coolant rods could not be raised.

Ansteel pointed. "Atop the death chamber! Robot revolt! Sabotage! There!"

Ansteel's ensign sounded the bugle-call from his suit amplifiers and ignited the standard in his gauntlets, so the hologram now flamed with battle-colors. This shimmering image was of a vulture-winged and ram-headed lioness, an ancient symbol of a monster whose questions it was death not to answer. This emblem of the Inquisitional Deathtroopers blazed into view above the cohort, rearing, wings spread, shaking her horns, and uttering a raspy, groaning shriek, halfway between roar and wail.

Shocklances and other nerve weapons would have no effect on robots, but some firing squads in the maniple were armed with jammers and scramblers meant for positronic brains. And blaster rifles worked on any target.

The troopers of the other cohorts were startled by the sudden alarm. The Plague Troopers in white and the Locust Troopers in black broke ranks, scattered or hit the deck, blasters out and scanning for sources of threat. The Shocktroopers in red, whose cyborg brains were wired into radio links and swimming with neurochemicals to improve reaction time, fell into fire teams and directed fire where the Deathguard were firing.

Meanwhile, the regulars stood frozen, buzzing with radio traffic, while the auxiliary troops broke ranks and milled about, trying to prevent the civilians from stampeding. The Proconsul's bodyguards, huge shields held high, were hustling him up the landing ramp, which was already beginning to trundle closed. Where was the Templar? Where was the tailor? Then Ansteel saw them: the Templar was standing as he had been, as if paralyzed, hood bowed, hands folding on his shining sword, which was still planted point-first between his boots. His frame was rigid, muscles locked, as if he strained at some impossible effort. The tailor was standing before him, metal limbs splayed, politely leading or rudely pushing panicky dignitaries to the left and right around the standing man, so they did not bump or trample him.

Ansteel shouldered his weapon, thumbed it to longrange, and switched his goggle viewpoint into the sniper scope. One ray of energy smiting the crowd of officers and high-ranked civilians would not be seen. And if he struck a politician or desk warrior in the throng, no great loss...

An outcry interrupted him. He felt the ground tremble beneath his feet. An earthquake? An enemy landing?

He jerked his goggle view back to normal, raised his head, and looked up. The robots atop the death chamber had been blasted, or damaged, or had taken cover. He saw one slender metal body topple slowly from the brink, speeding through a hundred yards of empty air to smash spectacularly on the fused surface of the parade ground. Any robot struck by Deathguard was twitching and flopping in an epileptic spasm, positronic brain jammed and haywire.

The cyborgs of the Praetorian Guard, however, had heavier weapons, including guided grenades and beam propelled jellied flammables, which could arc nicely over the brink of the rooftop, and drench the cowering robots in flame or high-energy pulse explosions. When their synchronized salvo arrived, the remaining robots, as well as the switches, control rod winches, coolant boxes, and other mechanisms of the atomic pile were reduce to flaming wreckage. The roof armor, however, was unscratched. No handheld weapon could puncture it.

But the shaking of the ground increased. Slowly, majestically, impossibly, the vast black cube-shaped death chamber of metal, the countless tons of mass, with all the prisoners trapped inside, now rose into the air. Slowly at first, and then with greater speed, the huge bulk lifted off from the base on which it stood, pulling free the clamps sunk into the concrete. Rubble and dust trailed from the lower corners of the great cube as it sailed aloft, solid as a battleship, and just as weightless.

The Praetorians roared and howled in rage. The hologram emblem of their cohort, a wolflike monster with saber fangs and savage, saw-toothed ram horns, led the roaring and howling. Again and again the many squads of the red-armored company fired their heavy weapons. Many of the Praetorians had been issued weapons that were normally vehicle mounted, but which their mighty, mechanized limbs could tote and wield with ease.

High energy beams and high explosive shells flamed and thundered against the armored sides of the death chamber, and bullets clattered like hail.

The black cube rose above the fiery commotion, serene, silent, unharmed. The prisoners within were perfectly safe. No radiation, no impact, could penetrate the heavy shielding.

The officials, officers, and men stood on the parade ground, staring and gaping upward, and the crowd fell silent, awed. Little pools of incendiary fire clinging to the unscathed cube sent trails of smoke skyward from the wrecked machinery atop. The control rod mechanisms were slag. Nothing would ever draw those rods up from the pile: no lethal energy would be released into the helpless prisoners.

The brighter sun chose that moment to come from behind the dimmer sun, and colored light swept across the scene, glancing off the big black cube, and making it glitter.

Silent as a black ship crewed by archangels, the square shape of the chamber entered a large, gray storm-cloud and disappeared from sight.

The storm cloud sailed grandly out to sea, growing larger as it went.

3. Phantom Paladin Vanishes

Some ambitious jetpackers among the regular legionnaires ignited their flight gear and took off with thundercracks of acceleration, speeding after in pursuit. Their fuel reserves were limited, and their flight ceiling was low, so they returned emptyhanded after ten or fifteen minutes. By that time, flitters and rotor-craft joined the search, closing the distance to the growing storm cloud, and diving in. Not long after, the *Omnipotent* released a squadron of atmospheric fighter-bombers from her starboard flight catapults. By that time, the dark cloudbanks had expanded to the horizon, and the storm had broken, and it was raining over the sea. Visibility was poor, and lightning strokes were interfering with scanning gear.

Expel spoke in his ear. His voice held no note of amazement. Ansteel was impressed with his decurion's nonchalance. "Giant object, flat and reflective, slowly moving, and metallic? No way sensor sweep can miss it."

A cold intuition told Ansteel that the chamber would not be found. Sensor beams would somehow fail, or be pointed the wrong way, or robots would disobey orders, or men hitherto loyal would suddenly be confused, or frightened, or asleep, as if struck down by an unseen warlock's charm. Or if the thing merely dropped into the sea with the rainfall, there were no submersible units at hand to conduct any sort of search.

So all he said back to Expel was, "We'll see."

The Proconsul and the other dignitaries had boarded. The ramp being used as a reviewing stand was retracted, the pinnace was sealed for flight. The Proconsul's pinnace was now taking off.

Ansteel was alarmed. The Templar warlock-knight was about to be carried up to the *Omnipotent*, and board the superdreadnaught. Who knows what havoc a man with freakish mind powers could accomplish?

Ansteel gritted his teeth. Quick action could still save the situation. An antispace battery could blast the pinnace before it cleared the atmosphere! No, belay that — the Proconsul was aboard. Even if he did not realize it himself, the Proconsul, and all aboard, were hostages.

Ansteel raised his oxygen gain to blow cold, sharp air into his mask, and clear his thoughts. The answer was simpler than that. The Templar was trapped. If a squad of heavy marines met the pinnace as it docked, the Templar could be caught in the airlock, as easily as any man.

No. Not marines. Men armed and trained for this. The Deathguard. The unit he served.

Ansteel spent frantic minutes trying to reach the colonel, the brigadier, or the commadore on the comm, or someone in the civilian Inquisition office who could warn the *Omnipotent*. All the channels were blocked. A mere centurion did not have the priority to get through, not during an emergency.

When the comm did clatter to life again, it was one-way: a command to restore order. Some people in the native crowd were laughing and cheering at the sight of the escape, or singing illegal songs of praise.

The buzzing fiery scream of blasterfire echoed over the scene, silencing the disloyal mirth, and replacing it with human screams.

Ansteel wanted to find an aircraft, to chase after the receding pinnace, to seek out and find the hooded figure. Ansteel wanted to throw him into an oxywater-filled inquiry torture coffin, paralyzed, helpless, tubes in his veins and wires in his brain. He wanted to find some answers.

The desire, the need, was like a fire in his heart, burning.

Face immobile, he quenched that fire. He was a soldier of the Empire. Orders were orders. Ansteel trotted toward the gathering riot, double-time, calling his men to fall in as he went, and deploying them in a picket line of four-man firing teams.

4. The Honor of the Regiment

Later, the official story given out was that rebels among the natives had shot first, with an improvised direction-energy weapon made from a car battery. Not likely, but it was better not to question the official story.

During a quiet moment in the house-to-house fighting that came next, Expel and Ansteel were hunkered down behind a burning metal shape of what had once been brightly-colored playground equipment. They were waiting for mobile armor to shell a children's hospital across the way, and clear out a gunner's nest. The head of a fanciful penguin, from whose mouth issued a children's slide, glared at Ansteel with one eye, wreathed in smoke. The other half of the face had been reduced to slag. Ansteel knew how he felt.

Expel opened his faceplate, which was against regulation. His mask mike was no longer recording his speech. The chin of his mask hung over his brow like a visor.

Like Ansteel, Expel was a Sphingali, or, rather, the gene sample from a mother he would never know had been Sphingali. This race was blue-skinned, with pale palms and footsoles. Expel was sky-blue, the hue of a clear lake, for the ancestral lands of his genetic forebears were from near the poles of long-lost Algol. Ansteel's forebears were from the equatorial regions, so his hue was a blue as dark as jet.

"Better shut that, legionnaire," Ansteel said. "Don't want a pan full of shrapnel."

Expel passed him a joss stick. "Our time is a very shadow that passes away, Centurion. Let no flower of the spring pass us by."

With a toss of his head, Ansteel retracted his faceplate and took the joss stick. It was not one of the self-igniting kinds, but hand-rolled. Ansteel, without looking, put his blaster hand over the top of the wreckage, let a few wild shots fly free. He drew back his hand. The mouth of the weapon shed a smoky wisp. He bent his face over it. The tip of the joss stick clenched in his teeth touched the hot metal. He puffed it to a red glow.

Ansteel bore the handsome, chiseled features of the nameless sorcerers and ancient kings who carved their visages into mountainsides, moons, and asteroids still seen in the abandoned Sphingali star systems. His nose was a narrow hook, his lips firm, his jaw a jut. His good eye was an eerie gray-green, seeming to hold depth upon depth. His bad eye was an inch-wide appliance of chrome, with a gleaming milky lens, surrounded by a fine net of scars.

"What did you want to say?" asked Ansteel. Expel normally did not share his smokes. He just wanted both helmets open, both mikes offline.

"How did you know, sir? What tipped you off?"

Ansteel was not about to tell anyone he saw a Templar. That was a quick flit to a court martial. Or worse places. So he said, "Good situational awareness."

"So … need to know? Is that is, sir?"

"More like none of your business, soldier." Ansteel was not in the mood for a smoke, and he heard the whirring ground-effect murmur of armored vehicles approaching. "Our support. Late as always." He tossed the joss stick away, and tossed his head. His faceplate slid back into place with a click, and his suit hissed and pressurized. "Ready to ash some trash?"

Expel raised his blast-rifle and made a show of chambering a round with a loud clack. "Ready in the bottle, before I was born. For the glory of the Empire."

"And the honor of the regiment."

Those were the last words he ever spoke to Decurion Tufir Expel, who did not survive the engagement. The medics, during triage, of course put a clone trooper at a lower priority than a naturally born man, or an expensive cyborg. He had no family, no home world to which to ship the body, so he was dissected for organ and tissue transplant, without any ceremony.

Eventually, the full-scale riot was suppressed. City blocks were ablaze, and Ansteel had lost several more men, including Corporal Dee, his best sharpshooter. There was no sign and no rumor of any unusual men in hooded robes with shining swords doing any unusual things, or nattily-dressed robots in top hats.

CHAPTER 11:
THE MASTER OF DARKNESS

Galactic Year 12813, Planet Mira

1. House of the Golden Order

It was six years after her world died when Lyra Centauri beheld the Great Tree for the first time. Six years, that is, according to the galactic calendar, reckoned by the frame of reference of the ruling world of Septentrion, in Inner Core. Thanks to time dilation, it had only been five years for her.

Her first view of the famous tree was just after sunset. The upper branches caught the red and level rays of sunset while the trunk, and all the world below, was shadow. The planet Ksora, from which she had so recently come, boasted only one evening star, a sullen red gas giant huddled close to the system's twin suns. Mira had a single sun, and Lyra was not yet used to having but one shadow chasing her feet. However, Mira had a score of interior planets, so a dozen evening stars were twinkling just above the red and black horizon, like a line of jewels floating entangled among the burning elf-lamps of the upper branches.

These were bioluminescent flowers, bright as festive lanterns, glowing and growing along the countless branches and infinite twigs of the mile-high lamprose tree. The tree was so tall, that the crown was in another season: the many-colored leaves of autumn were high in the atmosphere, whereas the green leaves of summer lower down, in warmer air, were spread like a miniature sky above the campus. Colored blooms from these upper branches, dying, had broken free, and were sailing on the wind as they fell, shining like motes of fairy dust.

On a knoll north of the Great Tree was the Grandmaster's manor. This was a long, low, rambling building of pale wood built in a severe, classical style. It was the first building Lyra had ever seen with chimneys.

At age eleven, the chimney smoke spooked her. She thought the building was on fire, and at first she refused to go in, tugging on the Matron's grip, and trying to get away. The tall man in a hooded robe, walking silently, came out to meet her. He was frightening and stern to look on, but his eyes were deep and wise. His voice was deep and kind.

His silver hair shined in the shadows of his hood like a hidden crown. The short beard framing his face was silver, but his mustachios and marionette lines by his mouth were black.

She remembered how he took her hand. He raised a finger, and a songbird landed on it, and he put the bird gently on her finger. And, just like that, she was not afraid. For the first time since childhood, she was not afraid.

Inside, the manor was big, but the rooms were simple. He kept no servants, and only one robot: a B9-NGL model tailor named Buttons. Buttons was a golden android wearing a formal coat with a cravat and a high collar, with a top hat. The robot sat crossed-legged on the floor, mending a seam in his master's robes, saying nothing.

Lyra showed the Grandmaster all the knives and needles she had hidden in her robes, despite the Matrons' searches. He smiled and brought down his ghostblade in its scabbard from its charging rack above the mantelpiece, and unsheathed it for her.

"Little lassie, this be Galadlang, the Ironflame. 'Tis the blade what slew the Dark Emperor, Rodomont Lord Death, and freed our galaxy. I have not lifted it in anger since."

And his deep eyes grew deeper yet, and the blade lit up with white fire. Just like her father's.

" 'Tis the same blade that, before, was shattered in me hand by Ganelon Lord Doomshadow, when he and I were met in brutal battle beneath the haunted stones standing upright on the moors of Matar, the world of unceasing rain. The shards I took in secret from world to world, dressed in beggar's rags, seeking the art to re-forge them, and all told me the art had been lost centuries ago when the last of the Arcadian ghost-smiths were slain by the Empire. But there was one ghost-smith yet alive... "

So he had said.

"If it was broken, how did you mend it?" Young Lyra had asked.

"As anything is done. With help from faithful friends, and help from on high."

"You overthrew the ... " she began, but she could not bring herself to say the words. She did not want to say the name of the people who killed her mother and father.

"The Empire ...? You want to hear my part I played in the war?" He smiled. The blade went dark, and he sheathed it again. "Aye! That tale is long in telling, and I tell it only to my friends. I would offer you my handclasp in pledge ... but ..."

"But what?" she said anxiously, because now she was curious about the story.

" 'Tis not a thing done lightly. A pledge cannot be taken back, not ever."

She thrust out her hand with an impatient motion, but the man in the hood did not take it.

He said "Little miss, I have heard you refuse to sleep in my dormitory, and will not eat what my cook puts before you, but climb under the table."

She rolled her eyes, and patiently explained the obvious to the old man. "It is not safe to sleep in the same place twice, especially out in the open. The closet is safer. The other girls in the dorm might slit my throat while I am sleeping, and take my shoes."

He nodded gravely. "And the food of my table?"

"Oh, I don't mind the food at all, but you can't eat with older kids around. They will swipe my bowl."

He said, "The murder rate between ten-year-old Star Maiden aspirants has been on the decline for, lo, many a year. We can hide your shoes with your civilian clothes in a safe box, I warrant, which none will dare break into. I will see you are shod, and give you a white robe to wear. I cannot speak to the bowl stealing. Nonetheless, you will have to brave these dangers with a big heart and a smooth face, showing no fear, or else the great work of my house cannot go forward."

"Your house? The manor house?"

"All this is my house, restored and rebuilt after the Empire crushed and scattered all the lore-masters of Arcadia, burned the Third Temple on Septentrion, and slew the Templars. For four hundred years, it stood empty. It is a house of learning. *The* house of learning! Come again to me in a weeks' time, and if I hear good report of you from the Matrons, I will know you are my friend, and clasp your hand, and, aye, you shall have the tale in full. I weary not in the telling."

She understood now what she had not, then: the house of the Grandmaster was not the manor house with its smoking chimneys. It was the House of Learning for the Golden Order, all four branches of it: the Academy of the Arcadian Lore, the Reliquary of Pilgrims, the Nunnery of the Star Maidens tending the Temple of Mira, and the training camp of Templars who guarded it.

Jaywind Starquest was the last Templar Knight, the last living link to a legendary and largely forgotten past.

Where was he now? Where were any who had vowed the quest?

Lyra Centauri was on Elgafar, just opening her eyes. She blinked, and tears began the creep down her cheeks, hot and tinkling. She sniffed back a sob, and raised her sleeve to wipe her cheek.

A cold voice spoke, but not in her ears. "Sister! Why do you weep?"

2. The Lake of Fire

Galactic Year 12820, Shrine Planetoid Elgafar

Lyra opened her eyes, drew a breath. The shadowy silhouette of the being called Nightshadow was in the meditation chamber, watching over her. It was day. The three tiny but blindingly bright pinpoint lights of this system's distant triple suns sent a slanting rectangle of light in through the eastern window. The smoky substance of Nightshadow's image was washed out where the light passed through him, so that he seemed even less solid than was his wont. He cast no shadow on the floor. There was no reflection of him in the Kirlian mirror.

She finished wiping her cheeks on her sleeve. In a silken rustle of her wide-hemmed, midnight-blue pantaloons, she rose to her feet. Anger and sorrow were swirling in her heart. Angry words came from her lips with no warning. "Why don't you have an aura? It's rude! All living things have auras. Worlds and stars are surrounded by energy fields. How are you hiding yours?"

His voice was mild. "Call it Duck Witchery."

"Ducks?"

"The Fuliguline. The species that used to be indentured to the Hominids, who were supposed to guide them to civilization. It turns out that they had a psychic talent after all, but it was hard to find, because it is the psychic ability to hide psychic ability. It is called Incognition. Surely you studied it at the Arcadian Academy on Mira."

Lyra spoke absentmindedly. "The Matrons do not teach it to the novices. They do not want us hiding from them."

Her anger was less now, but her sorrow was more. She looked at the memorial shelf hanging on the wall. It was nearly blank. She knew none of her ancestors. Only her father and mother, dead these many years.

And the third figurine between them…

Her eyes swam again with tears, blurring her vision. She blinked. "So unfair! Templars teach the squires, I think. To hide from foes, I suppose..." her voice trailed off.

Nightshadow said, "My reason is likewise. For I, too, have foes. They are mighty, and terrible, and hidden. A certain degree of discretion is needed. Hence this dark disguise. Also, it looks imposing."

That made her giggle in surprise. "What? Was that a joke?" She looked up at him, but the smoky oval beneath the wide brim of his hat showed no features, no expression.

"Opinions differ." Then his tone sobered. "Your are in grief. What happened?"

"The depot was destroyed. Everything gone. Everyone."

"Athos?"

She was startled by the snap in his voice. The cloaked silhouette stood with shoulders hunched, gloves like claws, a posture of shock. The edges of his silhouette flayed and flickered, as if unknitting.

"How did you know his name? He was there. He is dead. They are all dead."

"You saw his corpse?"

"No. I assume he is dead … there was fire … I …"

The smoky being regained his composure. His spine grew straight once more, and his smoky outline more crisp. His voice was still tense. "What precisely did you see? Did you look behind every floor and wall of the ship?"

She described her painstaking search on the pirate ship, and, later of the spaceboat that descended to the planet; her sense of something alive in a coffin shot from the ship's torpedo tube; her discovery of a patrolman, buried alive; and her rescue of him during his re-entry and splashdown.

She described her incomplete first examination of the Living Mountain of Death. She had been interrupted by alarms when the patrolman, who had apparently gone insane, and decided to attack the whole pirate base himself, unarmed. She disabled the tracking system with her arrows, so the Weasel manning the base could not simply kill the intruder with a remote weapon.

Then she had to follow the Weasel in his walking tank to rescue the insane patrolman yet again. And, to make matters worse, she then had to return to the base and disable and destroy more machines with her sacred arrows, to prevent the automatic anti-personnel systems, run by a Weasel robot, from destroying the mad patrolman. Then the robot departed in person, seeking to kill the patrolman, and she had to follow it.

"He turned out to be a nobleman traveling in secret. You will never guess who. He is the son of a galactic hero, Raphean Lone!"

The shadowy head nodded. "That family has done much. They spring from the line of Ar Arislan, who led the Nemean revolt, and slew an Emperor in the senate. They are not to be underestimated. The daughters of Lone are noble and fair, and the sons brave and handsome, or so it is said."

"He had the code hidden in a secret compartment of his signet ring, and he used it on the robot to turn into a person, a machine-man, not a machine. But I had to tell him how to talk to it. The robot recited its lading list from its memory banks."

Painstakingly, she repeated as best she could the conversation between Athos and the robot. She recited as much of the list the robot had repeated to her she could recall. It was not a long list, because the names, dates, and crate numbers meant nothing to her, and because she did not have a robotic memory.

The shadow being asked, "What happened next?"

"Nothing happened next! I listened to the Weasel robot reciting its list. I could not talk to it to tell it to speed up or go back. It was helping us because Athos gave it free will. Set it free."

"*He*," said Nightshadow absentmindedly. "Emancipated robots are called *he*."

Lyra was annoyed. That particular grammar slip was one she never made. "Pay attention! The list said all the 8R models shipped in were stored in a vault in a sub-basement, so I rushed in there, looking for a crate with the number you told me."

"But the item was not present?"

"Don't call him an item! Emancipated robots are called *he!*"

"Did you see the crate?"

"I don't know. It does not matter, now, does it? If he was there, he was burned to nothing! If he was not there, then all this was for nothing! Two years of looking!"

"How can you *not* know, Sister? Either you saw the crate or you did not."

"The place was messed up: some crates were on their sides, some broken open, some were just stacked every which way, not in any order. I found some expensive R8R speech-making robots out of their crates, just idling on standby, and an NSTZ8R med-bot, but I could not question them or pluck out their memory pins. Then … then …"

"Then what?"

Her eyes were hot with tears once more. Her heart ached. She wiped her cheek on her sleave. "Nothing is supposed to hurt you when you are in the astral form. I was not expecting to be hurt! A blast came. The shock knocked me out."

"How can that be? An electromagnetic pulse cannot hurt you."

"No. The pain of all the others; the terrible pain." She gathered up her sleeves and wiped her face. Her voice was muffled. A sob escaped her. "I felt them all burn up: fish and forests and birds and beasts, men, women, children. They all screamed and died. I was flung back into space. I came to myself at my last orientation point. To get back I had to gather my concentration, but my visualization no longer connected to anything. The carved mountain was gone. I tried using my memory of the landscape outside as a focus. First one spot, then a spot farther away. Still nothing. I tried using a memory from the pirate ship, but it had left."

"*She,*" muttered Nightshadow. "Ships are *she.*"

"Then I remembered the ocean. I could manifest my astral form above the waves where the dinosaur-fish were sporting and writhing. I flew toward shore. The whole horizon was on fire. Everything was flame. I went over sea and land in an eyeblink, as fast as I could think my thought.

"I dove into the fire. Below was ash, above was ash, and the in-between was red and roaring. It was like walking around the inside of a trash incinerator during a burn. But the whole forest was inside the incinerator, flocks and herds of every kind, all bellowing and screaming, all running madly, all scorched or scalded.

"I saw some moths flying into the firelight, and I batted at them to shoo them away before they burned, but my hands and fingers just passed through them. But I could feel their little lives flicker out like sparks.

"Finally, I reach the very middle. There was a lake of liquid rock. It was so hot that the air above it was glowing like a plasma gun and giving off a lightning blasts like something I have never seen."

She shivered at the memory.

"There were so many forks of lightning, it was like a river delta. Like a forest of thorns, winking in and out. The thunder was like a waterfall, a roar that never paused."

Nightshadow said, "The heat had ionized the air. Such weapons are normally not used in atmosphere. Why did the pirates open fire on the planet? They never destroy loot, certainly not their own."

She perhaps did not hear, but hid her face in her elbow. Then she said, "How long I floated through the mess I do not know. I flew upward, to get above the dazzle of the lightning-storm, the clouds of ash. Up and up I went, but it was as if the whole sky was stained with soot. Finally, above the atmosphere, I saw something coming over the limb of the horizon. It was a ship. I saw the shape: like an arrowhead, but huge. I saw the size: immense. And I saw the markings on the prow. An

Imperial battleship. She was flying the sign of the Black Cogwheel. The battleflag of the Empire."

She fell silent.

"After so long … " he muttered. "The shadows gather…" Then dark, wide-brimmed hat shook slowly back and forth. "It almost makes me sorry to be so right, so often…"

Then, in a louder voice, he said, "What next?"

She snapped, "What do you mean *what next*? There is no *what next*! The Empire yet lives! They are slaying people on that planet just as they slew the people on mine! Why does no one believe me!"

"Of course I believe you. Otherwise we would not be doing this, you and I. Did you form a search pattern around the area of ground zero? Did you search for survivors? The patrolman — he is important."

"What? No! What are you talking about?" Her head bobbed back into view. Her voice grew shrill with outrage. "The Greatest Empire leaves no survivors! They kill everyone! There was a tribe living in that forest! They were burned alive! By these *terrible* people! Why are you sending me out on these *terrible* missions to look at these *terrible* things?!"

The yellow eyes glinted beneath the rim of the hat, looking upon her steadily, but he said nothing.

Her voice dropped again to a whisper. "So many corpses! So many. Too many for the birds to eat. The birds were dead, too. It was like, when I was young: The waste yard behind Skinner's Row after tanning day, where they throw the bones and scraps, all wrong-colored with tanning salts and toxins! The crows would gather there, too, the dumb ones, and die from eating the poison in the corpses."

Anger returned. "Maybe I should just go back to Mira, and give up on these *terrible* things! These missions and adventures and endless searching! I should live my life sweeping shrines, polishing relics, singing psalms, and dancing dances! Calligraphy! Lighting candles! Every All Saints' Eve, I can shoot ceremonial arrows to scare bad spirits away, arrows that won't hurt anyone …."

Her mouth became a red circle of shock. Her dark, wet eyes grew hot with fear. Lyra snatched up her golden shrinebow and stepped toward the Kirlian mirror, holding the eight-foot length of polished bamboo and cherry-birch wood up high, so she could see its reflection.

In the amber surface, the golden bowshaft was stained red. Her fingers were dark, and stains ran up her wrists and arms.

"I've killed a man," she whispered. "Vranko. That was his name. I prayed for him, but that was not enough…"

Nightshadow said, "You must return as quickly as possible in astral form to Zavijava, and conduct a proper search."

She said sharply, "A mortal being, formed by the stars just as you or I have been, was slain there by my hand, using a sacred instrument never meant for such a deed! I cannot go back. You go!"

She held up her hand. Red sparks began to flicker along her pale fingers, and little red forks of energy played between her knuckles and nails. It was an inner rage made visible.

Lyra scowled, staring at her hand, muttering a prayer under her breath. Slowly, ever so slowly, the red sparks crackling between her fingers grew dimmer and winked out.

The black vaporous figure said nothing. The hat brim was turned slightly down, as if he were lost in thought.

Both were silent for a minute, then several minutes, then for so long, that the three suns of this rapidly turning asteroid passed overhead, and now were shining sparks in the western windows of the chamber.

Eventually Nightshadow spoke. "Sister, we walk dark paths through many a dire way before we reach the promised light at the end of all roads. We seek hidden remnants of an evil Empire."

"I seek Arcadia, where the secret of slaying the sun-slayer rests."

"We cannot find either without finding the lost world of your youth. To do that, we must find …."

"Find what? Everything and everyone are buried beneath a lake of molten lava on Zavijava! The Weasel robot recited all the outgoing shipment numbers to me! That crate number was not listed! It was not there! The crate was shipped in and never shipped out! That means it was burned and melted and the ashes and slag buried under a lake of radioactive lava!"

Lyra, strength gone, sank to her knees. Her face was a mask of grief.

His calm voice came out of the shadows. "You also said the storage vault was in disarray. Pirates do not keep careful records. Perhaps the crate we seek was removed, or never arrived. If you will not return there, I will have Zavijava searched for survivors."

She looked up. She saw no expression on the faceless shadow being, of course, aside from the glint of his eyes.

"There could be no survivors! It is impossible!"

Nightshadow said, "Do not underestimate the sons of Raphean Lone. What is impossible for other men, they can do. Athos Lone will be found alive."

She said, "You told me it was well outside your astral projection range. That is why you had me go."

His deep, cool voice issued from his cloudy silhouette. "I need not send myself. I have another asset in that star system. The question is, what of you?"

Lyra straightened her spine. She took a deep breath in through her nose, and let it escape from her red lips. Her pretty face became placid. "I must pray and do penance and cleanse myself."

"And then—?"

Like a snapping eel rising to the surface of a calm pond, a look of anger broke through her serene expression and sent a red spark crackling through her eyes. Her irises flashed crimson. "You think I will give up? The Empire slew my world. Everyone I knew. My house. Other children I played with. Everything I owned, everyone I love. All gone." Her little fists were white at the knuckles. She was shivering with rage. "I will find Starquest. He will overcome the Empire! He did it before."

"Everyone else in the galaxy has given up, Sister. No one thinks the Empire still lives. No one else believes the Syndicate is still active. Only you. Only I."

"*The Empire has put out the sun.* Those were my father's dying words. And I saw them. The Deathtroopers in their pale armor. Lord Doomshadow's special cohort. The Inquisition. The forbidden weapons. I saw it all. A dark centurion, he boasted that the Dark Overlords still live. I heard it all. So I will not give up. I cannot!"

His voice was soft. A tear glinted in her long, black eyelashes. She looked up. Her eyes were once again as dark and lustrous as onyx, with no trace of red. "I will stop the Great Eye of Darkness. No other little girl will weep the tears I wept on that day. That was my vow. The stars heard me."

The cold voice said, "You cannot give up. Nor will I. We are alike in that."

Lyra wiped her eyes, which now were narrowed in a look of curiosity. "Who are you, really?"

"I am not at liberty to say."

"Are your parents alive? Are they shadows, too? Come now, what *are* you? Some secret government agent? A rogue Templar? A Dark Overlord who turned against his masters? A supernatural spirit of vengeance?"

That elicited a low chuckle. "Nothing so romantic. Call me the cat which curiosity could not kill. It carries its own curse."

"Curse...?"

"Of a kind. My curiosity uncovered dark knowledge, and this calls me into dark places, to fight secret struggles. If I fail to heed this call, there is no one else to go. I can share the danger, but not the secrets, not even with you, lest you be cursed as well."

That annoyed her. "I know the ten techniques of exorcism! I fear no curse!"

"Then you will do what must be done. If the cause of war be just, will not the stars forgive the blood the soldier sheds? Heaven knows how soon the soldier is willing to shed his own."

These words quelled her anger. She lowered her eyes pensively. Softly, Lyra said, "Very well! I will continue the search, with hope or without it! But we had two leads. Mine ended in a lake of fire. What of yours? I cannot return to Septentrion for reasons you know. That world is cursed with millennia of wickedness and sorrow. You followed your lead? You said there was a ship called the *Sorcerer* whose cargo might hold a clue. What did you find?"

Nightshadow's hatbrim lowered and his voice came out from beneath it. "The press of other matters constrains me. War is in the offing. The Septentrion investigation is not complete. I will have a full report on the merchantman *Sorcerer* and her captain, an evil monk named Mantis, when assets are available."

Anger inside her had been silent beneath a warm blanket of hope. Now that blanket was torn, and anger leapt free. Sparks started in her eyes. "What! You —!"

Words failed her.

She sputtered, then said, "We have a bargain. A compact. That means you keep your side of the deal! You keep your word!"

With his hat tilted low, his yellow eyes were not visible. His voice was deep and dispassionate. "Events cannot be rushed. We are menaced at every side, and must act with prudence. I will follow the clue trail on Septentrion. Yet you are not done following your own. Your report is neither complete nor conclusive."

Lyra was outraged. "I told you everything!"

"You have not thought through the implications. The investigation at Zavijava is incomplete. There is something you overlooked. So that lead is not dead yet. I will return with further instructions once the fates of any fugitives from Zavijava are identified. Now I must make haste."

"What? Incomplete how? What did I overlook?"

But he had already started to fade from view. She said, "Wait! I have more to say! Don't you have a comdisc channel? A post box? How do I reach you?"

But he was gone. She was speaking to the empty air.

The silence was deafening.

Athos was also gone. She had known the name of the brave young patrolman, and had saved his life more than once. And yet, in the end, all her efforts turned to empty air as well, and he perished.

Vranko was gone. She had murdered one man to save another, and that effort turned to nothing as well. All she had accomplished was to stain her hands with blood. It was not the first time she had committed crime, but it sickened her. Her purity was gone.

She gaze rested on the figurines on her shelf of ancestors. Everyone was gone.

3. The Silent Voice

Lyra's thoughts were chaos. Slowly she walked about the shrine asteroid, from dusk to dawn to dusk again, for an hour. She swept the ways and tended the garden and dried her tears.

The planetoid was so small, and the sky above so huge. She stared upward in wonder and sadness. Immense was the emptiness. Could anything fill such a void?

As if a silent voice were speaking to her, Lyra Centauri suddenly knew the young Patrolman would be found alive. How and why she knew, she could not say.

She saw that the immense void above her was filled with starlight. As for the void within her, perhaps that could be filled as well.

Lyra returned to her shrine. She had many prayers to pray.

****

Has the brave Captain Athos been obliterated? Will the Mask of the Ancient Mariner be found again?
What secret is behind the unearthly Nightshadow? Whose voice bespoke the Centurion of the Deathguard?
What star is next to perish when the Great Eye of Darkness opens? Where is Arcadia?

THESE THRILLING MYSTERIES AND MORE
IN OUR NEXT EXCITING INSTALLMENT !!!

STARQUEST:
SECRET AGENTS OF THE GALAXY

ABOUT THE AUTHOR

John C. Wright is a retired attorney, newspaperman and newspaper editor, who was only once on the lam and forced to hide from the police who did not admire his newspaper.

In 1984, he graduated from St. John's College in Annapolis, home of the "great books" program. In 1987, he graduated from the college and William and Mary's Law School (going from the third oldest to the second oldest school in continuous use in the United States), and was admitted to the practice of law in three jurisdictions (New York, May 1989; Maryland December 1990; D.C. January 1994). his law practice was unsuccessful enough to drive him into bankruptcy soon thereafter. his stint as a newspaperman for the St. Mary's Today was more rewarding spiritually, but, alas, also a failure financially. He presently works (successfully) as a writer in Virginia, where he lives in fairy-tale-like happiness with his wife, the authoress L. Jagi Lamplighter, and their three children: Orville, Wilbur, and Just Wright.

EXPLORE THE 4TH AGE OF STARQUEST!

Millenia ago, in the time between humanity's arrival in the Andromeda Galaxy and the adventures of Captain Athos, the human race had no knowledge of what had come before – or wait awaited them among the stars of Andromeda.

It was a time of intrigue. It was a time of empires – both good and ill – to arise… and fall. It was a time of heroes, heroines, and villains.

It was a time when one man – Galen Dwyn – would find his destiny – and his heart – and lead humanity forward.

Dragon Award Finalist Richard Paolinelli explores the 4th Age of John C. Wright's Starquest Universe in a series of thrilling sci-fi adventures. Come and explore this corner of humanity's journey today!

Galen's Way: https://www.amazon.com/dp/B08V6KR4CR
Galen's Blade: https://www.amazon.com/gp/product/B09M2W5JM2
Galen's Heart: Coming Soon!

SET SAIL ON YOUR NEXT GREAT ADVENTURE
WITH TUSCANY BAY BOOKS

Visit Tuscany Bay Books at our website: Tuscany Bay Books and browse our entire catalog of books by over a dozens incredible authors across multiple genres: sci-fi, fantasy, mystery, thriller, westerns, young adult, and even non-fiction.

In addition to John C. Wright's Starquest and Richard Paolinelli's Starquest 4th Age series, Tuscany Bay Books proudly publishes the works of:

Declan Finn's St. Tommy NYPD series and White Ops series,
Lori Janeski's The Carter Files series,
the 11-volume Planetary Anthology Series,
and Richard Paolinelli's Del Rio Mystery Series.

And many, many more standalone novels and short stories that you're sure to enjoy. All are available in e-book and print formats.

Printed in Great Britain
by Amazon

48585315R00169